Also by Elie Wiesel

The Night Trilogy

THE NIGHT TRILOGY

CONSISTING OF A MEMOIR, TRANSLATED BY MARION WIESEL, AND TWO NOVELS

Night · Dawn · Day

ELIE WIESEL

HILL AND WANG

A DIVISION OF FARRAR, STRAUS AND GIROUX

NEW YORK

Hill and Wang
A division of Farrar, Straus and Giroux
18 West 18th Street, New York 10011

Printed in the United States of America
This paperback edition, 2008

Library of Congress Cataloging-in-Publication Data
Wiesel, Elie, 1928–
 [Selections. English. 2008]
 The night trilogy : Night ; Dawn ; Day / Elie Wiesel.
  p. cm.
 "Consisting of a memoir, translated by Marion Wiesel, and two novels".
 ISBN-13: 978-0-8090-7364-1 (pbk. : alk. paper)
 ISBN-10: 0-8090-7364-1 (pbk. : alk. paper)
 1. Wiesel, Elie, 1928– —Translations into English. 2. Wiesel, Elie, 1928–
3. Authors, French—20th century—Biography. 4. Holocaust, Jewish (1939–1945)—
Personal narratives. I. Wiesel, Marion. II. Title.

PQ2683.I32 Z4613 2008
940.53'18092—dc22
[B]

                                             2007052727

Designed by Abby Kagan

www.fsgbooks.com

13 15 17 19 20 18 16 14

Contents

Night

TRANSLATED FROM THE FRENCH BY

MARION WIESEL

Preface to the New Translation

I F IN MY LIFETIME I WAS TO WRITE only one book, this would be the one. Just as the past lingers in the present, all my writings after *Night*, including those that deal with biblical, Talmudic, or Hasidic themes, profoundly bear its stamp, and cannot be understood if one has not read this very first of my works.

Why did I write it?

Did I write it so as *not* to go mad or, on the contrary, to *go* mad in order to understand the nature of madness, the immense, terrifying madness that had erupted in history and in the conscience of mankind?

Was it to leave behind a legacy of words, of memories, to help prevent history from repeating itself?

Or was it simply to preserve a record of the ordeal I endured as an adolescent, at an age when one's knowledge of death and evil should be limited to what one discovers in literature?

There are those who tell me that I survived in order to write this text. I am not convinced. I don't know *how* I survived; I was weak, rather shy; I did nothing to save myself. A miracle? Certainly not. If heaven could or would perform a miracle for me, why not for others more deserving than myself? It was nothing more than chance. However, having survived, I needed to give some meaning to my survival. Was it to protect that meaning that I set to paper an experience in which nothing made any sense?

In retrospect I must confess that I do not know, or no longer know, what I wanted to achieve with my words. I only know that without this testimony, my life as a writer—or my life, period—would not have become what it is: that of a witness who believes he has a moral obligation to try to prevent the enemy from enjoying one last victory by allowing his crimes to be erased from human memory.

For today, thanks to recently discovered documents, the evidence shows that in the early days of their accession to power, the Nazis in Germany set out to build a society in which there simply would be no room for Jews. Toward the end of their reign, their goal changed: they decided to leave behind a world in ruins in which Jews would seem never to have existed. That is why everywhere in Russia, in the Ukraine, and in Lithuania, the Einsatzgruppen carried out the Final Solution by turning their machine guns on more than a million Jews, men, women, and children, and throwing them into huge mass graves, dug just moments before by the victims themselves. Special units would then disinter the corpses and burn them. Thus, for the first time in history, Jews were not only killed twice but denied burial in a cemetery.

It is obvious that the war which Hitler and his accomplices waged was a war not only against Jewish men, women, and children, but also against Jewish religion, Jewish culture, Jewish tradition, therefore Jewish memory.

CONVINCED THAT THIS PERIOD in history would be judged one day, I knew that I must bear witness. I also knew that, while I had many things to say, I did not have the words to say them. Painfully aware of my limitations, I watched helplessly as language became an obstacle. It became clear that it would be necessary to invent a new language. But how was one to rehabilitate and transform words betrayed and perverted by the enemy? Hunger—thirst—fear—transport—selection—fire—chimney: these words all have intrinsic meaning, but in those times, they meant something else. Writing in my mother tongue—at that point close to extinction—I would pause at every sentence, and start over and over again. I would conjure up other verbs, other images, other silent cries. It still was not right. But what exactly was "it"? "It" was something elusive, darkly shrouded for fear of being usurped, profaned. All the dictionary had to offer seemed meager, pale, lifeless. Was there a way to describe the last journey in sealed cattle cars, the last voyage toward the unknown? Or the discovery of a demented and glacial universe where to be inhuman was human, where disciplined, educated men in uniform came to kill, and innocent children and weary old men came to die? Or the countless separations on a single fiery night, the tearing apart of entire families, entire communities? Or, incredibly, the vanishing of a beautiful, well-behaved little Jewish girl with golden hair and a sad smile, murdered with her mother the very night of their arrival? How was one to speak of them without trembling and a heart broken for all eternity?

Deep down, the witness knew then, as he does now, that his testimony would not be received. After all, it deals with an event that sprang from the darkest zone of man. Only those who experienced Auschwitz know what it was. Others will never know.

But would they at least understand?

Could men and women who consider it normal to assist the weak, to heal the sick, to protect small children, and to respect the wisdom of their elders understand what happened there? Would they be able to comprehend how, within that cursed universe, the masters tortured the weak and massacred the children, the sick, and the old?

And yet, having lived through this experience, one could not keep silent no matter how difficult, if not impossible, it was to speak.

And so I persevered. And trusted the silence that envelops and transcends words. Knowing all the while that any one of the fields of ashes in Birkenau carries more weight than all the testimonies about Birkenau. For, despite all my attempts to articulate the unspeakable, "it" is still not right.

Is that why my manuscript—written in Yiddish as "And the World Remained Silent" and translated first into French, then into English—was rejected by every major publisher, French and American, despite the tireless efforts of the great Catholic French writer and Nobel laureate François Mauriac? After months and months of personal visits, letters, and telephone calls, he finally succeeded in getting it into print.

Though I made numerous cuts, the original Yiddish version still was long. Jérôme Lindon, the legendary head of the small but prestigious Éditions de Minuit, edited and further cut the French version. I accepted his decision because I worried that some things might be superfluous. Substance alone mattered. I was more afraid of having said too much than too little.

Example: in the Yiddish version, the narrative opens with these cynical musings:

> In the beginning there was faith—which is childish; trust—which is vain; and illusion—which is dangerous.
> We believed in God, trusted in man, and lived with the illu-

sion that every one of us has been entrusted with a sacred spark from the Shekhinah's flame; that every one of us carries in his eyes and in his soul a reflection of God's image.

That was the source if not the cause of all our ordeals.

Other passages from the original Yiddish text had more on the death of my father and on the Liberation. Why not include those in this new translation? Too personal, too private, perhaps; they need to remain between the lines. And yet . . .

I remember that night, the most horrendous of my life:

". . . Eliezer, my son, come here . . . I want to tell you something . . . Only to you . . . Come, don't leave me alone . . . Eliezer . . ."

I heard his voice, grasped the meaning of his words and the tragic dimension of the moment, yet I did not move.

It had been his last wish to have me next to him in his agony, at the moment when his soul was tearing itself from his lacerated body—yet I did not let him have his wish.

I was afraid.

Afraid of the blows.

That was why I remained deaf to his cries.

Instead of sacrificing my miserable life and rushing to his side, taking his hand, reassuring him, showing him that he was not abandoned, that I was near him, that I felt his sorrow, instead of all that, I remained flat on my back, asking God to make my father stop calling my name, to make him stop crying. So afraid was I to incur the wrath of the SS.

In fact, my father was no longer conscious.

Yet his plaintive, harrowing voice went on piercing the silence and calling me, nobody but me.

"Well?" The SS had flown into a rage and was striking my father on the head: "Be quiet, old man! Be quiet!"

My father no longer felt the club's blows; I did. And yet I did not react. I let the SS beat my father, I left him alone in the clutches of death. Worse: I was angry with him for having been noisy, for having cried, for provoking the wrath of the SS.

"Eliezer! Eliezer! Come, don't leave me alone . . ."

His voice had reached me from so far away, from so close. But I had not moved.

I shall never forgive myself.

Nor shall I ever forgive the world for having pushed me against the wall, for having turned me into a stranger, for having awakened in me the basest, most primitive instincts.

His last word had been my name. A summons. And I had not responded.

In the Yiddish version, the narrative does not end with the image in the mirror, but with a gloomy meditation on the present:

And now, scarcely ten years after Buchenwald, I realize that the world forgets quickly. Today, Germany is a sovereign state. The German Army has been resuscitated. Ilse Koch, the notorious sadistic monster of Buchenwald, was allowed to have children and live happily ever after . . . War criminals stroll through the streets of Hamburg and Munich. The past seems to have been erased, relegated to oblivion.

Today, there are anti-Semites in Germany, France, and even the United States who tell the world that the "story" of six million assassinated Jews is nothing but a hoax, and many people, not knowing any better, may well believe them, if not today then tomorrow or the day after . . .

I am not so naïve as to believe that this slim volume will

change the course of history or shake the conscience of the world.

Books no longer have the power they once did.

Those who kept silent yesterday will remain silent tomorrow.

THE READER would be entitled to ask: Why this new translation, since the earlier one has been around for forty-five years? If it is not faithful or not good enough, why did I wait so long to replace it with one better and closer to the original?

In response, I would say only that back then, I was an unknown writer who was just getting started. My English was far from good. When my British publisher told me that he had found a translator, I was pleased. I later read the translation and it seemed all right. I never reread it. Since then, many of my other works have been translated by Marion, my wife, who knows my voice and how to transmit it better than anyone else. I am fortunate: when Farrar, Straus and Giroux asked her to prepare a new translation, she accepted. I am convinced that the readers will appreciate her work. In fact, as a result of her rigorous editing, I was able to correct and revise a number of important details.

And so, as I reread this text written so long ago, I am glad that I did not wait any longer. And yet, I still wonder: Have I used the right words? I speak of my first night *over there*. The discovery of the reality inside the barbed wire. The warnings of a "veteran" inmate, counseling my father and myself to lie about our ages: my father was to make himself younger, and I older. The selection. The march toward the chimneys looming in the distance under an indifferent sky. The infants thrown into fiery ditches . . . I did not say that they *were alive*, but that was what I thought. But then I convinced myself: no, they were dead, otherwise I surely would have lost my mind. And yet fellow inmates also saw them; they *were alive* when they were thrown into the flames. Historians, among them Telford Taylor, confirmed it. And yet somehow I did not lose my mind.

BEFORE CONCLUDING this introduction, I believe it important to emphasize how strongly I feel that books, just like people, have a destiny. Some invite sorrow, others joy, some both.

Earlier, I described the difficulties encountered by *Night* before its publication in French, forty-seven years ago. Despite overwhelmingly favorable reviews, the book sold poorly. The subject was considered morbid and interested no one. If a rabbi happened to mention the book in his sermon, there were always people ready to complain that it was senseless to "burden our children with the tragedies of the Jewish past."

Since then, much has changed. *Night* has been received in ways that I never expected. Today, students in high schools and colleges in the United States and elsewhere read it as part of their curriculum.

How to explain this phenomenon? First of all, there has been a powerful change in the public's attitude. In the fifties and sixties, adults born before or during World War II showed a careless and patronizing indifference toward what is so inadequately called the Holocaust. That is no longer true.

Back then, few publishers had the courage to publish books on that subject.

Today, such works are on most book lists. The same is true in academia. Back then, few schools offered courses on the subject. Today, many do. And, strangely, those courses are particularly popular. The topic of Auschwitz has become part of mainstream culture. There are films, plays, novels, international conferences, exhibitions, annual ceremonies with the participation of the nation's officialdom. The most striking example is that of the United States Holocaust Memorial Museum in Washington, D.C.; it has received more than twenty-two million visitors since its inauguration in 1993.

This may be because the public knows that the number of survivors is shrinking daily, and is fascinated by the idea of sharing memories that will soon be lost. For in the end, it is all about memory, its sources and its magnitude, and, of course, its consequences.

For the survivor who chooses to testify, it is clear: his duty is to bear witness for the dead *and* for the living. He has no right to deprive future generations of a past that belongs to our collective memory. To forget would be not only dangerous but offensive; to forget the dead would be akin to killing them a second time.

SOMETIMES I AM ASKED if I know "the response to Auschwitz"; I answer that not only do I not know it, but that I don't even know if a tragedy of this magnitude *has* a response. What I do know is that there is "response" in responsibility. When we speak of this era of evil and darkness, so close and yet so distant, "responsibility" is the key word.

The witness has forced himself to testify. For the youth of today, for the children who will be born tomorrow. He does not want his past to become their future.

—ELIE WIESEL

Foreword by
François Mauriac

F OREIGN JOURNALISTS frequently come to see me. I am
wary of them, torn as I am between my desire to speak to
them freely and the fear of putting weapons into the
hands of interviewers whose attitude toward France I do not
know. During these encounters, I tend to be on my guard.

That particular morning, the young Jew who came to inter-
view me on behalf of a Tel Aviv daily won me over from the first
moment. Our conversation very quickly became more personal.
Soon I was sharing with him memories from the time of the Occupation. It is not always the events that have touched us personally
that affect us the most. I confided to my young visitor that nothing I had witnessed during that dark period had marked me as
deeply as the image of cattle cars filled with Jewish children at
the Austerlitz train station . . . Yet I did not even see them with
my own eyes. It was my wife who described them to me, still under the shock of the horror she had felt. At that time we knew
nothing about the Nazis' extermination methods. And who could
have imagined such things! But these lambs torn from their
mothers, that was an outrage far beyond anything we would have

thought possible. I believe that on that day, I first became aware of the mystery of the iniquity whose exposure marked the end of an era and the beginning of another. The dream conceived by Western man in the eighteenth century, whose dawn he thought he had glimpsed in 1789, and which until August 2, 1914, had become stronger with the advent of the Enlightenment and scientific discoveries—that dream finally vanished for me before those trainloads of small children. And yet I was still thousands of miles away from imagining that these children were destined to feed the gas chambers and crematoria.

This, then, was what I probably told this journalist. And when I said, with a sigh, "I have thought of these children so many times!" he told me, "I was one of them." He was one of them! He had seen his mother, a beloved little sister, and most of his family, except his father and two other sisters, disappear in a furnace fueled by living creatures. As for his father, the boy had to witness his martyrdom day after day and, finally, his agony and death. And what a death! The circumstances of it are narrated in this book, and I shall allow readers—who should be as numerous as those reading *The Diary of Anne Frank*—to discover them for themselves as well as by what miracle the child himself escaped.

I maintain therefore that this personal record, coming as it does after so many others and describing an abomination such as we might have thought no longer had any secrets for us, is different, distinct, and unique nevertheless. The fate of the Jews of the small town in Transylvania called Sighet; their blindness as they confronted a destiny from which they would still have had time to flee; the inconceivable passivity with which they surrendered to it, deaf to the warnings and pleas of a witness who, having escaped the massacre, relates to them what he has seen with his own eyes, but they refuse to believe him and call him a madman—this set of circumstances would surely have sufficed to inspire a book to which, I believe, no other can be compared.

It is, however, another aspect of this extraordinary book that has held my attention. The child who tells us his story here was one of God's chosen. From the time he began to think, he lived only for God, studying the Talmud, eager to be initiated into the Kabbalah, wholly dedicated to the Almighty. Have we ever considered the consequence of a less visible, less striking abomination, yet the worst of all, for those of us who have faith: the death of God in the soul of a child who suddenly faces absolute evil?

Let us try to imagine what goes on in his mind as his eyes watch rings of black smoke unfurl in the sky, smoke that emanates from the furnaces into which his little sister and his mother had been thrown after thousands of other victims:

> Never shall I forget that night, the first night in camp, that turned my life into one long night seven times sealed.
>
> Never shall I forget that smoke.
>
> Never shall I forget the small faces of the children whose bodies I saw transformed into smoke under a silent sky.
>
> Never shall I forget those flames that consumed my faith forever.
>
> Never shall I forget the nocturnal silence that deprived me for all eternity of the desire to live.
>
> Never shall I forget those moments that murdered my God and my soul and turned my dreams to ashes.
>
> Never shall I forget those things, even were I condemned to live as long as God Himself.
>
> Never.

It was then that I understood what had first appealed to me about this young Jew: the gaze of a Lazarus risen from the dead yet still held captive in the somber regions into which he had strayed, stumbling over desecrated corpses. For him, Nietzsche's cry articulated an almost physical reality: God is dead, the God of love, of gentleness and consolation, the God of Abraham, Isaac, and Jacob had, under the watchful gaze of this child, vanished forever into the smoke of the human holocaust demanded by the Race, the most voracious of all idols.

And how many devout Jews endured such a death? On that most horrible day, even among all those other bad days, when the child witnessed the hanging (yes!) of another child who, he tells us, had the face of a sad angel, he heard someone behind him groan:

> "For God's sake, where is God?"
> And from within me, I heard a voice answer:
> "Where He is? This is where—hanging here from this gallows."

On the last day of the Jewish year, the child is present at the solemn ceremony of Rosh Hashanah. He hears thousands of slaves cry out in unison, "Blessed be the Almighty!" Not so long ago, he too would have knelt down, and with such worship, such awe, such love! But this day, he does not kneel, he stands. The human creature, humiliated and offended in ways that are inconceivable to the mind or the heart, defies the blind and deaf divinity.

> I no longer pleaded for anything. I was no longer able to lament. On the contrary, I felt very strong. I was the accuser, God the accused. My eyes had opened and I was alone, terribly alone in a world without God, without man. Without love or mercy. I was nothing but ashes now, but I felt myself to be stronger than this

Almighty to whom my life had been bound for so long. In the midst of these men assembled for prayer, I felt like an observer, a stranger.

And I, who believe that God is love, what answer was there to give my young interlocutor whose dark eyes still held the reflection of the angelic sadness that had appeared one day on the face of a hanged child? What did I say to him? Did I speak to him of that other Jew, this crucified brother who perhaps resembled him and whose cross conquered the world? Did I explain to him that what had been a stumbling block for *his* faith had become a cornerstone for *mine*? And that the connection between the cross and human suffering remains, in my view, the key to the unfathomable mystery in which the faith of his childhood was lost? And yet, Zion has risen up again out of the crematoria and the slaughterhouses. The Jewish nation has been resurrected from among its thousands of dead. It is they who have given it new life. We do not know the worth of one single drop of blood, one single tear. All is grace. If the Almighty is the Almighty, the last word for each of us belongs to Him. That is what I should have said to the Jewish child. But all I could do was embrace him and weep.

T HEY CALLED HIM Moishe the Beadle, as if his entire life he had never had a surname. He was the jack-of-all-trades in a Hasidic house of prayer, a *shtibl*. The Jews of Sighet—the little town in Transylvania where I spent my childhood—were fond of him. He was poor and lived in utter penury. As a rule, our townspeople, while they did help the needy, did not particularly like them. Moishe the Beadle was the exception. He stayed out of people's way. His presence bothered no one. He had mastered the art of rendering himself insignificant, invisible.

Physically, he was as awkward as a clown. His waiflike shyness made people smile. As for me, I liked his wide, dreamy eyes, gazing off into the distance. He spoke little. He sang, or rather he chanted, and the few snatches I caught here and there spoke of divine suffering, of the Shekhinah in Exile, where, according to Kabbalah, it awaits its redemption linked to that of man.

I met him in 1941. I was almost thirteen and deeply observant. By day I studied Talmud and by night I would run to the synagogue to weep over the destruction of the Temple.

One day I asked my father to find me a master who could guide me in my studies of Kabbalah. "You are too young for that. Maimonides tells us that one must be thirty before venturing into the world of mysticism, a world fraught with peril. First you must study the basic subjects, those you are able to comprehend."

My father was a cultured man, rather unsentimental. He rarely displayed his feelings, not even within his family, and was more involved with the welfare of others than with that of his own kin. The Jewish community of Sighet held him in highest esteem; his advice on public and even private matters was frequently sought. There were four of us children. Hilda, the eldest; then Bea; I was the third and the only son; Tzipora was the youngest.

My parents ran a store. Hilda and Bea helped with the work. As for me, my place was in the house of study, or so they said.

"There are no Kabbalists in Sighet," my father would often tell me.

He wanted to drive the idea of studying Kabbalah from my mind. In vain. I succeeded on my own in finding a master for myself in the person of Moishe the Beadle.

He had watched me one day as I prayed at dusk.

"Why do you cry when you pray?" he asked, as though he knew me well.

"I don't know," I answered, troubled.

I had never asked myself that question. I cried because . . . because something inside me felt the need to cry. That was all I knew.

"Why do you pray?" he asked after a moment.

Why did I pray? Strange question. Why did I live? Why did I breathe?

"I don't know," I told him, even more troubled and ill at ease. "I don't know."

From that day on, I saw him often. He explained to me, with

great emphasis, that every question possessed a power that was lost in the answer . . .

Man comes closer to God through the questions he asks Him, he liked to say. Therein lies true dialogue. Man asks and God replies. But we don't understand His replies. We cannot understand them. Because they dwell in the depths of our souls and remain there until we die. The real answers, Eliezer, you will find only within yourself.

"And why do you pray, Moishe?" I asked him.

"I pray to the God within me for the strength to ask Him the real questions."

We spoke that way almost every evening, remaining in the synagogue long after all the faithful had gone, sitting in the semi-darkness where only a few half-burnt candles provided a flickering light.

One evening, I told him how unhappy I was not to be able to find in Sighet a master to teach me the Zohar, the Kabbalistic works, the secrets of Jewish mysticism. He smiled indulgently. After a long silence, he said, "There are a thousand and one gates allowing entry into the orchard of mystical truth. Every human being has his own gate. He must not err and wish to enter the orchard through a gate other than his own. That would present a danger not only for the one entering but also for those who are already inside."

And Moishe the Beadle, the poorest of the poor of Sighet, spoke to me for hours on end about the Kabbalah's revelations and its mysteries. Thus began my initiation. Together we would read, over and over again, the same page of the Zohar. Not to learn it by heart but to discover within the very essence of divinity.

And in the course of those evenings I became convinced that Moishe the Beadle would help me enter eternity, into that time when question and answer would become ONE.

AND THEN, one day all foreign Jews were expelled from Sighet. And Moishe the Beadle was a foreigner.

Crammed into cattle cars by the Hungarian police, they cried silently. Standing on the station platform, we too were crying. The train disappeared over the horizon; all that was left was thick, dirty smoke.

Behind me, someone said, sighing, "What do you expect? That's war . . ."

The deportees were quickly forgotten. A few days after they left, it was rumored that they were in Galicia, working, and even that they were content with their fate.

Days went by. Then weeks and months. Life was normal again. A calm, reassuring wind blew through our homes. The shopkeepers were doing good business, the students lived among their books, and the children played in the streets.

One day, as I was about to enter the synagogue, I saw Moishe the Beadle sitting on a bench near the entrance.

He told me what had happened to him and his companions. The train with the deportees had crossed the Hungarian border and, once in Polish territory, had been taken over by the Gestapo. The train had stopped. The Jews were ordered to get off and onto waiting trucks. The trucks headed toward a forest. There everybody was ordered to get out. They were forced to dig huge trenches. When they had finished their work, the men from the Gestapo began theirs. Without passion or haste, they shot their prisoners, who were forced to approach the trench one by one and offer their necks. Infants were tossed into the air and used as targets for the machine guns. This took place in the Galician forest, near Kolomay. How had he, Moishe the Beadle, been able to escape? By a miracle. He was wounded in the leg and left for dead . . .

Day after day, night after night, he went from one Jewish house to the next, telling his story and that of Malka, the young girl who lay dying for three days, and that of Tobie, the tailor who begged to die before his sons were killed.

Moishe was not the same. The joy in his eyes was gone. He no longer sang. He no longer mentioned either God or Kabbalah. He spoke only of what he had seen. But people not only refused to believe his tales, they refused to listen. Some even insinuated that he only wanted their pity, that he was imagining things. Others flatly said that he had gone mad.

As for Moishe, he wept and pleaded:

"Jews, listen to me! That's all I ask of you. No money. No pity. Just listen to me!" he kept shouting in synagogue, between the prayer at dusk and the evening prayer.

Even I did not believe him. I often sat with him, after services, and listened to his tales, trying to understand his grief. But all I felt was pity.

"They think I'm mad," he whispered, and tears, like drops of wax, flowed from his eyes.

Once, I asked him the question: "Why do you want people to believe you so much? In your place I would not care whether they believed me or not . . ."

He closed his eyes, as if to escape time.

"You don't understand," he said in despair. "You cannot understand. I was saved miraculously. I succeeded in coming back. Where did I get my strength? I wanted to return to Sighet to describe to you my death so that you might ready yourselves while there is still time. Life? I no longer care to live. I am alone. But I wanted to come back to warn you. Only no one is listening to me . . ."

This was toward the end of 1942.

Thereafter, life seemed normal once again. London radio, which we listened to every evening, announced encouraging news: the daily bombings of Germany and Stalingrad, the preparation of the Second Front. And so we, the Jews of Sighet, waited for better days that surely were soon to come.

I continued to devote myself to my studies, Talmud during the day and Kabbalah at night. My father took care of his business and the community. My grandfather came to spend Rosh Hashanah with us so as to attend the services of the celebrated Rebbe of Borsche. My mother was beginning to think it was high time to find an appropriate match for Hilda.

Thus passed the year 1943.

SPRING 1944. Splendid news from the Russian Front. There could no longer be any doubt: Germany would be defeated. It was only a matter of time, months or weeks, perhaps.

The trees were in bloom. It was a year like so many others, with its spring, its engagements, its weddings, and its births.

The people were saying, "The Red Army is advancing with giant strides . . . Hitler will not be able to harm us, even if he wants to . . ."

Yes, we even doubted his resolve to exterminate us.

Annihilate an entire people? Wipe out a population dispersed throughout so many nations? So many millions of people! By what means? In the middle of the twentieth century!

And thus my elders concerned themselves with all manner of things—strategy, diplomacy, politics, and Zionism—but not with their own fate.

Even Moishe the Beadle had fallen silent. He was weary of talking. He would drift through synagogue or through the streets, hunched over, eyes cast down, avoiding people's gaze.

In those days it was still possible to buy emigration certificates to Palestine. I had asked my father to sell everything, to liquidate everything, and to leave.

"I am too old, my son," he answered. "Too old to start a new life. Too old to start from scratch in some distant land . . ."

Budapest radio announced that the Fascist party had seized power. The regent Miklós Horthy was forced to ask a leader of the pro-Nazi *Nyilas* party to form a new government.

Yet we still were not worried. Of course we had heard of the Fascists, but it was all in the abstract. It meant nothing more to us than a change of ministry.

The next day brought really disquieting news: German troops had penetrated Hungarian territory with the government's approval.

Finally, people began to worry in earnest. One of my friends, Moishe Chaim Berkowitz, returned from the capital for Passover and told us, "The Jews of Budapest live in an atmosphere of fear and terror. Anti-Semitic acts take place every day, in the streets, on the trains. The Fascists attack Jewish stores, synagogues. The situation is becoming very serious . . ."

The news spread through Sighet like wildfire. Soon that was all people talked about. But not for long. Optimism soon revived: The Germans will not come this far. They will stay in Budapest. For strategic reasons, for political reasons . . .

In less than three days, German Army vehicles made their appearance on our streets.

ANGUISH. German soldiers—with their steel helmets and their death's-head emblem. Still, our first impressions of the Germans were rather reassuring. The officers were billeted in private homes, even in Jewish homes. Their attitude toward their hosts was distant but polite. They never demanded the impossible, made no offensive remarks, and sometimes even smiled at the lady of the house. A German officer lodged in the Kahns' house across the street from us. We were told he was a charming man, calm, likable, and polite. Three days after he moved in, he brought Mrs. Kahn a box of chocolates. The optimists were jubilant: "Well? What did we tell you? You wouldn't believe us. There they are, *your* Germans. What do you say now? Where is their famous cruelty?"

The Germans were already in our town, the Fascists were already in power, the verdict was already out—and the Jews of Sighet were still smiling.

THE EIGHT DAYS of Passover.

The weather was sublime. My mother was busy in the kitchen. The synagogues were no longer open. People gathered in private homes: no need to provoke the Germans.

Almost every rabbi's home became a house of prayer.

We drank, we ate, we sang. The Bible commands us to rejoice during the eight days of celebration, but our hearts were not in it. We wished the holiday would end so as not to have to pretend.

On the seventh day of Passover, the curtain finally rose: the Germans arrested the leaders of the Jewish community.

From that moment on, everything happened very quickly. The race toward death had begun.

First edict: Jews were prohibited from leaving their residences for three days, under penalty of death.

Moishe the Beadle came running to our house.

"I warned you," he shouted. And left without waiting for a response.

The same day, the Hungarian police burst into every Jewish home in town: a Jew was henceforth forbidden to own gold, jewelry, or any valuables. Everything had to be handed over to the authorities, under penalty of death. My father went down to the cellar and buried our savings.

As for my mother, she went on tending to the many chores in the house. Sometimes she would stop and gaze at us in silence.

Three days later, a new decree: every Jew had to wear the yellow star.

Some prominent members of the community came to consult with my father, who had connections at the upper levels of the Hungarian police; they wanted to know what he thought of the situation. My father's view was that it was not all bleak, or perhaps he just did not want to discourage the others, to throw salt on their wounds:

"The yellow star? So what? It's not lethal . . ."

(Poor Father! Of what then did you die?)

But new edicts were already being issued. We no longer had the right to frequent restaurants or cafés, to travel by rail, to attend synagogue, to be on the streets after six o'clock in the evening.

Then came the ghettos.

TWO GHETTOS were created in Sighet. A large one in the center of town occupied four streets, and another smaller one extended over several alleyways on the outskirts of town. The street we lived on, Serpent Street, was in the first ghetto. We therefore could remain in our house. But, as it occupied a corner, the windows facing the street outside the ghetto had to be sealed. We gave some of our rooms to relatives who had been driven out of their homes.

Little by little life returned to "normal." The barbed wire that encircled us like a wall did not fill us with real fear. In fact, we felt this was not a bad thing; we were entirely among ourselves. A small Jewish republic . . . A Jewish Council was appointed, as well as a Jewish police force, a welfare agency, a labor committee, a health agency—a whole governmental apparatus.

People thought this was a good thing. We would no longer have to look at all those hostile faces, endure those hate-filled stares. No more fear. No more anguish. We would live among Jews, among brothers . . .

Of course, there still were unpleasant moments. Every day, the Germans came looking for men to load coal into the military trains. Volunteers for this kind of work were few. But apart from that, the atmosphere was oddly peaceful and reassuring.

Most people thought that we would remain in the ghetto until the end of the war, until the arrival of the Red Army. Afterward everything would be as before. The ghetto was ruled by neither German nor Jew; it was ruled by delusion.

SOME TWO WEEKS before Shavuot. A sunny spring day, people strolled seemingly carefree through the crowded streets. They exchanged cheerful greetings. Children played games, rolling hazelnuts on the sidewalks. Some schoolmates and I were in Ezra Malik's garden studying a Talmudic treatise.

Night fell. Some twenty people had gathered in our courtyard. My father was sharing some anecdotes and holding forth on his opinion of the situation. He was a good storyteller.

Suddenly, the gate opened, and Stern, a former shopkeeper who now was a policeman, entered and took my father aside. Despite the growing darkness, I could see my father turn pale.

"What's wrong?" we asked.

"I don't know. I have been summoned to a special meeting of the Council. Something must have happened."

The story he had interrupted would remain unfinished.

"I'm going right now," he said. "I'll return as soon as possible. I'll tell you everything. Wait for me."

We were ready to wait as long as necessary. The courtyard turned into something like an antechamber to an operating room. We stood, waiting for the door to open. Neighbors, hearing the rumors, had joined us. We stared at our watches. Time had slowed down. What was the meaning of such a long session?

"I have a bad feeling," said my mother. "This afternoon I saw new faces in the ghetto. Two German officers, I believe they were Gestapo. Since we've been here, we have not seen a single officer . . ."

It was close to midnight. Nobody felt like going to sleep, though some people briefly went to check on their homes. Others left but asked to be called as soon as my father returned.

At last, the door opened and he appeared. His face was drained of color. He was quickly surrounded.

"Tell us. Tell us what's happening! Say something . . ."

At that moment, we were so anxious to hear something encouraging, a few words telling us that there was nothing to worry about, that the meeting had been routine, just a review of welfare and health problems . . . But one glance at my father's face left no doubt.

"The news is terrible," he said at last. And then one word: "Transports."

The ghetto was to be liquidated entirely. Departures were to take place street by street, starting the next day.

We wanted to know everything, every detail. We were stunned, yet we wanted to fully absorb the bitter news.

"Where will they take us?"

That was a secret. A secret for all, except one: the president of the Jewish Council. But he would not tell, or *could* not tell. The Gestapo had threatened to shoot him if he talked.

"There are rumors," my father said, his voice breaking, "that we are being taken somewhere in Hungary to work in the brick factories. It seems that here, we are too close to the front . . ."

After a moment's silence, he added:

"Each of us will be allowed to bring his personal belongings. A backpack, some food, a few items of clothing. Nothing else."

Again, heavy silence.

"Go and wake the neighbors," said my father. "They must get ready . . ."

The shadows around me roused themselves as if from a deep sleep and left silently in every direction.

FOR A MOMENT, we remained alone. Suddenly Batia Reich, a relative who lived with us, entered the room: "Someone is knocking at the sealed window, the one that faces outside!"

It was only after the war that I found out who had knocked that night. It was an inspector of the Hungarian police, a friend of my father's. Before we entered the ghetto, he had told us, "Don't worry. I'll warn you if there is danger." Had he been able to speak to us that night, we might still have been able to flee . . . But by the time we succeeded in opening the window, it was too late. There was nobody outside.

THE GHETTO was awake. One after the other, the lights were going on behind the windows.

I went into the house of one of my father's friends. I woke the head of the household, a man with a gray beard and the gaze of a dreamer. His back was hunched over from untold nights spent studying.

"Get up, sir, get up! You must ready yourself for the journey. Tomorrow you will be expelled, you and your family, you and all the other Jews. Where to? Please don't ask me, sir, don't ask questions. God alone could answer you. For heaven's sake, get up . . ."

He had no idea what I was talking about. He probably thought I had lost my mind.

"What are you saying? Get ready for the journey? What journey? Why? What is happening? Have you gone mad?"

Half asleep, he was staring at me, his eyes filled with terror, as though he expected me to burst out laughing and tell him to go back to bed. To sleep. To dream. That nothing had happened. It was all in jest . . .

My throat was dry and the words were choking me, paralyzing my lips. There was nothing else to say.

At last he understood. He got out of bed and began to dress, automatically. Then he went over to the bed where his wife lay sleeping and with infinite tenderness touched her forehead. She opened her eyes and it seemed to me that a smile crossed her lips. Then he went to wake his two children. They woke with a start, torn from their dreams. I fled.

Time went by quickly. It was already four o'clock in the morning. My father was running right and left, exhausted, consoling friends, checking with the Jewish Council just in case the order had been rescinded. To the last moment, people clung to hope.

The women were boiling eggs, roasting meat, preparing cakes, sewing backpacks. The children were wandering about aimlessly, not knowing what to do with themselves to stay out of the way of the grown-ups.

Our backyard looked like a marketplace. Valuable objects, precious rugs, silver candlesticks, Bibles and other ritual objects were strewn over the dusty grounds—pitiful relics that seemed never to have had a home. All this under a magnificent blue sky.

By eight o'clock in the morning, weariness had settled into our veins, our limbs, our brains, like molten lead. I was in the midst of prayer when suddenly there was shouting in the streets. I quickly unwound my phylacteries and ran to the window. Hungarian police had entered the ghetto and were yelling in the street nearby.

"All Jews, outside! Hurry!"

They were followed by Jewish police, who, their voices breaking, told us:

"The time has come . . . you must leave all this . . ."

The Hungarian police used their rifle butts, their clubs to indiscriminately strike old men and women, children and cripples.

One by one, the houses emptied and the streets filled with people carrying bundles. By ten o'clock, everyone was outside. The police were taking roll calls, once, twice, twenty times. The heat was oppressive. Sweat streamed from people's faces and bodies.

Children were crying for water.

Water! There was water close by inside the houses, the backyards, but it was forbidden to break rank.

"Water, Mother, I am thirsty!"

Some of the Jewish police surreptitiously went to fill a few jugs. My sisters and I were still allowed to move about, as we were destined for the last convoy, and so we helped as best we could.

AT LAST, at one o'clock in the afternoon came the signal to leave.

There was joy, yes, joy. People must have thought there could be no greater torment in God's hell than that of being stranded here, on the sidewalk, among the bundles, in the middle of the street under a blazing sun. Anything seemed preferable to that. They began to walk without another glance at the abandoned streets, the dead, empty houses, the gardens, the tombstones . . .

On everyone's back, there was a sack. In everyone's eyes, tears and distress. Slowly, heavily, the procession advanced toward the gate of the ghetto.

And there I was, on the sidewalk, watching them file past, unable to move. Here came the Chief Rabbi, hunched over, his face strange looking without a beard, a bundle on his back. His very presence in the procession was enough to make the scene seem surreal. It was like a page torn from a book, a historical novel, perhaps, dealing with the captivity in Babylon or the Spanish Inquisition.

They passed me by, one after the other, my teachers, my friends, the others, some of whom I had once feared, some of whom I had found ridiculous, all those whose lives I had shared for years. There they went, defeated, their bundles, their lives in tow, having left behind their homes, their childhood.

They passed me by, like beaten dogs, with never a glance in my direction. They must have envied me.

The procession disappeared around the corner. A few steps more and they were beyond the ghetto walls.

The street resembled fairgrounds deserted in haste. There was a little of everything: suitcases, briefcases, bags, knives, dishes, banknotes, papers, faded portraits. All the things one planned to take along and finally left behind. They had ceased to matter.

Open rooms everywhere. Gaping doors and windows looked out into the void. It all belonged to everyone since it no longer belonged to anyone. It was there for the taking. An open tomb.

A summer sun.

WE HAD SPENT the day without food. But we were not really hungry. We were exhausted.

My father had accompanied the deportees as far as the ghetto's gate. They first had been herded through the main synagogue, where they were thoroughly searched to make sure they were not carrying away gold, silver, or any other valuables. There had been incidents of hysteria and harsh blows.

"When will it be our turn?" I asked my father.

"The day after tomorrow. Unless . . . things work out. A miracle, perhaps . . ."

Where were the people being taken? Did anyone know yet? No, the secret was well kept.

Night had fallen. That evening, we went to bed early. My father said:

"Sleep peacefully, children. Nothing will happen until the day after tomorrow, Tuesday."

Monday went by like a small summer cloud, like a dream in the first hours of dawn.

Intent on preparing our backpacks, on baking breads and cakes, we no longer thought about anything. The verdict had been delivered.

That evening, our mother made us go to bed early. To conserve our strength, she said.

It was to be the last night spent in our house.

I was up at dawn. I wanted to have time to pray before leaving.

My father had risen before all of us, to seek information in town. He returned around eight o'clock. Good news: we were not leaving town today; we were only moving to the small ghetto. That is where we were to wait for the last transport. We would be the last to leave.

At nine o'clock, the previous Sunday's scenes were repeated. Policemen wielding clubs were shouting:

"All Jews outside!"

We were ready. I went out first. I did not want to look at my parents' faces. I did not want to break into tears. We remained sitting in the middle of the street, like the others two days earlier. The same hellish sun. The same thirst. Only there was no one left to bring us water.

I looked at my house in which I had spent years seeking my God, fasting to hasten the coming of the Messiah, imagining what my life would be like later. Yet I felt little sadness. My mind was empty.

"Get up! Roll call!"

We stood. We were counted. We sat down. We got up again. Over and over. We waited impatiently to be taken away. What were they waiting for? Finally, the order came:

"Forward! March!"

My father was crying. It was the first time I saw him cry. I had never thought it possible. As for my mother, she was walking, her face a mask, without a word, deep in thought. I looked at my little sister, Tzipora, her blond hair neatly combed, her red coat over her arm: a little girl of seven. On her back a bag too heavy for her. She was clenching her teeth; she already knew it was useless to complain. Here and there, the police were lashing out with their clubs: "Faster!" I had no strength left. The journey had just begun and I already felt so weak . . .

"Faster! Faster! Move, you lazy good-for-nothings!" the Hungarian police were screaming.

That was when I began to hate them, and my hatred remains our only link today. They were our first oppressors. They were the first faces of hell and death.

They ordered us to run. We began to run. Who would have thought that we were so strong? From behind their windows, from behind their shutters, our fellow citizens watched as we passed.

We finally arrived at our destination. Throwing down our bundles, we dropped to the ground:

"Oh God, Master of the Universe, in your infinite compassion, have mercy on us . . ."

THE SMALL GHETTO. Only three days ago, people were living here. People who owned the things we were using now. They had been expelled. And we had already forgotten all about them.

The chaos was even greater here than in the large ghetto. Its inhabitants evidently had been caught by surprise. I visited the rooms that had been occupied by my Uncle Mendel's family. On the table, a half-finished bowl of soup. A platter of dough waiting to be baked. Everywhere on the floor there were books. Had my uncle meant to take them along?

We settled in. (What a word!) I went looking for wood, my sisters lit a fire. Despite her fatigue, my mother began to prepare a meal.

We cannot give up, we cannot give up, she kept repeating.

People's morale was not so bad: we were beginning to get used to the situation. There were those who even voiced optimism. The Germans were running out of time to expel us, they argued . . . Tragically for those who had already been deported, it would be too late. As for us, chances were that we would be allowed to go on with our miserable little lives until the end of the war.

The ghetto was not guarded. One could enter and leave as one pleased. Maria, our former maid, came to see us. Sobbing, she begged us to come with her to her village where she had prepared a safe shelter.

My father wouldn't hear of it. He told me and my big sisters, "If you wish, go there. I shall stay here with your mother and the little one . . ."

Naturally, we refused to be separated.

NIGHT. No one was praying for the night to pass quickly. The stars were but sparks of the immense conflagration that was consuming us. Were this conflagration to be extinguished one day, nothing would be left in the sky but extinct stars and unseeing eyes.

There was nothing else to do but to go to bed, in the beds of those who had moved on. We needed to rest, to gather our strength.

At daybreak, the gloom had lifted. The mood was more confident. There were those who said:

"Who knows, they may be sending us away for our own good. The front is getting closer, we shall soon hear the guns. And then surely the civilian population will be evacuated . . ."

"They worry lest we join the partisans . . ."

"As far as I'm concerned, this whole business of deportation is nothing but a big farce. Don't laugh. They just want to steal our valuables and jewelry. They know that it has all been buried and that they will have to dig to find it; so much easier to do when the owners are on vacation . . ."

On vacation!

This kind of talk that nobody believed helped pass the time. The few days we spent here went by pleasantly enough, in relative calm. People rather got along. There no longer was any distinction between rich and poor, notables and the others; we were all people condemned to the same fate—still unknown.

SATURDAY, the day of rest, was the day chosen for our expulsion.

The night before, we had sat down to the traditional Friday night meal. We had said the customary blessings over the bread and the wine and swallowed the food in silence. We sensed that we were gathered around the familial table for the last time. I spent that night going over memories and ideas and was unable to fall asleep.

At dawn, we were in the street, ready to leave. This time, there were no Hungarian police. It had been agreed that the Jewish Council would handle everything by itself.

Our convoy headed toward the main synagogue. The town seemed deserted. But behind the shutters, our friends of yesterday were probably waiting for the moment when they could loot our homes.

The synagogue resembled a large railroad station: baggage and tears. The altar was shattered, the wall coverings shredded, the walls themselves bare. There were so many of us, we could hardly breathe. The twenty-four hours we spent there were horrendous. The men were downstairs, the women upstairs. It was Saturday—the Sabbath—and it was as though we were there to attend services. Forbidden to go outside, people relieved themselves in a corner.

The next morning, we walked toward the station, where a convoy of cattle cars was waiting. The Hungarian police made us climb into the cars, eighty persons in each one. They handed us some bread, a few pails of water. They checked the bars on the windows to make sure they would not come loose. The cars were sealed. One person was placed in charge of every car: if someone managed to escape, that person would be shot.

Two Gestapo officers strolled down the length of the platform. They were all smiles; all things considered, it had gone very smoothly.

A prolonged whistle pierced the air. The wheels began to grind. We were on our way.

L YING DOWN was not an option, nor could we all sit down. We decided to take turns sitting. There was little air. The lucky ones found themselves near a window; they could watch the blooming countryside flit by.

After two days of travel, thirst became intolerable, as did the heat.

Freed of normal constraints, some of the young let go of their inhibitions and, under cover of darkness, caressed one another, without any thought of others, alone in the world. The others pretended not to notice.

There was still some food left. But we never ate enough to satisfy our hunger. Our principle was to economize, to save for tomorrow. Tomorrow could be worse yet.

The train stopped in Kaschau, a small town on the Czechoslovakian border. We realized then that we were not staying in Hungary. Our eyes opened. Too late.

The door of the car slid aside. A German officer stepped in accompanied by a Hungarian lieutenant, acting as his interpreter.

"From this moment on, you are under the authority of the

German Army. Anyone who still owns gold, silver, or watches must hand them over now. Anyone who will be found to have kept any of these will be shot on the spot. Secondly, anyone who is ill should report to the hospital car. That's all."

The Hungarian lieutenant went around with a basket and retrieved the last possessions from those who chose not to go on tasting the bitterness of fear.

"There are eighty of you in the car," the German officer added. "If anyone goes missing, you will all be shot, like dogs."

The two disappeared. The doors clanked shut. We had fallen into the trap, up to our necks. The doors were nailed, the way back irrevocably cut off. The world had become a hermetically sealed cattle car.

THERE WAS A WOMAN among us, a certain Mrs. Schächter. She was in her fifties and her ten-year-old son was with her, crouched in a corner. Her husband and two older sons had been deported with the first transport, by mistake. The separation had totally shattered her.

I knew her well. A quiet, tense woman with piercing eyes, she had been a frequent guest in our house. Her husband was a pious man who spent most of his days and nights in the house of study. It was she who supported the family.

Mrs. Schächter had lost her mind. On the first day of the journey, she had already begun to moan. She kept asking why she had been separated from her family. Later, her sobs and screams became hysterical.

On the third night, as we were sleeping, some of us sitting, huddled against each other, some of us standing, a piercing cry broke the silence:

"Fire! I see a fire! I see a fire!"

There was a moment of panic. Who had screamed? It was Mrs. Schächter. Standing in the middle of the car, in the faint light filtering through the windows, she looked like a withered tree in a field of wheat. She was howling, pointing through the window:

"Look! Look at this fire! This terrible fire! Have mercy on me!"

Some pressed against the bars to see. There was nothing. Only the darkness of night.

It took us a long time to recover from this harsh awakening. We were still trembling, and with every screech of the wheels, we felt the abyss opening beneath us. Unable to still our anguish, we tried to reassure each other:

"She is mad, poor woman . . ."

Someone had placed a damp rag on her forehead. But she nevertheless continued to scream:

"Fire! I see a fire!"

Her little boy was crying, clinging to her skirt, trying to hold her hand:

"It's nothing, Mother! There's nothing there . . . Please sit down . . ." He pained me even more than did his mother's cries.

Some of the women tried to calm her:

"You'll see, you'll find your husband and sons again . . . In a few days . . ."

She continued to scream and sob fitfully.

"Jews, listen to me," she cried. "I see a fire! I see flames, huge flames!"

It was as though she were possessed by some evil spirit.

We tried to reason with her, more to calm ourselves, to catch our breath, than to soothe her:

"She is hallucinating because she is thirsty, poor woman . . . That's why she speaks of flames devouring her . . ."

But it was all in vain. Our terror could no longer be contained.

Our nerves had reached a breaking point. Our very skin was aching. It was as though madness had infected all of us. We gave up. A few young men forced her to sit down, then bound and gagged her.

Silence fell again. The small boy sat next to his mother, crying. I started to breathe normally again as I listened to the rhythmic pounding of the wheels on the tracks as the train raced through the night. We could begin to doze again, to rest, to dream . . .

And so an hour or two passed. Another scream jolted us. The woman had broken free of her bonds and was shouting louder than before:

"Look at the fire! Look at the flames! Flames everywhere . . ."

Once again, the young men bound and gagged her. When they actually struck her, people shouted their approval:

"Keep her quiet! Make that madwoman shut up. She's not the only one here . . ."

She received several blows to the head, blows that could have been lethal. Her son was clinging desperately to her, not uttering a word. He was no longer crying.

The night seemed endless. By daybreak, Mrs. Schächter had settled down. Crouching in her corner, her blank gaze fixed on some faraway place, she no longer saw us.

She remained like that all day, mute, absent, alone in the midst of us. Toward evening she began to shout again:

"The fire, over there!"

She was pointing somewhere in the distance, always the same place. No one felt like beating her anymore. The heat, the thirst, the stench, the lack of air, were suffocating us. Yet all that was nothing compared to her screams, which tore us apart. A few more days and all of us would have started to scream.

But we were pulling into a station. Someone near a window read to us:

"Auschwitz."

Nobody had ever heard that name.

THE TRAIN did not move again. The afternoon went by slowly. Then the doors of the wagon slid open. Two men were given permission to fetch water.

When they came back, they told us that they had learned, in exchange for a gold watch, that this was the final destination. We were to leave the train here. There was a labor camp on the site. The conditions were good. Families would not be separated. Only the young would work in the factories. The old and the sick would find work in the fields.

Confidence soared. Suddenly we felt free of the previous nights' terror. We gave thanks to God.

Mrs. Schächter remained huddled in her corner, mute, untouched by the optimism around her. Her little one was stroking her hand.

Dusk began to fill the wagon. We ate what was left of our food. At ten o'clock in the evening, we were all trying to find a position for a quick nap and soon we were dozing. Suddenly:

"Look at the fire! Look at the flames! Over there!"

With a start, we awoke and rushed to the window yet again. We had believed her, if only for an instant. But there was nothing outside but darkness. We returned to our places, shame in our souls but fear gnawing at us nevertheless. As she went on howling, she was struck again. Only with great difficulty did we succeed in quieting her down.

The man in charge of our wagon called out to a German officer strolling down the platform, asking him to have the sick woman moved to a hospital car.

"Patience," the German replied, "patience. She'll be taken there soon."

Around eleven o'clock, the train began to move again. We pressed against the windows. The convoy was rolling slowly. A quarter of an hour later, it began to slow down even more. Through the windows, we saw barbed wire; we understood that this was the camp.

We had forgotten Mrs. Schächter's existence. Suddenly there was a terrible scream:

"Jews, look! Look at the fire! Look at the flames!"

And as the train stopped, this time we saw flames rising from a tall chimney into a black sky.

Mrs. Schächter had fallen silent on her own. Mute again, indifferent, absent, she had returned to her corner.

We stared at the flames in the darkness. A wretched stench floated in the air. Abruptly, our doors opened. Strange-looking creatures, dressed in striped jackets and black pants, jumped into the wagon. Holding flashlights and sticks, they began to strike at us left and right, shouting:

"Everybody out! Leave everything inside. Hurry up!"

We jumped out. I glanced at Mrs. Schächter. Her little boy was still holding her hand.

In front of us, those flames. In the air, the smell of burning flesh. It must have been around midnight. We had arrived. In Birkenau.

THE BELOVED OBJECTS that we had carried with us from place to place were now left behind in the wagon and, with them, finally, our illusions.

Every few yards, there stood an SS man, his machine gun trained on us. Hand in hand we followed the throng.

An SS came toward us wielding a club. He commanded:

"Men to the left! Women to the right!"

Eight words spoken quietly, indifferently, without emotion. Eight simple, short words. Yet that was the moment when I left my mother. There was no time to think, and I already felt my father's hand press against mine: we were alone. In a fraction of a second I could see my mother, my sisters, move to the right. Tzipora was holding Mother's hand. I saw them walking farther and farther away; Mother was stroking my sister's blond hair, as if to protect her. And I walked on with my father, with the men. I didn't know that this was the moment in time and the place where I was leaving my mother and Tzipora forever. I kept walking, my father holding my hand.

Behind me, an old man fell to the ground. Nearby, an SS man replaced his revolver in its holster.

My hand tightened its grip on my father. All I could think of was not to lose him. Not to remain alone.

The SS officers gave the order.

"Form ranks of fives!"

There was a tumult. It was imperative to stay together.

"Hey, kid, how old are you?"

The man interrogating me was an inmate. I could not see his face, but his voice was weary and warm.

"Fifteen."

"No. You're eighteen."

"But I'm not," I said. "I'm fifteen."

"Fool. Listen to what *I* say."

Then he asked my father, who answered:

"I'm fifty."

"No." The man now sounded angry. "Not fifty. You're forty. Do you hear? Eighteen and forty."

He disappeared into the darkness. Another inmate appeared, unleashing a stream of invectives:

"Sons of bitches, why have you come here? Tell me, why?"

Someone dared to reply:

"What do you think? That we came here of our own free will? That we asked to come here?"

The other seemed ready to kill him:

"Shut up, you moron, or I'll tear you to pieces! You should have hanged yourselves rather than come here. Didn't you know what was in store for you here in Auschwitz? You didn't know? In 1944?"

True. We didn't know. Nobody had told us. He couldn't believe his ears. His tone became even harsher:

"Over there. Do you see the chimney over there? Do you see

it? And the flames, do you see them?" (Yes, we saw the flames.)
"Over there, that's where they will take you. Over there will be
your grave. You still don't understand? You sons of bitches. Don't
you understand anything? You will be burned! Burned to a cin-
der! Turned into ashes!"

His anger changed into fury. We stood stunned, petrified.
Could this be just a nightmare? An unimaginable nightmare?

I heard whispers around me:

"We must do something. We can't let them kill us like that,
like cattle in the slaughterhouse. We must revolt."

There were, among us, a few tough young men. They actually
had knives and were urging us to attack the armed guards. One of
them was muttering:

"Let the world learn about the existence of Auschwitz. Let
everybody find out about it while they still have a chance to escape . . ."

But the older men begged their sons not to be foolish:

"We mustn't give up hope, even now as the sword hangs over
our heads. So taught our sages . . ."

The wind of revolt died down. We continued to walk until we
came to a crossroads. Standing in the middle of it was, though I
didn't know it then, Dr. Mengele, the notorious Dr. Mengele. He
looked like the typical SS officer: a cruel, though not unintelli-
gent, face, complete with monocle. He was holding a conductor's
baton and was surrounded by officers. The baton was moving
constantly, sometimes to the right, sometimes to the left.

In no time, I stood before him.

"Your age?" he asked, perhaps trying to sound paternal.

"I'm eighteen." My voice was trembling.

"In good health?"

"Yes."

"Your profession?"

Tell him that I was a student?

"Farmer," I heard myself saying.

This conversation lasted no more than a few seconds. It seemed like an eternity.

The baton pointed to the left. I took half a step forward. I first wanted to see where they would send my father. Were he to have gone to the right, I would have run after him.

The baton, once more, moved to the left. A weight lifted from my heart.

We did not know, as yet, which was the better side, right or left, which road led to prison and which to the crematoria. Still, I was happy, I was near my father. Our procession continued slowly to move forward.

Another inmate came over to us:

"Satisfied?"

"Yes," someone answered.

"Poor devils, you are heading for the crematorium."

He seemed to be telling the truth. Not far from us, flames, huge flames, were rising from a ditch. Something was being burned there. A truck drew close and unloaded its hold: small children. Babies! Yes, I did see this, with my own eyes . . . children thrown into the flames. (Is it any wonder that ever since then, sleep tends to elude me?)

So that was where we were going. A little farther on, there was another, larger pit for adults.

I pinched myself: Was I still alive? Was I awake? How was it possible that men, women, and children were being burned and that the world kept silent? No. All this could not be real. A nightmare perhaps . . . Soon I would wake up with a start, my heart pounding, and find that I was back in the room of my childhood, with my books . . .

My father's voice tore me from my daydreams:

"What a shame, a shame that you did not go with your mother . . . I saw many children your age go with their mothers . . ."

His voice was terribly sad. I understood that he did not wish to see what they would do to me. He did not wish to see his only son go up in flames.

My forehead was covered with cold sweat. Still, I told him that I could not believe that human beings were being burned in our times; the world would never tolerate such crimes . . .

"The world? The world is not interested in us. Today, everything is possible, even the crematoria . . ." His voice broke.

"Father," I said. "If that is true, then I don't want to wait. I'll run into the electrified barbed wire. That would be easier than a slow death in the flames."

He didn't answer. He was weeping. His body was shaking. Everybody around us was weeping. Someone began to recite Kaddish, the prayer for the dead. I don't know whether, during the history of the Jewish people, men have ever before recited Kaddish for themselves.

"*Yisgadal, veyiskadash, shmey raba* . . . May His name be celebrated and sanctified . . ." whispered my father.

For the first time, I felt anger rising within me. Why should I sanctify His name? The Almighty, the eternal and terrible Master of the Universe, chose to be silent. What was there to thank Him for?

We continued our march. We were coming closer and closer to the pit, from which an infernal heat was rising. Twenty more steps. If I was going to kill myself, this was the time. Our column had only some fifteen steps to go. I bit my lips so that my father would not hear my teeth chattering. Ten more steps. Eight. Seven. We were walking slowly, as one follows a hearse, our own funeral procession. Only four more steps. Three. There it was now, very close to us, the pit and its flames. I gathered all that remained of my strength in order to break rank and throw myself onto the barbed wire. Deep down, I was saying good-bye to my father, to the whole universe, and, against my will, I found myself whispering the words: "*Yisgadal, veyiskadash, shmey raba* . . . May His name be exalted and sanctified . . ." My heart was about to burst. There. I was face-to-face with the Angel of Death . . .

No. Two steps from the pit, we were ordered to turn left and herded into barracks.

I squeezed my father's hand. He said:

"Do you remember Mrs. Schächter, in the train?"

NEVER SHALL I FORGET that night, the first night in camp, that turned my life into one long night seven times sealed.

Never shall I forget that smoke.

Never shall I forget the small faces of the children whose bodies I saw transformed into smoke under a silent sky.

Never shall I forget those flames that consumed my faith forever.

Never shall I forget the nocturnal silence that deprived me for all eternity of the desire to live.

Never shall I forget those moments that murdered my God and my soul and turned my dreams to ashes.

Never shall I forget those things, even were I condemned to live as long as God Himself.

Never.

THE BARRACK we had been assigned to was very long. On the roof, a few bluish skylights. I thought: This is what the antechamber of hell must look like. So many crazed men, so much shouting, so much brutality.

Dozens of inmates were there to receive us, sticks in hand, striking anywhere, anyone, without reason. The orders came:

"Strip! Hurry up! *Raus!* Hold on only to your belt and your shoes . . ."

Our clothes were to be thrown on the floor at the back of the barrack. There was a pile there already. New suits, old ones, torn overcoats, rags. For us it meant true equality: nakedness. We trembled in the cold.

A few SS officers wandered through the room, looking for strong men. If vigor was that appreciated, perhaps one should try to appear sturdy? My father thought the opposite. Better not to draw attention. (We later found out that he had been right. Those who were selected that day were incorporated into the Sonder-Kommando, the Kommando working in the crematoria. Béla Katz, the son of an important merchant of my town, had arrived in Birkenau with the first transport, one week ahead of us. When he found out that we were there, he succeeded in slipping us a note. He told us that having been chosen because of his strength, he had been forced to place his own father's body into the furnace.)

The blows continued to rain on us:

"To the barber!"

Belt and shoes in hand, I let myself be dragged along to the barbers. Their clippers tore out our hair, shaved every hair on our bodies. My head was buzzing; the same thought surfacing over and over: not to be separated from my father.

Freed from the barbers' clutches, we began to wander about the crowd, finding friends, acquaintances. Every encounter filled us with joy—yes, joy: Thank God! You are still alive!

Some were crying. They used whatever strength they had left to cry. Why had they let themselves be brought here? Why didn't they die in their beds? Their words were interspersed with sobs.

Suddenly someone threw his arms around me in a hug: Yehiel, the Sigheter rebbe's brother. He was weeping bitterly. I thought he was crying with joy at still being alive.

"Don't cry, Yehiel," I said. "Don't waste your tears . . ."

"Not cry? We're on the threshold of death. Soon, we shall be inside . . . Do you understand? Inside. How could I not cry?"

I watched darkness fade through the bluish skylights in the roof. I no longer was afraid. I was overcome by fatigue.

The absent no longer entered our thoughts. One spoke of them—who knows what happened to them?—but their fate was not on our minds. We were incapable of thinking. Our senses were numbed, everything was fading into a fog. We no longer clung to anything. The instincts of self-preservation, of self-defense, of pride, had all deserted us. In one terrifying moment of lucidity, I thought of us as damned souls wandering through the void, souls condemned to wander through space until the end of time, seeking redemption, seeking oblivion, without any hope of finding either.

AROUND FIVE O'CLOCK in the morning, we were expelled from the barrack. The Kapos were beating us again, but I no longer felt the pain. A glacial wind was enveloping us. We were naked, holding our shoes and belts. An order:

"Run!" And we ran. After a few minutes of running, a new barrack.

A barrel of foul-smelling liquid stood by the door. Disinfection. Everybody soaked in it. Then came a hot shower. All very fast. As we left the showers, we were chased outside. And ordered to run some more. Another barrack: the storeroom. Very long tables. Mountains of prison garb. As we ran, they threw the clothes at us: pants, jackets, shirts . . .

In a few seconds, we had ceased to be men. Had the situation not been so tragic, we might have laughed. We looked pretty strange! Meir Katz, a colossus, wore a child's pants, and Stern, a skinny little fellow, was floundering in a huge jacket. We immediately started to switch.

I glanced over at my father. How changed he looked! His eyes were veiled. I wanted to tell him something, but I didn't know what.

The night had passed completely. The morning star shone in the sky. I too had become a different person. The student of Talmud, the child I was, had been consumed by the flames. All that was left was a shape that resembled me. My soul had been invaded—and devoured—by a black flame.

So many events had taken place in just a few hours that I had completely lost all notion of time. When had we left our homes? And the ghetto? And the train? Only a week ago? One night? *One single night?*

How long had we been standing in the freezing wind? One hour? A single hour? Sixty minutes?

Surely it was a dream.

NOT FAR FROM US, prisoners were at work. Some were digging holes, others were carrying sand. None as much as glanced at us. We were withered trees in the heart of the desert. Behind me, people were talking. I had no desire to listen to what they were saying, or to know who was speaking and what about. Nobody dared raise his voice, even though there was no guard around. We whispered. Perhaps because of the thick smoke that poisoned the air and stung the throat.

We were herded into yet another barrack, inside the Gypsy camp. We fell into ranks of five.

"And now, stop moving!"

There was no floor. A roof and four walls. Our feet sank into the mud.

Again, the waiting. I fell asleep standing up. I dreamed of a bed, of my mother's hand on my face. I woke: I was standing, my feet in the mud. Some people collapsed, sliding into the mud. Others shouted:

"Are you crazy? We were told to stand. Do you want to get us all in trouble?"

As if all the troubles in the world were not already upon us.

Little by little, we all sat down in the mud. But we had to get up whenever a Kapo came in to check if, by chance, somebody had a new pair of shoes. If so, we had to hand them over. No use protesting; the blows multiplied and, in the end, one still had to hand them over.

I had new shoes myself. But as they were covered with a thick coat of mud, they had not been noticed. I thanked God, in an improvised prayer, for having created mud in His infinite and wondrous universe.

Suddenly, the silence became more oppressive. An SS officer had come in and, with him, the smell of the Angel of Death. We stared at his fleshy lips. He harangued us from the center of the barrack:

"You are in a concentration camp. In Auschwitz . . ."

A pause. He was observing the effect his words had produced. His face remains in my memory to this day. A tall man, in his thirties, crime written all over his forehead and his gaze. He looked at us as one would a pack of leprous dogs clinging to life.

"Remember," he went on. "Remember it always, let it be graven in your memories. You are in Auschwitz. And Auschwitz is not a convalescent home. It is a concentration camp. Here, you must work. If you don't you will go straight to the chimney. To the crematorium. Work or crematorium—the choice is yours."

We had already lived through a lot that night. We thought that nothing could frighten us anymore. But his harsh words sent shivers through us. The word "chimney" here was not an abstraction; it floated in the air, mingled with the smoke. It was, perhaps, the only word that had a real meaning in this place. He left the barrack. The Kapos arrived, shouting:

"All specialists—locksmiths, carpenters, electricians, watchmakers—one step forward!"

The rest of us were transferred to yet another barrack, this one of stone. We had permission to sit down. A Gypsy inmate was in charge.

My father suddenly had a colic attack. He got up and asked politely, in German, "Excuse me . . . Could you tell me where the toilets are located?"

The Gypsy stared at him for a long time, from head to toe. As if he wished to ascertain that the person addressing him was actually a creature of flesh and bone, a human being with a body and a belly. Then, as if waking from a deep sleep, he slapped my father with such force that he fell down and then crawled back to his place on all fours.

I stood petrified. What had happened to me? My father had just been struck, in front of me, and I had not even blinked. I had watched and kept silent. Only yesterday, I would have dug my nails into this criminal's flesh. Had I changed that much? So fast? Remorse began to gnaw at me. All I could think was: I shall never forgive them for this. My father must have guessed my thoughts, because he whispered in my ear:

"It doesn't hurt." His cheek still bore the red mark of the hand.

"EVERYBODY outside!"

A dozen or so Gypsies had come to join our guard. The clubs and whips were cracking around me. My feet were running on their own. I tried to protect myself from the blows by hiding behind others. It was spring. The sun was shining.

"Fall in, five by five!"

The prisoners I had glimpsed that morning were working nearby. No guard in sight, only the chimney's shadow . . . Lulled by the sunshine and my dreams, I felt someone pulling at my sleeve. It was my father: "Come on, son."

We marched. Gates opened and closed. We continued to march between the barbed wire. At every step, white signs with black skulls looked down on us. The inscription: WARNING! DANGER OF DEATH. What irony. Was there here a single place where one was *not* in danger of death?

The Gypsies had stopped next to a barrack. They were replaced by SS men, who encircled us with machine guns and police dogs.

The march had lasted half an hour. Looking around me, I noticed that the barbed wire was behind us. We had left the camp.

It was a beautiful day in May. The fragrances of spring were in the air. The sun was setting.

But no sooner had we taken a few more steps than we saw the barbed wire of another camp. This one had an iron gate with the overhead inscription: ARBEIT MACHT FREI. Work makes you free.

Auschwitz.

FIRST IMPRESSION: better than Birkenau. Cement buildings with two stories rather than wooden barracks. Little gardens here and there. We were led toward one of those "blocks." Seated on the ground by the entrance, we began to wait again. From time to time somebody was allowed to go in. These were the showers, a compulsory routine. Going from one camp to the other, several times a day, we had, each time, to go through them.

After the hot shower, we stood shivering in the darkness. Our clothes had been left behind; we had been promised other clothes.

Around midnight, we were told to run.

"Faster!" yelled our guards. "The faster you run, the faster you'll get to go to sleep."

After a few minutes of racing madly, we came to a new block. The man in charge was waiting. He was a young Pole, who was smiling at us. He began to talk to us and, despite our weariness, we listened attentively.

"Comrades, you are now in the concentration camp Auschwitz. Ahead of you lies a long road paved with suffering. Don't lose hope. You have already eluded the worst danger: the selection. Therefore, muster your strength and keep your faith. We shall all see the day of liberation. Have faith in life, a thousand times faith. By driving out despair, you will move away from death. Hell does not last forever . . . And now, here is a prayer, or rather a piece of advice: let there be camaraderie among you. We are all brothers and share the same fate. The same smoke hovers over all our heads. Help each other. That is the only way to survive. And now, enough said, you are tired. Listen: you are in Block 17; I am responsible for keeping order here. Anyone with a complaint may come to see me. That is all. Go to sleep. Two people to a bunk. Good night."

Those were the first human words.

NO SOONER HAD WE CLIMBED into our bunks than we fell into a deep sleep.

The next morning, the "veteran" inmates treated us without brutality. We went to wash. We were given new clothing. They brought us black coffee.

We left the block around ten o'clock so it could be cleaned. Outside, the sun warmed us. Our morale was much improved. A good night's sleep had done its work. Friends met, exchanged a few sentences. We spoke of everything without ever mentioning those who had disappeared. The prevailing opinion was that the war was about to end.

At about noon, we were brought some soup, one bowl of thick soup for each of us. I was terribly hungry, yet I refused to touch it. I was still the spoiled child of long ago. My father swallowed my ration.

We then had a short nap in the shade of the block. That SS officer in the muddy barrack must have been lying: Auschwitz was, after all, a convalescent home . . .

In the afternoon, they made us line up. Three prisoners brought a table and some medical instruments. We were told to roll up our left sleeves and file past the table. The three "veteran" prisoners, needles in hand, tattooed numbers on our left arms. I became A-7713. From then on, I had no other name.

At dusk, a roll call. The work Kommandos had returned. The orchestra played military marches near the camp entrance. Tens of thousands of inmates stood in rows while the SS checked their numbers.

After the roll call, the prisoners from all the blocks dispersed, looking for friends, relatives, or neighbors among the arrivals of the latest convoy.

DAYS WENT BY. In the mornings: black coffee. At midday: soup. By the third day, I was eagerly eating any kind of soup . . . At six o'clock in the afternoon: roll call. Followed by bread with something. At nine o'clock: bedtime.

We had already been in Auschwitz for eight days. It was after roll call. We stood waiting for the bell announcing its end. Suddenly I noticed someone passing between the rows. I heard him ask:

"Who among you is Wiesel from Sighet?"

The person looking for us was a small fellow with spectacles in a wizened face. My father answered:

"That's me. Wiesel from Sighet."

The fellow's eyes narrowed. He took a long look at my father.

"You don't know me? . . . You don't recognize me. I'm your relative, Stein. Already forgotten? Stein. Stein from Antwerp. Reizel's husband. Your wife was Reizel's aunt . . . She often wrote to us . . . and such letters!"

My father had not recognized him. He must have barely known him, always being up to his neck in communal affairs and not knowledgeable in family matters. He was always elsewhere, lost in thought. (Once, a cousin came to see us in Sighet. She had stayed at our house and eaten at our table for two weeks before my father noticed her presence for the first time.) No, he did not remember Stein. I recognized him right away. I had known Reizel, his wife, before she had left for Belgium.

He told us that he had been deported in 1942. He said, "I heard people say that a transport had arrived from your region and I came to look for you. I thought you might have some news of Reizel and my two small boys who stayed in Antwerp . . ."

I knew nothing about them . . . Since 1940, my mother had not received a single letter from them. But I lied:

"Yes, my mother did hear from them. Reizel is fine. So are the children . . ."

He was weeping with joy. He would have liked to stay longer, to learn more details, to soak up the good news, but an SS was heading in our direction and he had to go, telling us that he would come back the next day.

The bell announced that we were dismissed. We went to fetch the evening meal: bread and margarine. I was terribly hungry and swallowed my ration on the spot. My father told me, "You mustn't eat all at once. Tomorrow is another day . . ."

But seeing that his advice had come too late, and that there was nothing left of my ration, he didn't even start his own.

"Me, I'm not hungry," he said.

WE REMAINED IN AUSCHWITZ for three weeks. We had nothing to do. We slept a lot. In the afternoon and at night.

Our one goal was to avoid the transports, to stay here as long as possible. It wasn't difficult; it was enough never to sign up as a skilled worker. The unskilled were kept until the end.

At the start of the third week, our *Blockälteste* was removed; he was judged too humane. The new one was ferocious and his aides were veritable monsters. The good days were over. We began to wonder whether it wouldn't be better to let ourselves be chosen for the next transport.

Stein, our relative from Antwerp, continued to visit us and, from time to time, he would bring a half portion of bread:

"Here, this is for you, Eliezer."

Every time he came, tears would roll down his icy cheeks. He would often say to my father:

"Take care of your son. He is very weak, very dehydrated. Take care of yourselves, you must avoid selection. Eat! Anything, anytime. Eat all you can. The weak don't last very long around here . . ."

And he himself was so thin, so withered, so weak . . .

"The only thing that keeps me alive," he kept saying, "is to know that Reizel and the little ones are still alive. Were it not for them, I would give up."

One evening, he came to see us, his face radiant.

"A transport just arrived from Antwerp. I shall go to see them tomorrow. Surely they will have news . . ."

He left.

We never saw him again. He had been given the news. The *real* news.

EVENINGS, AS WE LAY on our cots, we sometimes tried to sing a few Hasidic melodies. Akiba Drumer would break our hearts with his deep, grave voice.

Some of the men spoke of God: His mysterious ways, the sins of the Jewish people, and the redemption to come. As for me, I had ceased to pray. I concurred with Job! I was not denying His existence, but I doubted His absolute justice.

Akiba Drumer said:

"God is testing us. He wants to see whether we are capable of overcoming our base instincts, of killing the Satan within ourselves. We have no right to despair. And if He punishes us mercilessly, it is a sign that He loves us that much more . . ."

Hersh Genud, well versed in Kabbalah, spoke of the end of the world and the coming of the Messiah.

From time to time, in the middle of all that talk, a thought crossed my mind: Where is Mother right now . . . and Tzipora . . .

"Mother is still a young woman," my father once said. "She must be in a labor camp. And Tzipora, she is a big girl now. She too must be in a camp . . ."

How we would have liked to believe that. We pretended, for what if one of us still *did* believe?

ALL THE SKILLED WORKERS had already been sent to other camps. Only about a hundred of us, simple laborers, were left.

"Today, it's your turn," announced the block secretary. "You are leaving with the next transport."

At ten o'clock, we were handed our daily ration of bread. A dozen or so SS surrounded us. At the gate, the sign proclaimed that work meant freedom. We were counted. And there we were, in the countryside, on a sunny road. In the sky, a few small white clouds.

We were walking slowly. The guards were in no hurry. We were glad of it. As we were passing through some of the villages, many Germans watched us, showing no surprise. No doubt they had seen quite a few of these processions . . .

On the way, we saw some young German girls. The guards began to tease them. The girls giggled. They allowed themselves to be kissed and tickled, bursting with laughter. They all were laughing, joking, and passing love notes to one another. At least, during all that time, we endured neither shouting nor blows.

After four hours, we arrived at the new camp: Buna. The iron gate closed behind us.

T HE CAMP looked as though it had been through an epidemic: empty and dead. Only a few "well-dressed" inmates were wandering between the blocks.

Of course, we first had to pass through the showers. The head of the camp joined us there. He was a stocky man with big shoulders, the neck of a bull, thick lips, and curly hair. He gave an impression of kindness. From time to time, a smile would linger in his gray-blue eyes. Our convoy included a few ten- and twelve-year-olds. The officer took an interest in them and gave orders to bring them food.

We were given new clothing and settled in two tents. We were to wait there until we could be incorporated into work Kommandos. Then we would be assigned to a block.

In the evening, the Kommandos returned from the work yards. Roll call. We began looking for people we knew, asking the "veterans" which work Kommandos were the best and which block one should try to enter. All the inmates agreed:

"Buna is a very good camp. One can hold one's own here. The

most important thing is not to be assigned to the construction
Kommando . . ."

As if we had a choice . . .

Our tent leader was a German. An assassin's face, fleshy lips,
hands resembling a wolf's paws. The camp's food had agreed
with him; he could hardly move, he was so fat. Like the head
of the camp, he liked children. Immediately after our arrival, he
had bread brought for them, some soup and margarine. (In fact,
this affection was not entirely altruistic; there existed here a veritable traffic of children among homosexuals, I learned later.) He
told us:

"You will stay with me for three days in quarantine. Afterward,
you will go to work. Tomorrow: medical checkup."

One of his aides—a tough-looking boy with shifty eyes—came
over to me:

"Would you like to get into a good Kommando?"

"Of course. But on one condition: I want to stay with my
father."

"All right," he said. "I can arrange it. For a pittance: your
shoes. I'll give you another pair."

I refused to give him my shoes. They were all I had left.

"I'll also give you a ration of bread with some margarine . . ."

He liked my shoes; I would not let him have them. Later,
they were taken from me anyway. In exchange for nothing, that
time.

The medical checkup took place outside, early in the morning, before three doctors seated on a bench.

The first hardly examined me. He just asked:

"Are you in good health?"

Who would have dared to admit the opposite?

On the other hand, the dentist seemed more conscientious: he
asked me to open my mouth wide. In fact, he was not looking for

decay but for gold teeth. Those who had gold in their mouths were listed by their number. I did have a gold crown.

The first three days went by quickly. On the fourth day, as we stood in front of our tent, the Kapos appeared. Each one began to choose the men he liked:

"You . . . you . . . you . . ." They pointed their fingers, the way one might choose cattle, or merchandise.

We followed our Kapo, a young man. He made us halt at the door of the first block, near the entrance to the camp. This was the orchestra's block. He motioned us inside. We were surprised; what had we to do with music?

The orchestra was playing a military march, always the same. Dozens of Kommandos were marching off, in step, to the work yards. The Kapos were beating the time:

"Left, right, left, right."

SS officers, pen in hand, recorded the number of men leaving. The orchestra continued to play the same march until the last Kommando had passed. Then the conductor's baton stopped moving and the orchestra fell silent. The Kapo yelled:

"Fall in!"

We fell into ranks of five, with the musicians. We left the camp without music but in step. We still had the march in our ears.

"Left, right, left, right!"

We struck up conversations with our neighbors, the musicians. Almost all of them were Jews. Juliek, a Pole with eyeglasses and a cynical smile in a pale face. Louis, a native of Holland, a well-known violinist. He complained that they would not let him play Beethoven; Jews were not allowed to play German music. Hans, the young man from Berlin, was full of wit. The foreman was a Pole: Franek, a former student in Warsaw.

Juliek explained to me, "We work in a warehouse of electrical materials, not far from here. The work is neither difficult nor dangerous. Only Idek, the Kapo, occasionally has fits of madness, and then you'd better stay out of his way."

"You are lucky, little fellow," said Hans, smiling. "You fell into a good Kommando . . ."

Ten minutes later, we stood in front of the warehouse. A German employee, a civilian, the *Meister*, came to meet us. He paid as much attention to us as would a shopkeeper receiving a delivery of old rags.

Our comrades were right. The work was not difficult. Sitting on the ground, we counted bolts, bulbs, and various small electrical parts. The Kapo launched into a lengthy explanation of the importance of this work, warning us that anyone who proved to be lazy would be held accountable. My new comrades reassured me:

"Don't worry. He has to say this because of the *Meister*."

There were many Polish civilians here and a few Frenchwomen as well. The women silently greeted the musicians with their eyes.

Franek, the foreman, assigned me to a corner:

"Don't kill yourself. There's no hurry. But watch out. Don't let an SS catch you."

"Please, sir . . . I'd like to be near my father."

"All right. Your father will work here, next to you."

We were lucky.

Two boys came to join our group: Yossi and Tibi, two brothers from Czechoslovakia whose parents had been exterminated in Birkenau. They lived for each other, body and soul.

They quickly became my friends. Having once belonged to a Zionist youth organization, they knew countless Hebrew songs. And so we would sometimes hum melodies evoking the gentle waters of the Jordan River and the majestic sanctity of Jerusalem. We also spoke often about Palestine. Their parents, like mine, had not had the courage to sell everything and emigrate while there was still time. We decided that if we were allowed to live until the Liberation, we would not stay another day in Europe. We would board the first ship to Haifa.

Still lost in his Kabbalistic dreams, Akiba Drumer had discovered a verse from the Bible which, translated into numbers, made it possible for him to predict Redemption in the weeks to come.

WE HAD LEFT THE TENTS for the musicians' block. We now were entitled to a blanket, a washbowl, and a bar of soap. The *Blockälteste* was a German Jew.

It was good to have a Jew as your leader. His name was Alphonse. A young man with a startlingly wizened face. He was totally devoted to defending "his" block. Whenever he could, he would "organize" a cauldron of soup for the young, for the weak, for all those who dreamed more of an extra portion of food than of liberty.

ONE DAY, when we had just returned from the warehouse, I was summoned by the block secretary:

"A-7713?"

"That's me."

"After your meal, you'll go to see the dentist."

"But . . . I don't have a toothache . . ."

"After your meal. Without fail."

I went to the infirmary block. Some twenty prisoners were waiting in line at the entrance. It didn't take long to learn the reason for our summons: our gold teeth were to be extracted.

The dentist, a Jew from Czechoslovakia, had a face not unlike a death mask. When he opened his mouth, one had a ghastly vision of yellow, rotten teeth. Seated in the chair, I asked meekly:

"What are you going to do, sir?"

"I shall remove your gold crown, that's all," he said, clearly indifferent.

I thought of pretending to be sick:

"Couldn't you wait a few days, sir? I don't feel well, I have a fever . . ."

He wrinkled his brow, thought for a moment, and took my pulse.

"All right, son. Come back to see me when you feel better. But don't wait for me to call you!"

I went back to see him a week later. With the same excuse: I still was not feeling better. He did not seem surprised, and I don't know whether he believed me. Yet he most likely was pleased that I had come back on my own, as I had promised. He granted me a further delay.

A few days after my visit, the dentist's office was shut down. He had been thrown into prison and was about to be hanged. It appeared that he had been dealing in the prisoners' gold teeth for his own benefit. I felt no pity for him. In fact, I was pleased with what was happening to him: my gold crown was safe. It could be useful to me one day, to buy something, some bread or even time to live. At that moment in time, all that mattered to me was my daily bowl of soup, my crust of stale bread. The bread, the soup—those were my entire life. I was nothing but a body. Perhaps even less: a famished stomach. The stomach alone was measuring time.

IN THE WAREHOUSE, I often worked next to a young Frenchwoman. We did not speak: she did not know German and I did not understand French.

I thought she looked Jewish, though she passed for "Aryan." She was a forced labor inmate.

One day when Idek was venting his fury, I happened to cross his path. He threw himself on me like a wild beast, beating me in the chest, on my head, throwing me to the ground and picking me up again, crushing me with ever more violent blows, until I was covered in blood. As I bit my lips in order not to howl with pain, he must have mistaken my silence for defiance and so he continued to hit me harder and harder.

Abruptly, he calmed down and sent me back to work as if nothing had happened. As if we had taken part in a game in which both roles were of equal importance.

I dragged myself to my corner. I was aching all over. I felt a cool hand wiping the blood from my forehead. It was the French girl. She was smiling her mournful smile as she slipped me a crust of bread. She looked straight into my eyes. I knew she wanted to talk to me but that she was paralyzed with fear. She remained like that for some time, and then her face lit up and she said, in almost perfect German:

"Bite your lips, little brother . . . Don't cry. Keep your anger, your hate, for another day, for later. The day will come but not now . . . Wait. Clench your teeth and wait . . ."

MANY YEARS LATER, in Paris, I sat in the Métro, reading my newspaper. Across the aisle, a beautiful woman with dark hair and dreamy eyes. I had seen those eyes before.

"Madame, don't you recognize me?"

"I don't know you, sir."

"In 1944, you were in Poland, in Buna, weren't you?"

"Yes, but . . ."

"You worked in a depot, a warehouse for electrical parts . . ."

"Yes," she said, looking troubled. And then, after a moment of silence: "Wait . . . I do remember . . ."

"Idek, the Kapo . . . the young Jewish boy . . . your sweet words . . ."

We left the Métro together and sat down at a café terrace. We spent the whole evening reminiscing. Before parting, I said, "May I ask one more question?"

"I know what it is: Am I Jewish . . . ? Yes, I am. From an observant family. During the Occupation, I had false papers and passed as Aryan. And that was how I was assigned to a forced labor unit. When they deported me to Germany, I eluded being sent to a concentration camp. At the depot, nobody knew that I spoke German; it would have aroused suspicion. It was imprudent of me to say those few words to you, but I knew that you would not betray me . . ."

ANOTHER TIME we were loading diesel motors onto freight cars under the supervision of some German soldiers. Idek was on edge, he had trouble restraining himself. Suddenly, he exploded. The victim this time was my father.

"You old loafer!" he started yelling. "Is this what you call working?"

And he began beating him with an iron bar. At first, my father simply doubled over under the blows, but then he seemed to break in two like an old tree struck by lightning.

I had watched it all happening without moving. I kept silent. In fact, I thought of stealing away in order not to suffer the blows. What's more, if I felt anger at that moment, it was not directed at the Kapo but at my father. Why couldn't he have avoided Idek's wrath? That was what life in a concentration camp had made of me . . .

Franek, the foreman, one day noticed the gold crown in my mouth:

"Let me have your crown, kid."

I answered that I could not because without that crown I could no longer eat.

"For what they give you to eat, kid . . ."

I found another answer: my crown had been listed in the register during the medical checkup; this could mean trouble for us both.

"If you don't give me your crown, it will cost you much more!"

All of a sudden, this pleasant and intelligent young man had changed. His eyes were shining with greed. I told him that I needed to get my father's advice.

"Go ahead, kid, ask. But I want the answer by tomorrow."

When I mentioned it to my father, he hesitated. After a long silence, he said:

"No, my son. We cannot do this."

"He will seek revenge!"

"He won't dare, my son."

Unfortunately, Franek knew how to handle this; he knew my weak spot. My father had never served in the military and could not march in step. But here, whenever we moved from one place to another, it was in step. That presented Franek with the opportunity to torment him and, on a daily basis, to thrash him savagely. Left, right: he punched him. Left, right: he slapped him.

I decided to give my father lessons in marching in step, in keeping time. We began practicing in front of our block. I would command: "Left, right!" and my father would try.

The inmates made fun of us: "Look at the little officer, teaching the old man to march . . . Hey, little general, how many rations of bread does the old man give you for this?"

But my father did not make sufficient progress, and the blows continued to rain on him.

"So! You still don't know how to march in step, you old good-for-nothing?"

This went on for two weeks. It was untenable. We had to give in. That day, Franek burst into savage laughter:

"I knew it, I knew that I would win, kid. Better late than never. And because you made me wait, it will also cost you a ration of bread. A ration of bread for one of my pals, a famous dentist from Warsaw. To pay him for pulling out your crown."

"What? My ration of bread so that you can have *my* crown?"

Franek smiled.

"What would you like? That I break your teeth by smashing your face?"

That evening, in the latrines, the dentist from Warsaw pulled my crown with the help of a rusty spoon.

Franek became pleasant again. From time to time, he even gave me extra soup. But it didn't last long. Two weeks later, all the Poles were transferred to another camp. I had lost my crown for nothing.

A FEW DAYS BEFORE the Poles left, I had a novel experience.

It was on a Sunday morning. Our Kommando was not required to work that day. Only Idek would not hear of staying in the camp. We had to go to the depot. This sudden enthusiasm for work astonished us. At the depot, Idek entrusted us to Franek, saying, "Do what you like. But do something. Or else, you'll hear from me . . ."

And he disappeared.

We didn't know what to do. Tired of huddling on the ground, we each took turns strolling through the warehouse, in the hope of finding something, a piece of bread, perhaps, that a civilian might have forgotten there.

When I reached the back of the building, I heard sounds coming from a small adjoining room. I moved closer and had a glimpse of Idek and a young Polish girl, half naked, on a straw mat. Now I understood why Idek refused to leave us in the camp. He moved one hundred prisoners so that he could copulate with this girl! It struck me as terribly funny and I burst out laughing.

Idek jumped, turned and saw me, while the girl tried to cover her breasts. I wanted to run away, but my feet were nailed to the floor. Idek grabbed me by the throat.

Hissing at me, he threatened:

"Just you wait, kid . . . You will see what it costs to leave your work . . . You'll pay for this later . . . And now go back to your place . . ."

A HALF HOUR BEFORE the usual time to stop work, the Kapo assembled the entire Kommando. Roll call. Nobody understood what was going on. A roll call at this hour? Here? Only I knew. The Kapo made a short speech:

"An ordinary inmate does not have the right to mix into other people's affairs. One of you does not seem to have understood this point. I shall therefore try to make him understand clearly, once and for all."

I felt the sweat running down my back.

"A-7713!"

I stepped forward.

"A crate!" he ordered.

They brought a crate.

"Lie down on it! On your belly!"

I obeyed.

I no longer felt anything except the lashes of the whip.

"One! . . . Two! . . ." he was counting.

He took his time between lashes. Only the first really hurt. I heard him count:

"Ten . . . eleven! . . ."

His voice was calm and reached me as through a thick wall.

"Twenty-three . . ."

Two more, I thought, half unconscious.

The Kapo was waiting.

"Twenty-four . . . twenty-five!"

It was over. I had not realized it, but I had fainted. I came to when they doused me with cold water. I was still lying on the crate. In a blur, I could see the wet ground next to me. Then I heard someone yell. It had to be the Kapo. I began to distinguish what he was shouting:

"Stand up!"

I must have made some movement to get up, but I felt myself fall back on the crate. How I wanted to get up!

"Stand up!" He was yelling even more loudly.

If only I could answer him, if only I could tell him that I could not move. But my mouth would not open.

At Idek's command, two inmates lifted me and led me to him.

"Look me in the eye!"

I looked at him without seeing him. I was thinking of my father. He would be suffering more than I.

"Listen to me, you son of a swine!" said Idek coldly. "So much for your curiosity. You shall receive five times more if you dare tell anyone what you saw! Understood?"

I nodded, once, ten times, endlessly. As if my head had decided to say yes for all eternity.

ONE SUNDAY, as half of our group, including my father, was at work, the others, including me, took the opportunity to stay and rest.

At around ten o'clock, the sirens started to go off. Alert. The

Blockälteste gathered us inside the blocks, while the SS took refuge in the shelters. As it was relatively easy to escape during an alert—the guards left the watchtowers and the electric current in the barbed wire was cut—the standing order to the SS was to shoot anyone found outside his block.

In no time, the camp had the look of an abandoned ship. No living soul in the alleys. Next to the kitchen, two cauldrons of hot, steaming soup had been left untended. Two cauldrons of soup! Smack in the middle of the road, two cauldrons of soup with no one to guard them! A royal feast going to waste! Supreme temptation! Hundreds of eyes were looking at them, shining with desire. Two lambs with hundreds of wolves lying in wait for them. Two lambs without a shepherd, free for the taking. But who would dare?

Fear was greater than hunger. Suddenly, we saw the door of Block 37 open slightly. A man appeared, crawling snakelike in the direction of the cauldrons.

Hundreds of eyes were watching his every move. Hundreds of men were crawling with him, scraping their bodies with his on the stones. All hearts trembled, but mostly with envy. He was the one who had dared.

He reached the first cauldron. Hearts were pounding harder: he had succeeded. Jealousy devoured us, consumed us. We never thought to admire him. Poor hero committing suicide for a ration or two or more of soup . . . In our minds, he was already dead.

Lying on the ground near the cauldron, he was trying to lift himself to the cauldron's rim. Either out of weakness or out of fear, he remained there, undoubtedly to muster his strength. At last he succeeded in pulling himself up to the rim. For a second, he seemed to be looking at himself in the soup, looking for his ghostly reflection there. Then, for no apparent reason, he let out a terrible scream, a death rattle such as I had never heard before and, with open mouth, thrust his head toward the still steaming liquid. We jumped at the sound of the shot. Falling to the ground, his face stained by the soup, the man writhed a few seconds at the base of the cauldron, and then he was still.

That was when we began to hear the planes. Almost at the same moment, the barrack began to shake.

"They're bombing the Buna factory," someone shouted.

I anxiously thought of my father, who was at work. But I was glad nevertheless. To watch that factory go up in flames—what revenge! While we had heard some talk of German military defeats on the various fronts, we were not sure if they were credible. But today, this was real!

We were not afraid. And yet, if a bomb had fallen on the blocks, it would have claimed hundreds of inmates' lives. But we no longer feared death, in any event not this particular death. Every bomb that hit filled us with joy, gave us renewed confidence.

The raid lasted more than one hour. If only it could have gone on for ten times ten hours . . . Then, once more, there was silence. The last sound of the American plane dissipated in the wind and there we were, in our cemetery. On the horizon we saw a long trail of black smoke. The sirens began to wail again. The end of the alert.

Everyone came out of the blocks. We breathed in air filled with fire and smoke, and our eyes shone with hope. A bomb had landed in the middle of the camp, near the *Appelplatz*, the assembly point, but had not exploded. We had to dispose of it outside the camp.

The head of the camp, the *Lagerälteste*, accompanied by his aide and by the chief Kapo, were on an inspection tour of the camp. The raid had left traces of great fear on his face.

In the very center of the camp lay the body of the man with

soup stains on his face, the only victim. The cauldrons were carried back to the kitchen.

The SS were back at their posts in the watchtowers, behind their machine guns. Intermission was over.

An hour later, we saw the Kommandos returning, in step as always. Happily, I caught sight of my father.

"Several buildings were flattened," he said, "but the depot was not touched . . ."

In the afternoon, we cheerfully went to clear the ruins.

ONE WEEK LATER, as we returned from work, there, in the middle of the camp, in the *Appelplatz*, stood a black gallows.

We learned that soup would be distributed only after roll call, which lasted longer than usual. The orders were given more harshly than on other days, and there were strange vibrations in the air.

"Caps off!" the *Lagerälteste* suddenly shouted.

Ten thousand caps came off at once.

"Cover your heads!"

Ten thousand caps were back on our heads, at lightning speed.

The camp gate opened. An SS unit appeared and encircled us: one SS every three paces. The machine guns on the watchtowers were pointed toward the *Appelplatz*.

"They're expecting trouble," whispered Juliek.

Two SS were headed toward the solitary confinement cell. They came back, the condemned man between them. He was a young boy from Warsaw. An inmate with three years in concentration camps behind him. He was tall and strong, a giant compared to me.

His back was to the gallows, his face turned toward his judge, the head of the camp. He was pale but seemed more solemn than frightened. His manacled hands did not tremble. His eyes were coolly assessing the hundreds of SS guards, the thousands of prisoners surrounding him.

The *Lagerälteste* began to read the verdict, emphasizing every word:

"In the name of Reichsführer Himmler . . . prisoner number . . . stole during the air raid . . . according to the law . . . prisoner number . . . is condemned to death. Let this be a warning and an example to all prisoners."

Nobody moved.

I heard the pounding of my heart. The thousands of people who died daily in Auschwitz and Birkenau, in the crematoria, no longer troubled me. But this boy, leaning against his gallows, upset me deeply.

"This ceremony, will it be over soon? I'm hungry . . ." whispered Juliek.

At a sign of the *Lagerälteste*, the *Lagerkapo* stepped up to the condemned youth. He was assisted by two prisoners. In exchange for two bowls of soup.

The Kapo wanted to blindfold the youth, but he refused.

After what seemed like a long moment, the hangman put the rope around his neck. He was about to signal his aides to pull the chair from under the young man's feet when the latter shouted, in a strong and calm voice:

"Long live liberty! My curse on Germany! My curse! My—"

The executioner had completed his work.

Like a sword, the order cut through the air:

"Caps off!"

Ten thousand prisoners paid their respects.

"Cover your heads!"

Then the entire camp, block after block, filed past the hanged boy and stared at his extinguished eyes, the tongue hanging from his gaping mouth. The Kapos forced everyone to look him squarely in the face.

Afterward, we were given permission to go back to our block and have our meal.

I remember that on that evening, the soup tasted better than ever . . .

I WATCHED other hangings. I never saw a single victim weep. These withered bodies had long forgotten the bitter taste of tears.

Except once. The *Oberkapo* of the Fifty-second Cable Kommando was a Dutchman: a giant of a man, well over six feet. He had some seven hundred prisoners under his command, and they all loved him like a brother. Nobody had ever endured a blow or even an insult from him.

In his "service" was a young boy, a *pipel*, as they were called. This one had a delicate and beautiful face—an incredible sight in this camp.

(In Buna, the *pipel* were hated; they often displayed greater cruelty than their elders. I once saw one of them, a boy of thirteen, beat his father for not making his bed properly. As the old man quietly wept, the boy was yelling: "If you don't stop crying instantly, I will no longer bring you bread. Understood?" But the Dutchman's little servant was beloved by all. His was the face of an angel in distress.)

One day the power failed at the central electric plant in Buna. The Gestapo, summoned to inspect the damage, concluded that it was sabotage. They found a trail. It led to the block of the Dutch *Oberkapo*. And after a search, they found a significant quantity of weapons.

The *Oberkapo* was arrested on the spot. He was tortured for weeks on end, in vain. He gave no names. He was transferred to Auschwitz. And never heard from again.

But his young *pipel* remained behind, in solitary confinement. He too was tortured, but he too remained silent. The SS then condemned him to death, him and two other inmates who had been found to possess arms.

One day, as we returned from work, we saw three gallows, three black ravens, erected on the *Appelplatz*. Roll call. The SS surrounding us, machine guns aimed at us: the usual ritual. Three prisoners in chains—and, among them, the little *pipel*, the sad-eyed angel.

The SS seemed more preoccupied, more worried, than usual. To hang a child in front of thousands of onlookers was not a small matter. The head of the camp read the verdict. All eyes were on the child. He was pale, almost calm, but he was biting his lips as he stood in the shadow of the gallows.

This time, the *Lagerkapo* refused to act as executioner. Three SS took his place.

The three condemned prisoners together stepped onto the chairs. In unison, the nooses were placed around their necks.

"Long live liberty!" shouted the two men.

But the boy was silent.

"Where is merciful God, where is He?" someone behind me was asking.

At the signal, the three chairs were tipped over.

Total silence in the camp. On the horizon, the sun was setting.

"Caps off!" screamed the *Lagerälteste*. His voice quivered. As for the rest of us, we were weeping.

"Cover your heads!"

Then came the march past the victims. The two men were no longer alive. Their tongues were hanging out, swollen and bluish.

But the third rope was still moving: the child, too light, was still breathing . . .

And so he remained for more than half an hour, lingering between life and death, writhing before our eyes. And we were forced to look at him at close range. He was still alive when I passed him. His tongue was still red, his eyes not yet extinguished.

Behind me, I heard the same man asking:

"For God's sake, where is God?"

And from within me, I heard a voice answer:

"Where He is? This is where—hanging here from this gallows . . ."

That night, the soup tasted of corpses.

THE SUMMER was coming to an end. The Jewish year was almost over. On the eve of Rosh Hashanah, the last day of that cursed year, the entire camp was agitated and every one of us felt the tension. After all, this was a day unlike all others. The last day of the year. The word "last" had an odd ring to it. What if it really were the last day?

The evening meal was distributed, an especially thick soup, but nobody touched it. We wanted to wait until after prayer. On the *Appelplatz*, surrounded by electrified barbed wire, thousands of Jews, anguish on their faces, gathered in silence.

Night was falling rapidly. And more and more prisoners kept coming, from every block, suddenly able to overcome time and space, to will both into submission.

What are You, my God? I thought angrily. How do You compare to this stricken mass gathered to affirm to You their faith, their anger, their defiance? What does Your grandeur mean, Master of the Universe, in the face of all this cowardice, this decay, and this misery? Why do you go on troubling these poor people's wounded minds, their ailing bodies?

SOME TEN THOUSAND MEN had come to participate in a solemn service, including the *Blockälteste*, the Kapos, all bureaucrats in the service of Death.

"Blessed be the Almighty . . ."

The voice of the officiating inmate had just become audible. At first I thought it was the wind.

"Blessed be God's name . . ."

Thousands of lips repeated the benediction, bent over like trees in a storm.

Blessed be God's name?

Why, but why would I bless Him? Every fiber in me rebelled. Because He caused thousands of children to burn in His mass graves? Because He kept six crematoria working day and night, including Sabbath and the Holy Days? Because in His great might, He had created Auschwitz, Birkenau, Buna, and so many other factories of death? How could I say to Him: Blessed be Thou, Almighty, Master of the Universe, who chose us among all nations to be tortured day and night, to watch as our fathers, our mothers, our brothers end up in the furnaces? Praised be Thy Holy Name, for having chosen us to be slaughtered on Thine altar?

I listened as the inmate's voice rose; it was powerful yet broken, amid the weeping, the sobbing, the sighing of the entire "congregation":

"All the earth and universe are God's!"

He kept pausing, as though he lacked the strength to uncover the meaning beneath the text. The melody was stifled in his throat.

And I, the former mystic, was thinking: Yes, man is stronger, greater than God. When Adam and Eve deceived You, You chased them from paradise. When You were displeased by Noah's generation, You brought down the Flood. When Sodom lost Your favor, You caused the heavens to rain down fire and damnation. But look at these men whom You have betrayed, allowing them to be tortured, slaughtered, gassed, and burned, what do they do? They pray before You! They praise Your name!

"All of creation bears witness to the Greatness of God!"

In days gone by, Rosh Hashanah had dominated my life. I knew that my sins grieved the Almighty and so I pleaded for forgiveness. In those days, I fully believed that the salvation of the world depended on every one of my deeds, on every one of my prayers.

But now, I no longer pleaded for anything. I was no longer able to lament. On the contrary, I felt very strong. I was the accuser, God the accused. My eyes had opened and I was alone, terribly alone in a world without God, without man. Without love or mercy. I was nothing but ashes now, but I felt myself to be stronger than this Almighty to whom my life had been bound for so long. In the midst of these men assembled for prayer, I felt like an observer, a stranger.

The service ended with Kaddish. Each of us recited Kaddish for his parents, for his children, and for himself.

We remained standing in the *Appelplatz* for a long time, unable to detach ourselves from this surreal moment. Then came the time to go to sleep, and slowly the inmates returned to their blocks. I thought I heard them wishing each other a Happy New Year!

I ran to look for my father. At the same time I was afraid of having to wish him a happy year in which I no longer believed. He was leaning against the wall, bent shoulders sagging as if under a heavy load. I went up to him, took his hand and kissed it. I felt a tear on my hand. Whose was it? Mine? His? I said nothing.

Nor did he. Never before had we understood each other so clearly.

The sound of the bell brought us back to reality. We had to go to bed. We came back from very far away. I looked up at my father's face, trying to glimpse a smile or something like it on his stricken face. But there was nothing. Not the shadow of an expression. Defeat.

YOM KIPPUR. The Day of Atonement. Should we fast? The question was hotly debated. To fast could mean a more certain, more rapid death. In this place, we were always fasting. It was Yom Kippur year-round. But there were those who said we should fast, precisely because it was dangerous to do so. We needed to show God that even here, locked in hell, we were capable of singing His praises.

I did not fast. First of all, to please my father who had forbidden me to do so. And then, there was no longer any reason for me to fast. I no longer accepted God's silence. As I swallowed my ration of soup, I turned that act into a symbol of rebellion, of protest against Him.

And I nibbled on my crust of bread.

Deep inside me, I felt a great void opening.

THE SS OFFERED us a beautiful present for the new year.

We had just returned from work. As soon as we passed the camp's entrance, we sensed something out of the ordinary in the air. The roll call was shorter than usual. The evening soup was distributed at great speed, swallowed as quickly. We were anxious.

I was no longer in the same block as my father. They had

transferred me to another Kommando, the construction one, where twelve hours a day I hauled heavy slabs of stone. The head of my new block was a German Jew, small with piercing eyes. That evening he announced to us that henceforth no one was allowed to leave the block after the evening soup. A terrible word began to circulate soon thereafter: selection.

We knew what it meant. An SS would examine us. Whenever he found someone extremely frail—a "Muselman" was what we called those inmates—he would write down his number: good for the crematorium.

After the soup, we gathered between the bunks. The veterans told us: "You're lucky to have been brought here so late. Today, this is paradise compared to what the camp was two years ago. Back then, Buna was a veritable hell. No water, no blankets, less soup and bread. At night, we slept almost naked and the temperature was thirty below. We were collecting corpses by the hundreds every day. Work was very hard. Today, this is a little paradise. The Kapos back then had orders to kill a certain number of prisoners every day. And every week, selection. A merciless selection . . . Yes, you are lucky."

"Enough! Be quiet!" I begged them. "Tell your stories tomorrow, or some other day."

They burst out laughing. They were not veterans for nothing.

"Are you scared? We too were scared. And, at that time, for good reason."

The old men stayed in their corner, silent, motionless, hunted-down creatures. Some were praying.

One more hour. Then we would know the verdict: death or reprieve.

And my father? I first thought of him now. How would he pass selection? He had aged so much . . .

Our *Blockälteste* had not been outside a concentration camp since 1933. He had already been through all the slaughterhouses, all the factories of death. Around nine o'clock, he came to stand in our midst:

"*Achtung!*"

There was instant silence.

"Listen carefully to what I am about to tell you." For the first time, his voice quivered. "In a few moments, selection will take place. You will have to undress completely. Then you will go, one by one, before the SS doctors. I hope you will all pass. But you must try to increase your chances. Before you go into the next room, try to move your limbs, give yourself some color. Don't walk slowly, run! Run as if you had the devil at your heels! Don't look at the SS. Run, straight in front of you!"

He paused and then added:

"And most important, don't be afraid!"

That was a piece of advice we would have loved to be able to follow.

I undressed, leaving my clothes on my cot. Tonight, there was no danger that they would be stolen.

Tibi and Yossi, who had changed Kommandos at the same time I did, came to urge me:

"Let's stay together. It will make us stronger."

Yossi was mumbling something. He probably was praying. I had never suspected that Yossi was religious. In fact, I had always believed the opposite. Tibi was silent and very pale. All the block inmates stood naked between the rows of bunks. This must be how one stands for the Last Judgment.

"They are coming!"

Three SS officers surrounded the notorious Dr. Mengele, the very same who had received us in Birkenau. The *Blockälteste* attempted a smile. He asked us:

"Ready?"

Yes, we were ready. So were the SS doctors. Dr. Mengele was holding a list: our numbers. He nodded to the *Blockälteste*: we can begin! As if this were a game.

The first to go were the "notables" of the block, the *Stubenälteste*, the Kapos, the foremen, all of whom were in perfect physical condition, of course! Then came the ordinary prisoners' turns. Dr. Mengele looked them over from head to toe. From time to time, he noted a number. I had but one thought: not to have my number taken down and not to show my left arm.

In front of me, there were only Tibi and Yossi. They passed. I had time to notice that Mengele had not written down their numbers. Someone pushed me. It was my turn. I ran without looking back. My head was spinning: you are too skinny . . . you are too weak . . . you are too skinny, you are good for the ovens . . . The race seemed endless; I felt as though I had been running for years . . . You are too skinny, you are too weak . . . At last I arrived. Exhausted. When I had caught my breath, I asked Yossi and Tibi:

"Did they write me down?"

"No," said Yossi. Smiling, he added, "Anyway, they couldn't have. You were running too fast . . ."

I began to laugh. I was happy. I felt like kissing him. At that moment, the others did not matter! They had not written me down.

Those whose numbers had been noted were standing apart, abandoned by the whole world. Some were silently weeping.

THE SS OFFICERS left. The *Blockälteste* appeared, his face reflecting our collective weariness.

"It all went well. Don't worry. Nothing will happen to anyone. Not to anyone . . ."

He was still trying to smile. A poor emaciated Jew questioned him anxiously, his voice trembling:

"But . . . sir. They *did* write me down!"

At that, the *Blockälteste* vented his anger: What! Someone refused to take his word?

"What is it now? Perhaps you think I'm lying? I'm telling you, once and for all: Nothing will happen to you! Nothing! You just like to wallow in your despair, you fools!"

The bell rang, signaling that the selection had ended in the entire camp.

With all my strength I began to race toward Block 36; midway, I met my father. He came toward me:

"So? Did you pass?"

"Yes. And you?"

"Also."

We were able to breathe again. My father had a present for me: a half ration of bread, bartered for something he had found at the depot, a piece of rubber that could be used to repair a shoe.

The bell. It was already time to part, to go to bed. The bell regulated everything. It gave me orders and I executed them blindly. I hated that bell. Whenever I happened to dream of a better world, I imagined a universe without a bell.

A FEW DAYS passed. We were no longer thinking about the selection. We went to work as usual and loaded the heavy stones onto the freight cars. The rations had grown smaller; that was the only change.

We had risen at dawn, as we did every day. We had received our black coffee, our ration of bread. We were about to head to the work yard as always. The *Blockälteste* came running:

"Let's have a moment of quiet. I have here a list of numbers. I shall read them to you. All those called will not go to work this morning; they will stay in camp."

Softly, he read some ten numbers. We understood. These were the numbers from the selection. Dr. Mengele had not forgotten.

The *Blockälteste* turned to go to his room. The ten prisoners surrounded him, clinging to his clothes:

"Save us! You promised . . . We want to go to the depot, we are strong enough to work. We are good workers. We can . . . we want . . ."

He tried to calm them, to reassure them about their fate, to explain to them that staying in the camp did not mean much, had no tragic significance: "After all, I stay here every day . . ."

The argument was more than flimsy. He realized it and, without another word, locked himself in his room.

The bell had just rung.

"Form ranks!"

Now, it no longer mattered that the work was hard. All that mattered was to be far from the block, far from the crucible of death, from the center of hell.

I saw my father running in my direction. Suddenly, I was afraid.

"What is happening?"

He was out of breath, hardly able to open his mouth.

"Me too, me too . . . They told me too to stay in the camp."

They had recorded his number without his noticing.

"What are we going to do?" I said anxiously.

But it was he who tried to reassure me:

"It's not certain yet. There's still a chance. Today, they will do another selection . . . a decisive one . . ."

I said nothing.

He felt time was running out. He was speaking rapidly, he wanted to tell me so many things. His speech became confused, his voice was choked. He knew that I had to leave in a few moments. He was going to remain alone, so alone . . .

"Here, take this knife," he said. "I won't need it anymore. You may find it useful. Also take this spoon. Don't sell it. Quickly! Go ahead, take what I'm giving you!"

My inheritance . . .

"Don't talk like that, Father." I was on the verge of breaking into sobs. "I don't want you to say such things. Keep the spoon and knife. You will need them as much as I. We'll see each other tonight, after work."

He looked at me with his tired eyes, veiled by despair. He insisted:

"I am asking you . . . Take it, do as I ask you, my son. Time is running out. Do as your father asks you . . ."

Our Kapo shouted the order to march.

The Kommando headed toward the camp gate. Left, right! I was biting my lips. My father had remained near the block, leaning against the wall. Then he began to run, to try to catch up with us. Perhaps he had forgotten to tell me something . . . But we were marching too fast . . . Left, right!

We were at the gate. We were being counted. Around us, the din of military music. Then we were outside.

ALL DAY, I PLODDED AROUND like a sleepwalker. Tibi and Yossi would call out to me, from time to time, trying to reassure me. As did the Kapo who had given me easier tasks that day. I felt sick at heart. How kindly they treated me. Like an orphan. I thought: Even now, my father is helping me.

I myself didn't know whether I wanted the day to go by

quickly or not. I was afraid of finding myself alone that evening. How good it would be to die right here!

At last, we began the return journey. How I longed for an order to run! The military march. The gate. The camp. I ran toward Block 36.

Were there still miracles on this earth? He was alive. He had passed the second selection. He had still proved his usefulness . . . I gave him back his knife and spoon.

AKIBA DRUMER HAS LEFT US, a victim of the selection. Lately, he had been wandering among us, his eyes glazed, telling everyone how weak he was: "I can't go on . . . It's over . . ." We tried to raise his spirits, but he wouldn't listen to anything we said. He just kept repeating that it was all over for him, that he could no longer fight, he had no more strength, no more faith. His eyes would suddenly go blank, leaving two gaping wounds, two wells of terror.

He was not alone in having lost his faith during those days of selection. I knew a rabbi, from a small town in Poland. He was old and bent, his lips constantly trembling. He was always praying, in the block, at work, in the ranks. He recited entire pages from the Talmud, arguing with himself, asking and answering himself endless questions. One day, he said to me:

"It's over. God is no longer with us."

And as though he regretted having uttered such words so coldly, so dryly, he added in his broken voice, "I know. No one has the right to say things like that. I know that very well. Man is too insignificant, too limited, to even try to comprehend God's mysterious ways. But what can someone like myself do? I'm neither a sage nor a just man. I am not a saint. I'm a simple creature of flesh and bone. I suffer hell in my soul and my flesh. I also have eyes and I see what is being done here. Where is God's mercy? Where's God? How can I believe, how can anyone believe in this God of Mercy?"

Poor Akiba Drumer, if only he could have kept his faith in God, if only he could have considered this suffering a divine test, he would not have been swept away by the selection. But as soon as he felt the first chinks in his faith, he lost all incentive to fight and opened the door to death.

When the selection came, he was doomed from the start, offering his neck to the executioner, as it were. All he asked of us was:

"In three days, I'll be gone . . . Say Kaddish for me."

We promised: In three days, when we would see the smoke rising from the chimney, we would think of him. We would gather ten men and hold a special service. All his friends would say Kaddish.

Then he left, in the direction of the hospital. His step was almost steady and he never looked back. An ambulance was waiting to take him to Birkenau.

There followed terrible days. We received more blows than food. The work was crushing. And three days after he left, we forgot to say Kaddish.

WINTER HAD ARRIVED. The days became short and the nights almost unbearable. From the first hours of dawn, a glacial wind lashed us like a whip. We were handed winter clothing: striped shirts that were a bit heavier. The veterans grabbed the opportunity for further sniggering:

"Now you'll really get a taste of camp!"

We went off to work as usual, our bodies frozen. The stones were so cold that touching them, we felt that our hands would remain stuck. But we got used to that too.

Christmas and New Year's we did not work. We were treated to a slightly less transparent soup.

Around the middle of January, my right foot began to swell from the cold. I could not stand on it. I went to the infirmary. The doctor, a great Jewish doctor, a prisoner like ourselves, was categorical: "We have to operate! If we wait, the toes and perhaps the leg will have to be amputated."

That was all I needed! But I had no choice. The doctor had decided to operate and there could be no discussion. In fact, I was rather glad that the decision had been his.

They put me in a bed with white sheets. I had forgotten that people slept in sheets.

Actually, being in the infirmary was not bad at all: we were entitled to good bread, a thicker soup. No more bell, no more roll call, no more work. From time to time, I was able to send a piece of bread to my father.

Next to me lay a Hungarian Jew suffering from dysentery. He was skin and bones, his eyes were dead. I could just hear his voice, the only indication that he was alive. Where did he get the strength to speak?

"Don't rejoice too soon, son. Here too there is selection. In fact, more often than outside. Germany has no need of sick Jews. Germany has no need of me. When the next transport arrives, you'll have a new neighbor. Therefore, listen to me: leave the infirmary before the next selection!"

These words, coming from the grave, as it were, from a faceless shape, filled me with terror. True, the infirmary was very small, and if new patients were to arrive, room would have to be made.

But then perhaps my faceless neighbor, afraid of being among the first displaced, simply wanted to get rid of me, to free my bed, to give himself a chance to survive . . . Perhaps he only wanted to frighten me. But then again, what if he was telling the truth? I decided to wait and see.

THE DOCTOR CAME TO TELL ME that he would operate the next day.

"Don't be afraid," he said. "Everything will be all right."

At ten o'clock in the morning, I was taken to the operating room. My doctor was there. That reassured me. I felt that in his presence, nothing serious could happen to me. Every one of his words was healing and every glance of his carried a message of hope. "It will hurt a little," he said, "but it will pass. Be brave."

The operation lasted one hour. They did not put me to sleep. I did not take my eyes off my doctor. Then I felt myself sink . . .

When I came to and opened my eyes, I first saw nothing but a huge expanse of white, my sheets, then I saw my doctor's face above me.

"Everything went well. You have spunk, my boy. Next, you'll stay here two weeks for some proper rest and that will be it. You'll eat well, you'll relax your body and your nerves . . ."

All I could do was follow the movements of his lips. I barely understood what he was telling me, but the inflection of his voice soothed me. Suddenly, I broke into a cold sweat; I couldn't feel my leg! Had they amputated it?

"Doctor," I stammered. "Doctor?"

"What is it, son?"

I didn't have the courage to ask him.

"Doctor, I'm thirsty . . ."

He had water brought to me . . . He was smiling. He was ready to walk out, to see other patients.

"Doctor?"

"Yes?"

"Will I be able to use my leg?"

He stopped smiling. I became very frightened. He said, "Listen, son. Do you trust me?"

"Very much, Doctor."

"Then listen well: In two weeks you'll be fully recovered. You'll be able to walk like the others. The sole of your foot was full of pus. I just had to open the sac. Your leg was not amputated. You'll see, in two weeks, you'll be walking around like everybody else."

All I had to do was wait two weeks.

BUT TWO DAYS AFTER my operation, rumors swept through the camp that the battlefront had suddenly drawn nearer. The Red Army was racing toward Buna: it was only a matter of hours.

We were quite used to this kind of rumor. It wasn't the first time that false prophets announced to us: peace-in-the-world, the-Red-Cross-negotiating-our-liberation, or other fables . . . And often we would believe them . . . It was like an injection of morphine.

Only this time, these prophecies seemed more founded. During the last nights we had heard the cannons in the distance.

My faceless neighbor spoke up:

"Don't be deluded. Hitler has made it clear that he will annihilate all Jews before the clock strikes twelve."

I exploded:

"What do you care what he said? Would you want us to consider him a prophet?"

His cold eyes stared at me. At last, he said wearily:

"I have more faith in Hitler than in anyone else. He alone has kept his promises, all his promises, to the Jewish people."

THAT AFTERNOON AT FOUR O'CLOCK, as usual, the bell called all the *Blockälteste* for their daily report.

They came back shattered. They had difficulty opening their mouths. All they could utter was one word: "Evacuation." The camp was going to be emptied and we would be sent to the rear. Where to? Somewhere in deepest Germany. To other camps; there was no shortage of them.

"When?"

"Tomorrow night."

"Perhaps the Russians will arrive before . . ."

"Perhaps."

We knew perfectly well they would not.

The camp had become a hive of activity. People were running, calling to one another. In every block, the inmates prepared for the journey ahead. I had forgotten about my lame foot. A doctor came into the room and announced:

"Tomorrow, right after nightfall, the camp will start on its march. Block by block. The sick can remain in the infirmary. They will not be evacuated."

That news made us wonder. Were the SS really going to leave hundreds of prisoners behind in the infirmaries, pending the arrival of their liberators? Were they really going to allow Jews to hear the clock strike twelve? Of course not.

"All the patients will be finished off on the spot," said the faceless one. "And in one last swoop, thrown into the furnaces."

"Surely, the camp will be mined," said another. "Right after the evacuation, it will all blow up."

As for me, I was thinking not about death but about not wanting to be separated from my father. We had already suffered so much, endured so much together. This was not the moment to separate.

I ran outside to look for him. The snow was piled high, the blocks' windows veiled in frost. Holding a shoe in my hand, for I could not put it on my right foot, I ran, feeling neither pain nor cold.

"What are we going to do?"

My father didn't answer.

"What are we going to do?"

He was lost in thought. The choice was in our hands. For once. We could decide our fate for ourselves. To stay, both of us, in the infirmary, where, thanks to my doctor, he could enter as either a patient or a medic.

I had made up my mind to accompany my father wherever he went.

"Well, Father, what do we do?"

He was silent.

"Let's be evacuated with the others," I said.

He didn't answer. He was looking at my foot.

"You think you'll be able to walk?"

"Yes, I think so."

"Let's hope we won't regret it, Eliezer."

AFTER THE WAR, I learned the fate of those who had remained at the infirmary. They were, quite simply, liberated by the Russians, two days after the evacuation.

I DID NOT RETURN to the infirmary. I went straight to my block. My wound had reopened and was bleeding: the snow under my feet turned red.

The *Blockälteste* distributed double rations of bread and margarine for the road. We could take as much clothing from the store as we wanted.

It was cold. We got into our bunks. The last night in Buna. Once more, the last night. The last night at home, the last night in the ghetto, the last night in the cattle car, and, now, the last night in Buna. How much longer would our lives be lived from one "last night" to the next?

I didn't sleep. Through the frosty windowpanes we could see flashes of red. Cannon shots broke the silence of night. How close the Russians were! Between them and us—one night—our last. There was whispering from one bunk to the other; with a little luck, the Russians would be here before the evacuation. Hope was still alive.

Someone called out:

"Try to sleep. Gather your strength for the journey."

It reminded me of my mother's last recommendations in the ghetto. But I couldn't fall asleep. My foot was on fire.

IN THE MORNING, the camp did not look the same. The prisoners showed up in all kinds of strange garb; it looked like a masquerade. We each had put on several garments, one over the other, to better protect ourselves from the cold. Poor clowns, wider than tall, more dead than alive, poor creatures whose ghostly faces peeked out from layers of prisoner's clothes! Poor clowns!

I tried to find a very large shoe. In vain. I tore my blanket and wrapped it around my foot. Then I went off to wander through the camp in search of a little more bread and a few potatoes. Some people said we would be going to Czechoslovakia. No: to Gros-Rosen. No: to Gleiwitz. No: to . . .

TWO O'CLOCK in the afternoon. The snow continued to fall heavily.

Now the hours were passing quickly. Dusk had fallen. Daylight disappeared into a gray mist.

Suddenly the *Blockälteste* remembered that we had forgotten to clean the block. He commanded four prisoners to mop the floor . . . One hour before leaving camp! Why? For whom?

"For the liberating army," he told us. "Let them know that here lived men and not pigs."

So we were men after all? The block was cleaned from top to bottom.

AT SIX O'CLOCK the bell rang. The death knell. The funeral. The procession was beginning its march.

"Fall in! Quickly!"

In a few moments, we stood in ranks. Block by block. Night had fallen. Everything was happening according to plan.

The searchlights came on. Hundreds of SS appeared out of the darkness, accompanied by police dogs. The snow continued to fall.

The gates of the camp opened. It seemed as though an even darker night was waiting for us on the other side.

The first blocks began to march. We waited. We had to await the exodus of the fifty-six blocks that preceded us. It was very cold. In my pocket, I had two pieces of bread. How I would have liked to eat them! But I knew I must not. Not yet.

Our turn was coming: Block 53 . . . Block 55 . . .

"Block 57, forward! March!"

It snowed on and on.

A N ICY WIND was blowing violently. But we marched without faltering.

The SS made us increase our pace. "Faster, you tramps, you flea-ridden dogs!" Why not? Moving fast made us a little warmer. The blood flowed more readily in our veins. We had the feeling of being alive . . .

"Faster, you filthy dogs!" We were no longer marching, we were running. Like automatons. The SS were running as well, weapons in hand. We looked as though we were running from them.

The night was pitch-black. From time to time, a shot exploded in the darkness. They had orders to shoot anyone who could not sustain the pace. Their fingers on the triggers, they did not deprive themselves of the pleasure. If one of us stopped for a second, a quick shot eliminated the filthy dog.

I was putting one foot in front of the other, like a machine. I was dragging this emaciated body that was still such a weight. If only I could have shed it! Though I tried to put it out of my mind, I couldn't help thinking that there were two of us: my body and I. And I hated that body. I kept repeating to myself:

"Don't think, don't stop, run!"

Near me, men were collapsing into the dirty snow. Gunshots.

A young boy from Poland was marching beside me. His name was Zalman. He had worked in the electrical material depot in Buna. People mocked him because he was forever praying or meditating on some Talmudic question. For him, it was an escape from reality, from feeling the blows . . .

All of a sudden, he had terrible stomach cramps.

"My stomach aches," he whispered to me. He couldn't go on. He had to stop a moment. I begged him: "Wait a little, Zalman. Soon, we will all come to a halt. We cannot run like this to the end of the world."

But, while running, he began to undo his buttons and yelled to me: "I can't go on. My stomach is bursting . . ."

"Make an effort, Zalman . . . Try . . ."

"I can't go on," he groaned.

He lowered his pants and fell to the ground.

That is the image I have of him.

I don't believe that he was finished off by an SS, for nobody had noticed. He must have died, trampled under the feet of the thousands of men who followed us.

I soon forgot him. I began to think of myself again. My foot was aching, I shivered with every step. Just a few more meters and it will be over. I'll fall. A small red flame . . . A shot . . . Death enveloped me, it suffocated me. It stuck to me like glue. I felt I could touch it. The idea of dying, of ceasing to be, began to fascinate me. To no longer exist. To no longer feel the excruciating pain of my foot. To no longer feel anything, neither fatigue nor cold, nothing. To break rank, to let myself slide to the side of the road . . .

My father's presence was the only thing that stopped me. He was running next to me, out of breath, out of strength, desperate.

I had no right to let myself die. What would he do without me? I was his sole support.

These thoughts were going through my mind as I continued to run, not feeling my numb foot, not even realizing that I was still running, that I still owned a body that galloped down the road among thousands of others.

When I became conscious of myself again, I tried to slow my pace somewhat. But there was no way. These human waves were rolling forward and would have crushed me like an ant.

By now, I moved like a sleepwalker. I sometimes closed my eyes and it was like running while asleep. Now and then, someone kicked me violently from behind and I would wake up. The man in back of me was screaming, "Run faster. If you don't want to move, let us pass you." But all I had to do was close my eyes to see a whole world pass before me, to dream of another life.

The road was endless. To allow oneself to be carried by the mob, to be swept away by blind fate. When the SS were tired, they were replaced. But no one replaced us. Chilled to the bone, our throats parched, famished, out of breath, we pressed on.

We were the masters of nature, the masters of the world. We had transcended everything—death, fatigue, our natural needs. We were stronger than cold and hunger, stronger than the guns and the desire to die, doomed and rootless, nothing but numbers, we were the only men on earth.

At last, the morning star appeared in the gray sky. A hesitant light began to hover on the horizon. We were exhausted, we had lost all strength, all illusion.

The Kommandant announced that we had already covered twenty kilometers since we left. Long since, we had exceeded the limits of fatigue. Our legs moved mechanically, in spite of us, without us.

We came to an abandoned village. Not a living soul. Not a single bark. Houses with gaping windows. A few people slipped out of the ranks, hoping to hide in some abandoned building.

One more hour of marching and, at last, the order to halt.

As one man, we let ourselves sink into the snow.

My father shook me. "Not here . . . Get up . . . A little farther down. There is a shed over there . . . Come . . ."

I had neither the desire nor the resolve to get up. Yet I obeyed. It was not really a shed, but a brick factory whose roof had fallen in. Its windowpanes were shattered, its walls covered in soot. It was not easy to get inside. Hundreds of prisoners jostled one another at the door.

We finally succeeded in entering. Inside too the snow was thick. I let myself slide to the ground. Only now did I feel the full extent of my weakness. The snow seemed to me like a very soft, very warm carpet. I fell asleep. I don't know how long I slept. A few minutes or one hour. When I woke up, a frigid hand was tapping my cheeks. I tried to open my eyes: it was my father.

How he had aged since last night! His body was completely twisted, shriveled up into himself. His eyes were glazed over, his lips parched, decayed. Everything about him expressed total exhaustion. His voice was damp from tears and snow.

"Don't let yourself be overcome by sleep, Eliezer. It's dangerous to fall asleep in snow. One falls asleep forever. Come, my son, come . . . Get up."

Get up? How could I? How was I to leave this warm blanket? I was hearing my father's words, but their meaning escaped me, as if he had asked me to carry the entire shed on my arms . . .

"Come, my son, come . . ."

I got up, with clenched teeth. Holding on to me with one arm, he led me outside. It was not easy. It was as difficult to go out as to come in. Beneath our feet there lay men, crushed, trampled underfoot, dying. Nobody paid attention to them.

We were outside. The icy wind whipped my face. I was constantly biting my lips so that they wouldn't freeze. All around me, what appeared to be a dance of death. My head was reeling. I was walking through a cemetery. Among the stiffened corpses, there were logs of wood. Not a sound of distress, not a plaintive cry, nothing but mass agony and silence. Nobody asked anyone for help. One died because one had to. No point in making trouble.

I saw myself in every stiffened corpse. Soon I wouldn't even be seeing them anymore; I would be one of them. A matter of hours.

"Come, Father, let's go back to the shed . . ."

He didn't answer. He was not even looking at the dead.

"Come, Father. It's better there. You'll be able to lie down. We'll take turns. I'll watch over you and you'll watch over me. We won't let each other fall asleep. We'll look after each other."

He accepted. After trampling over many bodies and corpses, we succeeded in getting inside. We let ourselves fall to the ground.

"Don't worry, son. Go to sleep. I'll watch over you."

"You first, Father. Sleep."

He refused. I stretched out and tried to sleep, to doze a little, but in vain. God knows what I would have given to be able to sleep a few moments. But deep inside, I knew that to sleep meant to die. And something in me rebelled against that death. Death, which was settling in all around me, silently, gently. It would seize upon a sleeping person, steal into him and devour him bit by bit. Next to me, someone was trying to awaken his neighbor, his brother, perhaps, or his comrade. In vain. Defeated, he lay down too, next to the corpse, and also fell asleep. Who would wake him up? Reaching out with my arm, I touched him:

"Wake up. One mustn't fall asleep here . . ."

He half opened his eyes.

"No advice," he said, his voice a whisper. "I'm exhausted. Mind your business, leave me alone."

My father too was gently dozing. I couldn't see his eyes. His cap was covering his face.

"Wake up," I whispered in his ear.

He awoke with a start. He sat up, bewildered, stunned, like an orphan. He looked all around him, taking it all in as if he had suddenly decided to make an inventory of his universe, to determine where he was and how and why he was there. Then he smiled.

I shall always remember that smile. What world did it come from?

Heavy snow continued to fall over the corpses.

The door of the shed opened. An old man appeared. His mustache was covered with ice, his lips were blue. It was Rabbi Eliahu, who had headed a small congregation in Poland. A very kind man, beloved by everyone in the camp, even by the Kapos and the *Blockälteste*. Despite the ordeals and deprivations, his face continued to radiate his innocence. He was the only rabbi whom nobody ever failed to address as "Rabbi" in Buna. He looked like one of those prophets of old, always in the midst of his people when they needed to be consoled. And, strangely, his words never provoked anyone. They did bring peace.

As he entered the shed, his eyes, brighter than ever, seemed to be searching for someone.

"Perhaps someone here has seen my son?"

He had lost his son in the commotion. He had searched for him among the dying, to no avail. Then he had dug through the snow to find his body. In vain.

For three years, they had stayed close to one another. Side by side, they had endured the suffering, the blows; they had waited for their ration of bread and they had prayed. Three years, from camp to camp, from selection to selection. And now—when the end seemed near—fate had separated them.

When he came near me, Rabbi Eliahu whispered, "It happened on the road. We lost sight of one another during the journey. I fell behind a little, at the rear of the column. I didn't have the strength to run anymore. And my son didn't notice. That's all I know. Where has he disappeared? Where can I find him? Perhaps you've seen him somewhere?"

"No, Rabbi Eliahu, I haven't seen him."

And so he left, as he had come: a shadow swept away by the wind.

He had already gone through the door when I remembered that I had noticed his son running beside me. I had forgotten and so had not mentioned it to Rabbi Eliahu!

But then I remembered something else: his son *had* seen him losing ground, sliding back to the rear of the column. He had seen him. And he had continued to run in front, letting the distance between them become greater.

A terrible thought crossed my mind: What if he had wanted to be rid of his father? He had felt his father growing weaker and, believing that the end was near, had thought by this separation to free himself of a burden that could diminish his own chance for survival.

It was good that I *had* forgotten all that. And I was glad that Rabbi Eliahu continued to search for his beloved son.

And in spite of myself, a prayer formed inside me, a prayer to this God in whom I no longer believed.

"Oh God, Master of the Universe, give me the strength never to do what Rabbi Eliahu's son has done."

There was shouting outside, in the courtyard. Night had fallen and the SS were ordering us to form ranks.

We started to march once more. The dead remained in the yard, under the snow without even a marker, like fallen guards. No one recited Kaddish over them. Sons abandoned the remains of their fathers without a tear.

On the road, it snowed and snowed, it snowed endlessly. We were marching more slowly. Even the guards seemed tired. My wounded foot no longer hurt, probably frozen. I felt I had lost that foot. It had become detached from me like a wheel fallen off a car. Never mind. I had to accept the fact: I would have to live with only one leg. The important thing was not to dwell on it. Especially now. Leave those thoughts for later.

Our column had lost all appearance of discipline. Everyone walked as he wished, as he could. No more gunshots. Our guards surely *were* tired.

But death hardly needed their help. The cold was conscientiously doing its work. At every step, somebody fell down and ceased to suffer.

From time to time, SS officers on motorcycles drove the length of the column to shake off the growing apathy:

"Hold on! We're almost there!"

"Courage! Just a few more hours!"

"We're arriving in Gleiwitz!"

These words of encouragement, even coming as they did from the mouths of our assassins, were of great help. Nobody wanted to give up now, just before the end, so close to our destination. Our eyes searched the horizon for the barbed wire of Gleiwitz. Our only wish was to arrive there quickly.

By now it was night. It had stopped snowing. We marched a few more hours before we arrived. We saw the camp only when we stood right in front of its gate.

The Kapos quickly settled us into the barrack. There was shoving and jostling as if this were the ultimate haven, the gateway to life. People trod over numbed bodies, trampled wounded faces. There were no cries, only a few moans. My father and I were thrown to the ground by this rolling tide. From beneath me came a desperate cry:

"You're crushing me . . . have mercy!"

The voice was familiar.

"You're crushing me . . . mercy, have mercy!"

The same faint voice, the same cry I had heard somewhere before. This voice had spoken to me one day. When? Years ago? No, it must have been in the camp.

"Mercy!"

Knowing that I was crushing him, preventing him from breathing, I wanted to get up and disengage myself to allow him to breathe. But I myself was crushed under the weight of other bodies. I had difficulty breathing. I dug my nails into unknown faces. I was biting my way through, searching for air. No one cried out.

Suddenly I remembered. Juliek! The boy from Warsaw who played the violin in the Buna orchestra . . .

"Juliek, is that you?"

"Eliezer . . . The twenty-five whiplashes . . . Yes . . . I remember."

He fell silent. A long moment went by.

"Juliek! Can you hear me, Juliek?"

"Yes . . ." he said feebly. "What do you want?"

He was not dead.

"Are you all right, Juliek?" I asked, less to know his answer than to hear him speak, to know he was alive.

"All right, Eliezer . . . All right . . . Not too much air . . . Tired. My feet are swollen. It's good to rest, but my violin . . ."

I thought he'd lost his mind. His violin? Here?

"What about your violin?"

He was gasping:

"I . . . I'm afraid . . . They'll break . . . my violin . . . I . . . I brought it with me."

I could not answer him. Someone had lain down on top of me, smothering me. I couldn't breathe through my mouth or my nose. Sweat was running down my forehead and my back. This was it; the end of the road. A silent death, suffocation. No way to scream, to call for help.

I tried to rid myself of my invisible assassin. My whole desire to live became concentrated in my nails. I scratched, I fought for a breath of air. I tore at decaying flesh that did not respond. I could not free myself of that mass weighing down my chest. Who knows? Was I struggling with a dead man?

I shall never know. All I can say is that I prevailed. I succeeded in digging a hole in that wall of dead and dying people, a small hole through which I could drink a little air.

"FATHER, ARE YOU THERE?" I asked as soon as I was able to utter a word.

I knew that he could not be far from me.

"Yes!" a voice replied from far away, as if from another world. "I am trying to sleep."

He was trying to sleep. Could one fall asleep here? Wasn't it dangerous to lower one's guard, even for a moment, when death could strike at any time?

Those were my thoughts when I heard the sound of a violin. A violin in a dark barrack where the dead were piled on top of the living? Who was this madman who played the violin here, at the edge of his own grave? Or was it a hallucination? It had to be Juliek.

He was playing a fragment of a Beethoven concerto. Never before had I heard such a beautiful sound. In such silence.

How had he succeeded in disengaging himself? To slip out from under my body without my feeling it?

The darkness enveloped us. All I could hear was the violin, and it was as if Juliek's soul had become his bow. He was playing his life. His whole being was gliding over the strings. His unfulfilled hopes. His charred past, his extinguished future. He played that which he would never play again.

I shall never forget Juliek. How could I forget this concert given before an audience of the dead and dying? Even today, when I hear that particular piece by Beethoven, my eyes close and out of the darkness emerges the pale and melancholy face of my Polish comrade bidding farewell to an audience of dying men.

I don't know how long he played. I was overcome by sleep. When I awoke at daybreak, I saw Juliek facing me, hunched over, dead. Next to him lay his violin, trampled, an eerily poignant little corpse.

WE STAYED IN GLEIWITZ for three days. Days without food or water. We were forbidden to leave the barrack. The door was guarded by the SS.

I was hungry and thirsty. I must have been very dirty and disheveled, to judge by what the others looked like. The bread we had brought from Buna had been devoured long since. And who knew when we would be given another ration?

The Front followed us. We could again hear the cannons very close by. But we no longer had the strength or the courage to think that the Germans would run out of time, that the Russians would reach us before we could be evacuated.

We learned that we would be moved to the center of Germany.

On the third day, at dawn, we were driven out of the barrack. We threw blankets over our shoulders, like prayer shawls. We were directed to a gate that divided the camp in two. A group of SS officers stood waiting. A word flew through our ranks: selection!

The SS officers were doing the selection: the weak, to the left; those who walked well, to the right.

My father was sent to the left. I ran after him. An SS officer shouted at my back:

"Come back!"

I inched my way through the crowd. Several SS men rushed to find me, creating such confusion that a number of people were able to switch over to the right—among them my father and I. Still, there were gunshots and some dead.

We were led out of the camp. After a half-hour march, we arrived in the very middle of a field crossed by railroad tracks. This was where we were to wait for the train's arrival.

Snow was falling heavily. We were forbidden to sit down or to move.

A thick layer of snow was accumulating on our blankets. We were given bread, the usual ration. We threw ourselves on it. Someone had the idea of quenching his thirst by eating snow. Soon, we were all imitating him. As we were not permitted to bend down, we took out our spoons and ate the snow off our neighbors' backs. A mouthful of bread and a spoonful of snow. The SS men who were watching were greatly amused by the spectacle.

The hours went by. Our eyes were tired from staring at the horizon, waiting for the liberating train to appear. It arrived only very late that evening. An infinitely long train, composed of roofless cattle cars. The SS shoved us inside, a hundred per car: we were so skinny! When everybody was on board, the convoy left.

P RESSED TIGHTLY AGAINST one another, in an effort to resist the cold, our heads empty and heavy, our brains a
whirlwind of decaying memories. Our minds numb with
indifference. Here or elsewhere, what did it matter? Die today
or tomorrow, or later? The night was growing longer, never-
ending.

When at last a grayish light appeared on the horizon, it revealed a tangle of human shapes, heads sunk deeply between the
shoulders, crouching, piled one on top of the other, like a cemetery covered with snow. In the early dawn light, I tried to distinguish between the living and those who were no more. But there
was barely a difference. My gaze remained fixed on someone
who, eyes wide open, stared into space. His colorless face was
covered with a layer of frost and snow.

My father had huddled near me, draped in his blanket, shoulders laden with snow. And what if he were dead, as well? I called
out to him. No response. I would have screamed if I could have.
He was not moving.

Suddenly, the evidence overwhelmed me: there was no longer any reason to live, any reason to fight.

The train stopped in an empty field. The abrupt halt had wakened a few sleepers. They stood, looking around, startled.

Outside, the SS walked by, shouting:

"Throw out all the dead! Outside, all the corpses!"

The living were glad. They would have more room. Volunteers began the task. They touched those who had remained on the ground.

"Here's one! Take him!"

The volunteers undressed him and eagerly shared his garments. Then, two "gravediggers" grabbed him by the head and feet and threw him from the wagon, like a sack of flour.

There was shouting all around:

"Come on! Here's another! My neighbor. He's not moving . . ."

I woke from my apathy only when two men approached my father. I threw myself on his body. He was cold. I slapped him. I rubbed his hands, crying:

"Father! Father! Wake up. They're going to throw you outside . . ."

His body remained inert.

The two "gravediggers" had grabbed me by the neck:

"Leave him alone. Can't you see that he's dead?"

"No!" I yelled. "He's not dead! Not yet!"

And I started to hit him harder and harder. At last, my father half opened his eyes. They were glassy. He was breathing faintly.

"You see," I cried.

The two men went away.

Twenty corpses were thrown from our wagon. Then the train resumed its journey, leaving in its wake, in a snowy field in Poland, hundreds of naked orphans without a tomb.

WE RECEIVED no food. We lived on snow; it took the place of bread. The days resembled the nights, and the nights left in our souls the dregs of their darkness. The train rolled slowly, often halted for a few hours, and continued. It never stopped snowing. We remained lying on the floor for days and nights, one on top of the other, never uttering a word. We were nothing but frozen bodies. Our eyes closed, we merely waited for the next stop, to unload our dead.

THERE FOLLOWED days and nights of traveling. Occasionally, we would pass through German towns. Usually, very early in the morning. German laborers were going to work. They would stop and look at us without surprise.

One day when we had come to a stop, a worker took a piece of bread out of his bag and threw it into a wagon. There was a stampede. Dozens of starving men fought desperately over a few crumbs. The worker watched the spectacle with great interest.

YEARS LATER, I witnessed a similar spectacle in Aden. Our ship's passengers amused themselves by throwing coins to the "natives," who dove to retrieve them. An elegant Parisian lady took great pleasure in this game. When I noticed two children desperately fighting in the water, one trying to strangle the other, I implored the lady:

"Please, don't throw any more coins!"

"Why not?" said she. "I like to give charity . . ."

IN THE WAGON where the bread had landed, a battle had ensued. Men were hurling themselves against each other, trampling, tearing at, and mauling each other. Beasts of prey unleashed, animal hate in their eyes. An extraordinary vitality possessed them, sharpening their teeth and nails.

A crowd of workmen and curious passersby had formed all along the train. They had undoubtedly never seen a train with this kind of cargo. Soon, pieces of bread were falling into the wagons from all sides. And the spectators observed these emaciated creatures ready to kill for a crust of bread.

A piece fell into our wagon. I decided not to move. Anyway, I knew that I would not be strong enough to fight off dozens of violent men! I saw, not far from me, an old man dragging himself on all fours. He had just detached himself from the struggling mob. He was holding one hand to his heart. At first I thought he had received a blow to his chest. Then I understood: he was hiding a piece of bread under his shirt. With lightning speed he pulled it out and put it to his mouth. His eyes lit up, a smile, like a grimace, illuminated his ashen face. And was immediately extinguished. A shadow had lain down beside him. And this shadow threw itself over him. Stunned by the blows, the old man was crying:

"Meir, my little Meir! Don't you recognize me . . . You're killing your father . . . I have bread . . . for you too . . . for you too . . ."

He collapsed. But his fist was still clutching a small crust. He wanted to raise it to his mouth. But the other threw himself on him. The old man mumbled something, groaned, and died. Nobody cared. His son searched him, took the crust of bread, and began to devour it. He didn't get far. Two men had been watching him. They jumped him. Others joined in. When they withdrew, there were two dead bodies next to me, the father and the son.

I was sixteen.

IN OUR WAGON, there was a friend of my father's, Meir Katz. He had worked as a gardener in Buna and from time to time had brought us some green vegetables. Less undernourished than the rest of us, detention had been easier on him. Because he was stronger than most of us, he had been put in charge of our wagon.

On the third night of our journey, I woke up with a start when I felt two hands on my throat, trying to strangle me. I barely had time to call out:

"Father!"

Just that one word. I was suffocating. But my father had awakened and grabbed my aggressor. Too weak to overwhelm him, he thought of calling Meir Katz:

"Come, come quickly! Someone is strangling my son!"

In a few moments, I was freed. I never did find out why this stranger had wanted to strangle me.

But days later, Meir Katz told my father:

"Shlomo, I am getting weak. My strength is gone. I won't make it . . ."

"Don't give in!" my father tried to encourage him. "You must resist! Don't lose faith in yourself!"

But Meir Katz only groaned in response:

"I can't go on, Shlomo! . . . I can't help it . . . I can't go on . . ."

My father took his arm. And Meir Katz, the strong one, the sturdiest of us all, began to cry. His son had been taken from him during the first selection but only now was he crying for him. Only now did he fall apart. He could not go on. He had reached the end.

On the last day of our journey, a terrible wind began to blow. And the snow kept falling. We sensed that the end was near; the real end. We could not hold out long in this glacial wind, this storm.

Somebody got up and yelled:

"We must not remain sitting. We shall freeze to death! Let's get up and move . . ."

We all got up. We all pulled our soaked blankets tighter around our shoulders. And we tried to take a few steps, to shuffle back and forth, in place.

Suddenly, a cry rose in the wagon, the cry of a wounded animal. Someone had just died.

Others, close to death, imitated his cry. And their cries seemed to come from beyond the grave. Soon everybody was crying. Groaning. Moaning. Cries of distress hurled into the wind and the snow.

The lament spread from wagon to wagon. It was contagious. And now hundreds of cries rose at once. The death rattle of an entire convoy with the end approaching. All boundaries had been crossed. Nobody had any strength left. And the night seemed endless.

Meir Katz was moaning:

"Why don't they just shoot us now?"

That same night, we reached our destination.

It was late. The guards came to unload us. The dead were left in the wagons. Only those who could stand could leave.

Meir Katz remained on the train. The last day had been the most lethal. We had been a hundred or so in this wagon. Twelve of us left it. Among them, my father and myself.

We had arrived in Buchenwald.

A T THE ENTRANCE TO THE CAMP, SS officers were waiting for us. We were counted. Then we were directed to the *Appelplatz*. The orders were given over the loudspeakers: "Form ranks of fives! Groups of one hundred! Five steps forward!"

I tightened my grip on my father's hand. The old, familiar fear: not to lose him.

Very close to us stood the tall chimney of the crematorium's furnace. It no longer impressed us. It barely drew our attention.

A veteran of Buchenwald told us that we would be taking a shower and afterward be sent to different blocks. The idea of a hot shower fascinated me. My father didn't say a word. He was breathing heavily beside me.

"Father," I said, "just another moment. Soon, we'll be able to lie down. You'll be able to rest . . ."

He didn't answer. I myself was so weary that his silence left me indifferent. My only wish was to take the shower as soon as possible and lie down on a cot.

Only it wasn't easy to reach the showers. Hundreds of prisoners crowded the area. The guards seemed unable to restore order. They were lashing out, left and right, to no avail. Some prisoners who didn't have the strength to jostle, or even to stand, sat down in the snow. My father wanted to do the same. He was moaning:

"I can't anymore . . . It's over . . . I shall die right here . . ."

He dragged me toward a pile of snow from which protruded human shapes, torn blankets.

"Leave me," he said. "I can't go on anymore . . . Have pity on me . . . I'll wait here until we can go into the showers . . . You'll come and get me."

I could have screamed in anger. To have lived and endured so much; was I going to let my father die now? Now that we would be able to take a good hot shower and lie down?

"Father!" I howled. "Father! Get up! Right now! You will kill yourself . . ."

And I grabbed his arm. He continued to moan:

"Don't yell, my son . . . Have pity on your old father . . . Let me rest here . . . a little . . . I beg of you, I'm so tired . . . no more strength . . ."

He had become childlike: weak, frightened, vulnerable.

"Father," I said, "you cannot stay here."

I pointed to the corpses around him; they too had wanted to rest here.

"I see, my son. I do see them. Let them sleep. They haven't closed an eye for so long . . . They're exhausted . . . exhausted . . ."

His voice was tender.

I howled into the wind:

"They're dead! They will never wake up! Never! Do you understand?"

This discussion continued for some time. I knew that I was no longer arguing with him but with Death itself, with Death that he had already chosen.

The sirens began to wail. Alert. The lights went out in the entire camp. The guards chased us toward the blocks. In a flash, there was no one left outside. We were only too glad not to have to stay outside any longer, in the freezing wind. We let ourselves sink into the floor. The cauldrons at the entrance found no takers. There were several tiers of bunks. To sleep was all that mattered.

WHEN I WOKE UP, it was daylight. That is when I remembered that I had a father. During the alert, I had followed the mob, not taking care of him. I knew he was running out of strength, close to death, and yet I had abandoned him.

I went to look for him.

Yet at the same time a thought crept into my mind: If only I didn't find him! If only I were relieved of this responsibility, I could use all my strength to fight for my own survival, to take care only of myself . . . Instantly, I felt ashamed, ashamed of myself forever.

I walked for hours without finding him. Then I came to a block where they were distributing black "coffee." People stood in line, quarreled.

A plaintive voice came from behind me:

"Eliezer, my son . . . bring me . . . a little coffee . . ."

I ran toward him.

"Father! I've been looking for you for so long . . . Where were you? Did you sleep? How are you feeling?"

He seemed to be burning with fever. I fought my way to the coffee cauldron like a wild beast. And I succeeded in bringing back a cup. I took one gulp. The rest was for him.

I shall never forget the gratitude that shone in his eyes when he swallowed this beverage. The gratitude of a wounded animal.

With these few mouthfuls of hot water, I had probably given him more satisfaction than during my entire childhood . . .

He was lying on the boards, ashen, his lips pale and dry, shivering. I couldn't stay with him any longer. We had been ordered to go outside to allow for cleaning of the blocks. Only the sick could remain inside.

We stayed outside for five hours. We were given soup. When they allowed us to return to the blocks, I rushed toward my father:

"Did you eat?"

"No."

"Why?"

"They didn't give us anything . . . They said that we were sick, that we would die soon, and that it would be a waste of food . . . I can't go on . . ."

I gave him what was left of my soup. But my heart was heavy. I was aware that I was doing it grudgingly.

Just like Rabbi Eliahu's son, I had not passed the test.

EVERY DAY, my father was getting weaker. His eyes were watery, his face the color of dead leaves. On the third day after we arrived in Buchenwald, everybody had to go to the showers. Even the sick, who were instructed to go last.

When we returned from the showers, we had to wait outside a long time. The cleaning of the blocks had not been completed.

From afar, I saw my father and ran to meet him. He went by me like a shadow, passing me without stopping, without a glance. I called to him, he did not turn around. I ran after him:

"Father, where are you running?"

He looked at me for a moment and his gaze was distant, otherworldly, the face of a stranger. It lasted only a moment and then he ran away.

SUFFERING FROM DYSENTERY, my father was prostrate on his cot, with another five sick inmates nearby. I sat next to him, watching him; I no longer dared to believe that he could still elude Death. I did all I could to give him hope.

All of a sudden, he sat up and placed his feverish lips against my ear:

"Eliezer . . . I must tell you where I buried the gold and silver . . . In the cellar . . . You know . . ."

And he began talking, faster and faster, afraid of running out of time before he could tell me everything. I tried to tell him that it was not over yet, that we would be going home together, but he no longer wanted to listen to me. He *could* no longer listen to me. He was worn out. Saliva mixed with blood was trickling from his lips. He had closed his eyes. He was gasping more than breathing.

FOR A RATION OF BREAD I was able to exchange cots to be next to my father. When the doctor arrived in the afternoon, I went to tell him that my father was very ill.

"Bring him here!"

I explained that he could not stand up, but the doctor would not listen. And so, with great difficulty, I brought my father to him. He stared at him, then asked curtly:

"What do you want?"

"My father is sick," I answered in his place. "Dysentery . . ."

"That's not my business. I'm a surgeon. Go on. Make room for the others!"

My protests were in vain.

"I can't go on, my son . . . Take me back to my bunk."

I took him back and helped him lie down. He was shivering.

"Try to get some sleep, Father. Try to fall asleep . . ."

His breathing was labored. His eyes were closed. But I was convinced that he was seeing everything. That he was seeing the truth in all things.

Another doctor came to the block. My father refused to get up. He knew that it would be of no use.

In fact, that doctor had come only to finish off the patients. I listened to him shouting at them that they were lazy good-for-nothings who only wanted to stay in bed . . . I considered jumping him, strangling him. But I had neither the courage nor the strength. I was riveted to my father's agony. My hands were aching, I was clenching them so hard. To strangle the doctor and the others! To set the whole world on fire! My father's murderers! But even the cry stuck in my throat.

ON MY RETURN from the bread distribution, I found my father crying like a child:

"My son, they are beating me!"

"Who?" I thought he was delirious.

"Him, the Frenchman . . . and the Pole . . . They beat me . . ."

One more stab to the heart, one more reason to hate. One less reason to live.

"Eliezer . . . Eliezer . . . tell them not to beat me . . . I haven't done anything . . . Why are they beating me?"

I began to insult his neighbors. They mocked me. I promised them bread, soup. They laughed. Then they got angry; they could not stand my father any longer, they said, because he no longer was able to drag himself outside to relieve himself.

THE FOLLOWING DAY, he complained that they had taken his ration of bread.

"While you were asleep?"

"No. I wasn't asleep. They threw themselves on me. They snatched it from me, my bread . . . And they beat me . . . Again . . . I can't go on, my son . . . Give me some water . . ."

I knew that he must not drink. But he pleaded with me so long that I gave in. Water was the worst poison for him, but what else could I do for him? With or without water, it would be over soon anyway . . .

"You, at least, have pity on me . . ."

Have pity on him! I, his only son . . .

A WEEK WENT BY like that.

"Is this your father?" asked the *Blockälteste*.

"Yes."

"He is very sick."

"The doctor won't do anything for him."

He looked me straight in the eye:

"The doctor *cannot* do anything more for him. And neither can you."

He placed his big, hairy hand on my shoulder and added:

"Listen to me, kid. Don't forget that you are in a concentration camp. In this place, it is every man for himself, and you cannot think of others. Not even your father. In this place, there is no such thing as father, brother, friend. Each of us lives and dies alone. Let me give you good advice: stop giving your ration of bread and soup to your old father. You cannot help him anymore.

And you are hurting yourself. In fact, you should be getting *his* rations . . ."

I listened to him without interrupting. He was right, I thought deep down, not daring to admit it to myself. Too late to save your old father . . . You could have two rations of bread, two rations of soup . . .

It was only a fraction of a second, but it left me feeling guilty. I ran to get some soup and brought it to my father. But he did not want it. All he wanted was water.

"Don't drink water, eat the soup . . ."

"I'm burning up . . . Why are you so mean to me, my son? . . . Water . . ."

I brought him water. Then I left the block for roll call. But I quickly turned back. I lay down on the upper bunk. The sick were allowed to stay in the block. So I would be sick. I didn't want to leave my father.

All around me, there was silence now, broken only by moaning. In front of the block, the SS were giving orders. An officer passed between the bunks. My father was pleading:

"My son, water . . . I'm burning up . . . My insides . . ."

"Silence over there!" barked the officer.

"Eliezer," continued my father, "water . . ."

The officer came closer and shouted to him to be silent. But my father did not hear. He continued to call me. The officer wielded his club and dealt him a violent blow to the head.

I didn't move. I was afraid, my body was afraid of another blow, this time to *my* head.

My father groaned once more, I heard:

"Eliezer . . ."

I could see that he was still breathing—in gasps. I didn't move.

When I came down from my bunk after roll call, I could see his lips trembling; he was murmuring something. I remained more than an hour leaning over him, looking at him, etching his bloody, broken face into my mind.

Then I had to go to sleep. I climbed into my bunk, above my father, who was still alive. The date was January 28, 1945.

I WOKE UP AT DAWN on January 29. On my father's cot there lay another sick person. They must have taken him away before daybreak and taken him to the crematorium. Perhaps he was still breathing . . .

No prayers were said over his tomb. No candle lit in his memory. His last word had been my name. He had called out to me and I had not answered.

I did not weep, and it pained me that I could not weep. But I was out of tears. And deep inside me, if I could have searched the recesses of my feeble conscience, I might have found something like: Free at last! . . .

I REMAINED IN BUCHENWALD until April 11. I shall not describe my life during that period. It no longer mattered. Since my father's death, nothing mattered to me anymore.

I was transferred to the children's block, where there were six hundred of us.

The Front was coming closer.

I spent my days in total idleness. With only one desire: to eat. I no longer thought of my father, or my mother.

From time to time, I would dream. But only about soup, an extra ration of soup.

ON APRIL 5, the wheel of history turned.

It was late afternoon. We were standing inside the block, waiting for an SS to come and count us. He was late. Such lateness was unprecedented in the history of Buchenwald. Something must have happened.

Two hours later, the loudspeakers transmitted an order from the camp Kommandant: all Jews were to gather in the *Appelplatz*.

This was the end! Hitler was about to keep his promise.

The children of our block did as ordered. There was no choice: Gustav, the *Blockälteste*, made it clear with his club . . . But on our way we met some prisoners who whispered to us:

"Go back to your block. The Germans plan to shoot you. Go back and don't move."

We returned to the block. On our way there, we learned that the underground resistance of the camp had made the decision not to abandon the Jews and to prevent their liquidation.

As it was getting late and the confusion was great—countless Jews had been passing as non-Jews—the *Lagerälteste* had decided that a general roll call would take place the next day. Everybody would have to be present.

The roll call took place. The *Lagerkommandant* announced that the Buchenwald camp would be liquidated. Ten blocks of inmates would be evacuated every day. From that moment on, there was no further distribution of bread and soup. And the evacuation began. Every day, a few thousand inmates passed the camp's gate and did not return.

ON APRIL 10, there were still some twenty thousand prisoners in the camp, among them a few hundred children. It was decided to evacuate all of us at once. By evening. Afterward, they would blow up the camp.

And so we were herded onto the huge *Appelplatz*, in ranks of five, waiting for the gate to open. Suddenly, the sirens began to scream. Alert. We went back to the blocks. It was too late to evacuate us that evening. The evacuation was postponed to the next day.

Hunger was tormenting us; we had not eaten for nearly six

days except for a few stalks of grass and some potato peels found on the grounds of the kitchens.

At ten o'clock in the morning, the SS took positions throughout the camp and began to herd the last of us toward the *Appelplatz*.

The resistance movement decided at that point to act. Armed men appeared from everywhere. Bursts of gunshots. Grenades exploding. We, the children, remained flat on the floor of the block.

The battle did not last long. Around noon, everything was calm again. The SS had fled and the resistance had taken charge of the camp.

At six o'clock that afternoon, the first American tank stood at the gates of Buchenwald.

OUR FIRST ACT AS FREE MEN was to throw ourselves onto the provisions. That's all we thought about. No thought of revenge, or of parents. Only of bread.

And even when we were no longer hungry, not one of us thought of revenge. The next day, a few of the young men ran into Weimar to bring back some potatoes and clothes—and to sleep with girls. But still no trace of revenge.

Three days after the liberation of Buchenwald, I became very ill: some form of poisoning. I was transferred to a hospital and spent two weeks between life and death.

One day when I was able to get up, I decided to look at myself in the mirror on the opposite wall. I had not seen myself since the ghetto.

From the depths of the mirror, a corpse was contemplating me.

The look in his eyes as he gazed at me has never left me.

Dawn

TRANSLATED FROM THE FRENCH BY

FRANCES FRENAYE

to François Mauriac

Preface

THIS NOVEL, MY FIRST, may be surprising for its sudden relevance to our present times. Does it not have to do with hostage taking, violence, and clandestine rebellion?

Yet the action of the novel is set in a past at once recent and far away, in a Palestine that is still Jewish, ruled by Great Britain, before the creation of the state of Israel.

Elisha, a young survivor of the death camps—an orphan bereft not only of his father and mother, but of hope—is recruited by members of the Resistance. At this point the enemy is not Arab but English. The power is in London, not Jerusalem. The tribunals are overburdened, the prisons overflowing. The executioner is working full-time. His justice is draconian.

A Jewish combatant is condemned to death. His superiors in the Resistance order Elisha to execute one of His Majesty's officials in retaliation. Both men are to die at dawn.

Dawn is purely a work of fiction, but I wrote it to look at myself in a new way. Obviously I did not live this tale, but I was implicated in its ethical dilemma from the moment that I assumed my character's place. Difficult? Not really. Suppose the American army, instead of sending me to France, had handed me a visa to the Holy Land—would I have had the courage to join one of the movements that fought for the right of the Jewish people to form an independent state in their ancestral homeland? And if so, could I have gone all the way in my commitment and killed a man, a stranger? Would I have had the strength to claim him as my victim?

So I wrote this novel in order to explore distant memories and buried doubts: What would have become of me if I had spent not just one year in the camps, but two or four? If I had been appointed Kapo? Could I have struck a friend? Humiliated an old man?

And taking the questions further within the context of the narrative: How are we ever to disarm evil and abolish death as a means to an end? How are we ever to break the cycle of violence and rage? Can terror coexist with justice? Does murder call for murder, despair for revenge? Can hate engender anything but hate?

The young hero spends an entire night preparing himself. He looks back on his blighted childhood, his open wounds. At the core of his being, he rejects the new part he is to play. He is afraid of betraying the dead who, as judges and witnesses, observe the living but are unable to come to their aid. And yet . . .

What will dawn bring for him? More darkness, or the light of the coming day?

This is where we see two men, albeit enemies, pursue a simple and inevitable dialogue illuminating the human truth that hatred is never an answer, and that death nullifies all answers. There is nothing sacred, nothing uplifting, in hatred or in death.

In this story, which calls religious and cultural ideas into question, I evoke the ultimate violence: murder. It aims to put on guard all of those who, in the name of their faith or of some ideal, commit cruel acts of terrorism against innocent victims.

And yet, this tale about despair becomes a story against despair.

—ELIE WIESEL

SOMEWHERE A CHILD began to cry. In the house across the way an old woman closed the shutters. It was hot with all the heat of an autumn evening in Palestine.

Standing near the window I looked out at the transparent twilight whose descent made the city seem silent, motionless, unreal, and very far away. Tomorrow, I thought for the hundredth time, I shall kill a man, and I wondered if the crying child and the woman across the way knew.

I did not know the man. To my eyes he had no face; he did not even exist, for I knew nothing about him. I did not know whether he scratched his nose when he ate, whether he talked or kept quiet when he was making love, whether he gloried in his hate, whether he betrayed his wife or his God or his own future. All I knew was that he was an Englishman and my enemy. The two terms were synonymous.

"Don't torture yourself," said Gad in a low voice. "This is war."

His words were scarcely audible, and I was tempted to tell him to speak louder, because no one could possibly hear. The child's crying covered all other sounds. But I could not open my mouth, because I was thinking of the man who was doomed to die. Tomorrow, I said to myself, we shall be bound together for all eternity by the tie that binds a victim and his executioner.

"It's getting dark," said Gad. "Shall I put on the light?"

I shook my head. The darkness was not yet complete. As yet there was no face at the window to mark the exact moment when day changed into night.

A beggar had taught me, a long time ago, how to distinguish night from day. I met him one evening in my hometown when I was saying my prayers in the overheated synagogue, a gaunt, shadowy fellow, dressed in shabby black clothes, with a look in his eyes that was not of this world. It was at the beginning of the war. I was twelve years old, my parents were still alive, and God still dwelt in our town.

"Are you a stranger?" I asked him.

"I'm not from around here," he said in a voice that seemed to listen rather than speak.

Beggars inspired me with mingled feelings of love and fear. I knew that I ought to be kind to them, for they might not be what they seemed. Hassidic literature tells us that a beggar may be the prophet Elijah in disguise, come to visit the earth and the hearts of men and to offer the reward of eternal life to those who treat him well. Nor is the prophet Elijah the only one to put on the garb of a beggar. The Angel of Death delights in frightening men in the same way. To do him wrong is more dangerous; he may take a man's life or his soul in return.

And so the stranger in the synagogue inspired me with fear. I asked him if he was hungry and he said no. I tried to find out if there was anything he wanted, but without success. I had an urge to do something for him, but did not know what.

The synagogue was empty and the candles had begun to burn low. We were quite alone, and I was overcome by increasing anxiety. I knew that I shouldn't be there with him at midnight, for that is the hour when the dead rise up from their graves and come to say their prayers. Anyone they find in the synagogue risks being carried away, for fear he betray their secret.

"Come to my house," I said to the beggar. "There you can find food to eat and a bed in which to sleep."

"I never sleep," he replied.

I was quite sure then that he was not a real beggar. I told him that I had to go home and he offered to keep me company. As we walked along the snow-covered streets he asked me if I was ever afraid of the dark.

"Yes, I am," I said. I wanted to add that I was afraid of him too, but I felt he knew that already.

"You mustn't be afraid of the dark," he said, gently grasping my arm and making me shudder. "Night is purer than day; it is better for thinking and loving and dreaming. At night everything is more intense, more true. The echo of words that have been spoken during the day takes on a new and deeper meaning. The tragedy of man is that he doesn't know how to distinguish between day and night. He says things at night that should only be said by day."

He came to a halt in front of my house. I asked him again if he didn't want to come in, but he said no, he must be on his way. That's it, I thought; he's going back to the synagogue to welcome the dead.

"Listen," he said, digging his fingers into my arm. "I'm going to teach you the art of distinguishing between day and night. Always look at a window, and failing that look into the eyes of a man. If you see a face, any face, then you can be sure that night has succeeded day. For, believe me, night has a face."

Then, without giving me time to answer, he said good-bye and disappeared into the snow.

Every evening since then I had made a point of standing near a window to witness the arrival of night. And every evening I saw a face outside. It was not always the same face, for no one night was like another. In the beginning I saw the face of the beggar. Then, after my father's death, I saw his face, with the eyes grown large with death and memory. Sometimes total strangers lent the night their tearful face or their forgotten smile. I knew nothing about them except that they were dead.

"Don't torture yourself in the dark," said Gad. "This is war."

I thought of the man I was to kill at dawn, and of the beggar. Suddenly I had an absurd thought: What if the beggar was the man I was to kill?

Outside, the twilight faded abruptly away as it so often does in the Middle East. The child was still crying, it seemed to me more plaintively than before. The city was like a ghost ship, noiselessly swallowed up by the darkness.

I looked out the window, where a shadowy face was taking shape out of the deep of the night. A sharp pain caught my throat. I could not take my eyes off the face. It was my own.

AN HOUR EARLIER Gad had told me the Old Man's decision. The execution was to take place, as executions always do, at dawn. His message was no surprise; like everyone else I was expecting it. Everyone in Palestine knew that the Movement always kept its word. And the English knew it too.

A month earlier one of our fighters, wounded during a terrorist operation, had been hauled in by the police and weapons had been found on him. A military tribunal had chosen to exact the penalty stipulated by martial law: death by hanging. This was the tenth death sentence the mandatory power in Palestine had imposed upon us. The Old Man decided that things had gone far enough; he was not going to allow the English to transform the Holy Land into a scaffold. And so he announced a new line of action—reprisals.

By means of posters and underground-radio broadcasts he issued a solemn warning: Do not hang David ben Moshe; his death will cost you dear. From now on, for the hanging of every Jewish fighter an English mother will mourn the death of her son. To add weight to his words the Old Man ordered us to take a hostage, preferably an army officer. Fate willed that our victim should be Captain John Dawson. He was out walking alone one night, and this made him an easy prey, for our men were on the lookout for English officers who walked alone in the night.

John Dawson's kidnapping plunged the whole country into a state of nervous tension. The English army proclaimed a forty-eight-hour curfew, every house was searched, and hundreds of suspects were arrested. Tanks were stationed at the crossroads, machine guns set up on the rooftops, and barbed-wire barricades erected at the street corners. The whole of Palestine was one great prison, and within it there was another, smaller prison where the hostage was successfully hidden.

In a brief, horrifying proclamation the High Commissioner of Palestine announced that the entire population would be held responsible if His Majesty's Captain John Dawson were to be killed by the terrorists. Fear reigned, and the ugly word "pogrom" was on everyone's lips.

"Do you really think they'd do it?"

"Why not?"

"The English? Could the *English* ever organize a pogrom?"

"Why not?"

"They wouldn't dare."

"Why not?"

"World opinion wouldn't tolerate it."

"Why not? Just remember Hitler; world opinion tolerated him for quite some time."

The situation was grave. The Zionist leaders recommended prudence; they got in touch with the Old Man and begged him, for the sake of the nation, not to go too far: there was talk of vengeance, of a pogrom, and this meant that innocent men and women would have to pay.

The Old Man answered: If David ben Moshe is hanged, John Dawson must die. If the Movement were to give in the English would score a triumph. They would take it for a sign of weakness and impotence on our part, as if we were saying to them: Go ahead and hang all the young Jews who are holding out against you. No, the Movement cannot give in. Violence is the only language the English can understand. Man for man. Death for death.

Soon the whole world was alerted. The major newspapers of London, Paris, and New York headlined the story, with David ben Moshe sharing the honors, and a dozen special correspondents flew into Lydda. Once more Jerusalem was the center of the universe.

In London, John Dawson's mother paid a visit to the Colonial Office and requested a pardon for David ben Moshe, whose life was bound up with that of her son. With a grave smile the Secretary of State for Colonial Affairs told her: Have no fear. The Jews will never do it. You know how they are; they shout and cry and make a big fuss, but they are frightened by the meaning of their own words. Don't worry; your son isn't going to die.

The High Commissioner was less optimistic. He sent a cable to the Colonial Office, recommending clemency. Such a gesture, he said, would dispose worldwide public opinion in England's favor.

The Secretary personally telephoned his reply. The recommendation had been studied at a Cabinet meeting. Two members of the Cabinet had approved it, but the others said no. They alleged not only political reasons but the prestige of the Crown as well. A pardon would be interpreted as a sign of weakness; it might give ideas to young, self-styled idealists in other parts of the Empire. People would say: "In Palestine a group of terrorists has told Great Britain where to get off." And the Secretary added, on his own behalf: "We should be the laughingstock of the world. And think of the repercussions in the House of Commons. The opposition are waiting for just such a chance to sweep us away."

"So the answer is no?" asked the High Commissioner.

"It is."

"And what about John Dawson, sir?"

"They won't go through with it."

"Sir, I beg to disagree."

"You're entitled to your opinion."

A few hours later the official Jerusalem radio announced that David ben Moshe's execution would take place in the prison at Acre at dawn the next day. The condemned man's family had been authorized to pay him a farewell visit and the population was enjoined to remain calm.

After this came the other news of the day. At the United Nations a debate on Palestine was in the offing. In the Mediterranean two ships carrying illegal immigrants had been detained and the passengers taken to internment on Cyprus. An automobile accident at Netanya: one man dead, two injured. The weather forecast for the following day: warm, clear, visibility unlimited . . . We repeat the first bulletin: David ben Moshe, condemned to death for terroristic activities, will be hanged . . .

The announcer made no mention of John Dawson. But his anguished listeners knew. John Dawson, as well as David ben Moshe, would die. The Movement would keep its word.

"Who is to kill him?" I asked Gad.

"You are," he replied.

"Me?" I said, unable to believe my own ears.

"You," Gad repeated. "Those are the Old Man's orders."

I felt as if a fist had been thrust into my face. The earth yawned beneath my feet and I seemed to be falling into a bottomless pit, where existence was a nightmare.

"This is war," Gad was saying.

His voice sounded as if it came from very far away; I could barely hear it.

"This is war. Don't torture yourself."

"Tomorrow I shall kill a man," I said to myself, reeling in my fall. "I shall kill a man, tomorrow."

E LISHA IS MY NAME. At the time of this story I was eighteen years old. Gad had recruited me for the Movement and brought me to Palestine. He had made me into a terrorist.

I had met Gad in Paris, where I went, straight from Buchenwald, immediately after the war. When the Americans liberated Buchenwald they offered to send me home, but I rejected the offer. I didn't want to relive my childhood, to see our house in foreign hands. I knew that my parents were dead and my native town was occupied by the Russians. What was the use of going back? "No thanks," I said; "I don't want to go home."

"Then where do you want to go?"

I said I didn't know; it didn't really matter.

After staying on for five weeks in Buchenwald I was put aboard a train for Paris. France had offered me asylum, and as soon as I reached Paris a rescue committee sent me for a month to a youth camp in Normandy.

When I came back from Normandy the same organization got me a furnished room on the rue de Marois and gave me a grant which covered my living expenses and the cost of the French lessons which I took every day of the week except Saturday and Sunday from a gentleman with a mustache whose name I have forgotten. I wanted to master the language sufficiently to sign up for a philosophy course at the Sorbonne.

The study of philosophy attracted me because I wanted to understand the meaning of the events of which I had been the victim. In the concentration camp I had cried out in sorrow and anger against God and also against man, who seemed to have inherited only the cruelty of his creator. I was anxious to reevaluate my revolt in an atmosphere of detachment, to view it in terms of the present.

So many questions obsessed me. Where is God to be found? In suffering or in rebellion? When is a man most truly a man? When he submits or when he refuses? Where does suffering lead him? To purification or to bestiality? Philosophy, I hoped, would give me an answer. It would free me from my memories, my doubts, my feeling of guilt. It would drive them away or at least bring them out in concrete form into the light of day. My purpose was to enroll at the Sorbonne and devote myself to this endeavor.

But I did nothing of the sort, and Gad was the one who caused me to abandon my original aim. If today I am only a question mark, he is responsible.

One evening there was a knock at my door. I went to open it, wondering who it could be. I had no friends or acquaintances in Paris and spent most of the time in my room, reading a book or sitting with my hand over my eyes, thinking about the past.

"I would like to talk with you."

The man who stood in the doorway was young, tall, and slender. Wearing a raincoat, he had the appearance of a detective or an adventurer.

"Come in," I said after he had already entered.

He didn't take off his coat. Silently he walked over to the table, picked up the few books that were there, riffled their pages, and then put them down. Then he turned to me.

"I know who you are," he said. "I know everything about you."

His face was tanned, expressive. His hair was unruly, one strand perpetually on his forehead. His mouth was hard, almost cruel, thus accentuating the kindness, the intensity, and warm intelligence in his eyes.

"You are more fortunate than I, for I know very little about myself."

A smile came to his lips. "I didn't come to talk about your past."

"The future," I answered, "is of limited interest to me."

He continued to smile.

"The future," he asked, "are you attached to it?"

I felt uneasy. I didn't understand him. The meaning of his questions escaped me. Something in him set me on edge. Perhaps it was the advantage of his superior knowledge, for he knew who I was, although I didn't even know his name. He looked at me with such familiarity, such expectation, that for a moment I thought he had mistaken me for someone else, that it wasn't me he had come to see.

"Who are you?" I asked. "What do you want with me?"

"I am Gad," he said in a resonant voice, as if he were uttering some Kabbalistic sentence which contained an answer to every question. He said "I am Gad" in the same way that Jehovah said "I am that I am."

"Very good," I said with mingled curiosity and fear. "Your name is Gad. Happy to know you. And now that you've introduced yourself, may I ask the purpose of your call? What do you want of me?"

His piercing eyes seemed to look straight through me. After several moments of this penetrating stare he said in a quite matter-of-fact way:

"I want you to give me your future."

Having been brought up in the Hasidic tradition, I had heard strange stories about the Meshulah, the mysterious messenger of fate to whom nothing is impossible. His voice is such as to make a man tremble, for the message it brings is more powerful than either the bearer or the recipient. His every word seems to come from the absolute, the infinite, and its significance is at the same time fearful and fascinating. Gad is a Meshulah, I said to myself. It was not his physical appearance that gave me this impression, but rather what he said and the way he said it.

"Who are you?" I asked again, in terror.

Something told me that at the end of the road we were to travel together I should find another man, very much like myself, whom I should hate.

"I am a messenger," he said.

I felt myself grow pale. My premonition was correct. He was a messenger, a man sent by fate, to whom I could refuse nothing. I must sacrifice everything to him, even hope, if he asked it.

"You want my future?" I asked. "What will you do with it?"

He smiled again, but in a cold, distant manner, as one who possesses a power over men.

"I'll make it into an outcry," he said, and there was a strange light in his dark eyes. "An outcry first of despair and then of hope. And finally a shout of triumph."

I sat down on my bed, offering him the only chair in the room, but he remained standing. In the Hasidic legends the messenger is always portrayed standing, as if his body must at all times serve as a connecting link between heaven and earth. Standing thus, in a trench coat which seemed as if it had never been taken off and were an integral part of his body, with his head inclined toward his right shoulder and a fiery expression in his eyes, he proceeded to tell me about the Movement.

He smoked incessantly. But even when he paused to light a cigarette he continued to stare obliquely at me and never stopped talking. He talked until dawn, and I listened with my eyes and mind wide open. Just so I had listened as a child to the grizzled master who revealed to me the mysterious universe of the Kabbala, where every idea is a story and every story, even one concerned with the life of a ghost, is a spark from eternity.

That night Gad told me about Palestine and the age-old Jewish dream of re-creating an independent homeland, one where every human act would be free. He told me also of the Movement's desperate struggle with the English.

"The English government has sent a hundred thousand soldiers to maintain so-called order. We of the Movement are no more than a hundred strong, but we strike fear into their hearts. Do you understand what I am saying? We cause the English—yes, the English—to tremble!" The sparks in his dark eyes lit up the fear of a hundred thousand uniformed men.

This was the first story I had ever heard in which the Jews were not the ones to be afraid. Until this moment I had believed that the mission of the Jews was to represent the trembling of history rather than the wind which made it tremble.

"The paratroopers, the police dogs, the tanks, the planes, the tommy guns, the executioners—they are all afraid. The Holy Land has become, for them, a land of fear. They don't dare walk out on the streets at night, or look a young girl in the eye for fear that she may shoot them in the belly, or stroke the head of a child for fear that he may throw a hand grenade in their face. They dare neither to speak nor to be silent. They are afraid."

Hour after hour Gad spoke to me of the blue nights of Palestine, of their calm and serene beauty. You walk out in the evening with a woman, you tell her that she is beautiful and you love her, and twenty centuries hear what you are saying. But for the English the night holds no beauty. For them every night opens and shuts like a tomb. Every night two, three, a dozen soldiers are swallowed up by the darkness and never seen again.

Then Gad told me the part he expected me to play. I was to give up everything and go with him to join the struggle. The Movement needed fresh recruits and reinforcements. It needed young men who were willing to offer it their futures. The sum of their futures would be the freedom of Israel, the future of Palestine.

It was the first time that I had heard of any of these things. My parents had not been Zionists. To me Zion was a sacred ideal, a Messianic hope, a prayer, a heartbeat, but not a place on the map or a political slogan, a cause for which men killed and died.

Gad's stories were utterly fascinating. I saw in him a prince of Jewish history, a legendary messenger sent by fate to awaken my imagination, to tell the people whose past was now their religion: Come, come; the future is waiting for you with open arms. From now on you will no longer be humiliated, persecuted, or even pitied. You will not be strangers encamped in an age and a place that are not yours. Come, brothers, come!

Gad stopped talking and went to look out the window at the approaching dawn. The shadows melted away and a pale, prematurely weary light the color of stagnant water invaded my small room.

"I accept your offer," I said.

I said it so softly that Gad seemed not to hear. He remained standing by the window and after a moment of silence turned around to say:

"Here is the dawn. In our land it is very different. Here the dawn is gray; in Palestine it is red like fire."

"I accept, Gad," I repeated.

"I heard you," he said, with a smile the color of the Paris dawn. "You'll be leaving in three weeks."

The autumn breeze blowing in through the window made me shiver. Three weeks, I reflected, before I plunge into the unknown. Perhaps my shiver was caused not so much by the breeze as by this reflection. I believe that even then unconsciously I knew that at the end of the road I was to travel with Gad, a man was waiting, a man who would be called upon to kill another man, myself.

Radio Jerusalem . . . Last-minute news flashes. David ben Moshe's execution will take place at dawn tomorrow. The High Commissioner has issued an appeal for calm. Curfew at nine o'clock. No one will be allowed on the streets. I repeat, no one will be allowed on the streets. The army has orders to shoot on sight . . .

The announcer's voice betrayed his emotion. As he said the name David ben Moshe there must have been tears in his eyes.

All over the world the young Jewish fighter was the hero of the day. All the wartime resistance movements of Europe held rallies in front of the British embassies; the chief rabbis of the capital cities sent a joint petition to His Majesty the King. Their telegram—with some thirty signatures at the bottom—ran: "Do not hang a young man whose only crime is fidelity to his ideal." A Jewish delegation was received at the White House and the President promised to intercede. That day the heart of humanity was one with that of David ben Moshe.

It was eight o'clock in the evening and completely dark. Gad switched on the light. Outside the child was still crying.

"The dirty dogs," said Gad; "they're going to hang him."

His face and hands were red and perspiring. He paced up and down the room, lighting one cigarette after another, only to throw each one away.

"They're going to hang him," he repeated. "The bastards!"

The news broadcast came to an end and a program of choral singing followed. I started to turn the radio off but Gad held me back.

"It's a quarter past eight," he said. "See if you can get our station."

I was too nervous to turn the dial.

"I'll find it," said Gad.

The broadcast had just begun. The announcer was a girl with a resonant, grave voice familiar to every one of us. Every evening at this hour men, women, and children paused in their work or play to listen to the vibrant, mysterious voice which always began with the same eight words: *You are listening to the Voice of Freedom* . . .

The Jews of Palestine loved this girl or young woman without knowing who she was. The English would have given anything to lay hands upon her. In their eyes she was as dangerous as the Old Man; she too was a part of the Legend. Only a very few people, no more than five, knew her identity, and Gad and I were among them. Her name was Ilana; she and Gad were in love and I was a friend to both of them. Their love was an essential part of my life. I needed to know that there was such a thing as love and that it brought smiles and joy in its wake.

You are listening to the Voice of Freedom, Ilana repeated.

Gad's dark face quivered. He was bent almost double over the radio, as if he wanted to touch with his hands and eyes the clear, deeply moving voice of Ilana, which tonight was his voice and mine and that of the whole country.

"Two men are preparing to meet death at dawn tomorrow," said Ilana, as if she were reading a passage from the Bible. "One of them deserves our admiration, the other our pity. Our brother and guide, David ben Moshe, knows why he is dying; John Dawson does not know. Both of them are vigorous and intelligent, on the threshold of life and happiness. They might have been friends, but now this can never be. At dawn tomorrow at the same hour, the same minute, they will die—but not together, for there is an abyss between them. David ben Moshe's death is meaningful; John Dawson's is not. David is a hero, John a victim . . ."

For twenty minutes Ilana went on talking. The last part of her broadcast was dedicated exclusively to John Dawson, because he had the greater need of comfort and consolation.

I knew neither David nor John, but I felt bound to them and their fates. It flashed across my mind that in speaking of John Dawson's imminent death Ilana was speaking of me also, since I was his killer. Who was to kill David ben Moshe? For a moment I had the impression that I was to kill both of them and all the other Johns and Davids on earth. I was the executioner. And I was eighteen years old. Eighteen years of searching and suffering, of study and rebellion, and they all added up to this. I wanted to understand the pure, unadulterated essence of human nature, the path to the understanding of man. I had sought after the truth, and here I was about to become a killer, a participant in the work of death and God. I went over to the mirror hanging on the wall and looked into my face. I almost cried out, for everywhere I saw my own eyes.

As a child I was afraid of death. I was not afraid to die, but every time I thought of death I shuddered.

"Death," Kalman, the grizzled master, told me, "is a being without arms or legs or mouth or head; it is all eyes. If ever you meet a creature with eyes everywhere, you can be sure that it is death."

Gad was still leaning over the radio.

"Look at me," I said, but he did not hear.

"John Dawson, you have a mother," Ilana was saying. "At this hour she must be crying, or eating her heart out in silent despair. She will not go to bed tonight. She will sit in a chair near the window, watch in hand, waiting for dawn. Her heart will skip a beat when yours stops beating forever. 'They've killed my son,' she will say. 'Those murderers!' But we are not murderers, Mrs. Dawson . . ."

"Look at me, Gad," I repeated.

He raised his eyes, shot me a glance, shrugged his shoulders, and went back to the voice of Ilana. Gad doesn't know that I am death, I thought to myself. But John Dawson's mother, sitting near the window of her London flat, must surely know. She is gazing out into the night, and the night has a thousand eyes, which are mine.

"No, Mrs. Dawson, we are not murderers. Your Cabinet ministers are murderers; they are responsible for the death of your son. We should have preferred to receive him as a brother, to offer him bread and milk and show him the beauties of our country. But your government made him our enemy and by the same token signed his death warrant. No, we are not murderers."

I buried my head in my hands. The child outside had stopped crying.

I N ALL PROBABILITY I had killed before, but under entirely different circumstances. The act had other dimensions, other witnesses. Since my arrival in Palestine several months before, I had taken part in various tangles with the police, in sabotage operations, in attacks on military convoys making their way across the green fields of Galilee or the white desert. There had been casualties on both sides, but the odds were in our favor because the night was our ally. Under cover of darkness we took the enemy by surprise; we set fire to an army encampment, killed a dozen soldiers, and disappeared without leaving any traces behind us. The Movement's objective was to kill the greatest number of soldiers possible. It was that simple.

Ever since the day of my arrival, my first steps on the soil of Palestine, this idea had been imprinted upon my brain. As I stepped off the ship at Haifa two comrades picked me up in their car and took me to a two-story house somewhere between Ramat-Gan and Tel Aviv. This house was ostensibly occupied by a professor of languages, to justify the comings and goings of a large number of young people who were actually, like myself, apprentices of a school of terrorist techniques. The cellar served as a dungeon where we kept prisoners, hostages, and those of our comrades who were wanted by the police. Here it was that John Dawson was awaiting execution. The hiding place was absolutely secure. Several times English soldiers had searched the house from top to bottom; their police dogs had come within a few inches of John Dawson, but there was a wall between them.

Gad directed our terrorist instruction. Other masked teachers taught us the use of a revolver, a machine gun, a hand grenade. We learned also to wield a dagger, to strangle a man from behind without making a sound, and to get out of practically any prison. The course lasted for six weeks. For two hours every day Gad indoctrinated us with the Movement's ideology. The goal was simply to get the English out; the method, intimidation, terror, and sudden death.

"On the day when the English understand that their occupation will cost them blood they won't want to stay," Gad told us. "It's cruel—inhuman, if you like. But we have no other choice. For generations we've wanted to be better, more pure in heart than those who persecuted us. You've all seen the result: Hitler and the extermination camps in Germany. We've had enough of trying to be more just than those who claim to speak in the name of justice. When the Nazis killed a third of our people just men found nothing to say. If ever it's a question of killing off Jews, everyone is silent; there are twenty centuries of history to prove it. We can rely only on ourselves. If we must become more unjust and inhuman than those who have been unjust and inhuman to us, then we shall do so. We don't like to be bearers of death; heretofore we've chosen to be victims rather than executioners. The commandment *Thou shalt not kill* was given from the summit of one of the mountains here in Palestine, and we were the only ones to obey it. But that's all over; we must be like everybody else. Murder will be not our profession but our duty. In the days and weeks and months to come you will have only one purpose: to kill those who have made us killers. We shall kill in order that once more we may be men . . ."

On the last day of the course a masked stranger addressed us. He spoke of what our leaders called the eleventh commandment: *Hate your enemy.* He had a soft, timid, romantic voice, and I think he was the Old Man. I'm not quite sure, but his words fired our enthusiasm and made us tremble with emotion. Long after he had gone away I felt them vibrate within me. Thanks to him I became part of a Messianic world where destiny had the face of a masked beggar, where not a single act was lost or a single glance wasted.

I remembered how the grizzled master had explained the sixth commandment to me. Why has a man no right to commit murder? Because in so doing he takes upon himself the function of God. And this must not be done too easily. Well, I said to myself, if in order to change the course of our history we have to become God, we shall become Him. How easy that is we shall see. No, it was not easy.

The first time I took part in a terrorist operation I had to make a superhuman effort not be sick at my stomach. I found myself utterly hateful. Seeing myself with the eyes of the past I imagined that I was in the dark gray uniform of an SS officer. The first time . . .

THEY RAN LIKE RABBITS, like drunken rabbits, looking for the shelter of a tree. They seemed to have neither heads nor hands, but only legs. And these legs ran like rabbits sotted with wine and sorrow. But we were all around them, forming a circle of fire from which there was no escape. We were there with our tommy guns, and our bullets were a flaming wall on which their lives were shattered to the accompaniment of agonized cries which I shall hear until the last day of my life.

There were six of us. I don't remember the names of the five others, but Gad was not among them. That day he stayed at the school, as if to show that he had complete confidence in us, as if he were saying: "Go to it; you can get along without me." My five comrades and I set out either to kill or to be killed.

"Good luck!" said Gad as he shook hands with us before we went away. "I'll wait here for your return."

This was the first time that I had been assigned to any operation, and I knew that when I came back—if I came back—I should be another man. I should have undergone my baptism of fire, my baptism of blood. I knew that I should feel very differently, but I had no idea that I should be ready to vomit.

Our mission was to attack a military convoy on the road between Haifa and Tel Aviv. The exact spot was the curve near the village of Hedera; the time late afternoon. In the disguise of workmen coming home from their job we arrived at the chosen place thirty minutes before H-hour. If we had come any earlier our presence might have attracted attention. We set mines on either side of the curve and moved into planned positions. A car was waiting fifty yards away to take us to Petach Tivka, where we were to split up and be driven in three other cars back to our base at the school.

The convoy arrived punctually upon the scene: three open trucks carrying about twenty soldiers. The wind ruffled their hair and the sun shone upon their faces. At the curve the first truck was exploded by one of our mines and the others came to an abrupt halt with screeching brakes. The soldiers leaped to the ground and were caught in the crossfire of our guns. They ran with lowered heads in every direction, but their legs were cut by our bullets, as if by an immense scythe, and they fell shrieking to the ground.

The whole episode lasted no more than a single minute. We withdrew in good order and everything went according to plan. Our mission was accomplished. Gad was waiting at the school and we made our report to him. His face glowed with pride.

"Good work," he said. "The Old Man won't believe it."

It was then that nausea overcame me. I saw the legs running like frightened rabbits and I found myself utterly hateful. I remembered the dreaded SS guards in the Polish ghettos. Day after day, night after night, they slaughtered the Jews in just the same way. Tommy guns were scattered here and there, and an officer, laughing or distractedly eating, barked out the order: *Fire!* Then the scythe went to work. A few Jews tried to break through the circle of fire, but they only rammed their heads against its insurmountable wall. They too ran like rabbits, like rabbits sotted with wine and sorrow, and death mowed them down.

NO, IT WAS NOT EASY to play the part of God, especially when it meant putting on the field-gray uniform of the SS. But it was easier than killing a hostage.

In the first operation and those that followed I was not alone. I killed, to be sure, but I was one of a group. With John Dawson I would be on my own. I would look into his face and he would look into mine and see that I was all eyes.

"Don't torture yourself, Elisha," said Gad. He had turned off the radio and was scrutinizing me intently. "This is war."

I wanted to ask him whether God, the God of war, wore a uniform. But I chose to keep silent. God doesn't wear a uniform, I said to myself. God is a member of the Resistance Movement, a terrorist.

ILANA ARRIVED a few minutes before the curfew with her two bodyguards, Gideon and Joab. She was restless and somber, more beautiful than ever. Her delicate features seemed chiseled out of brown marble and there was an expression of heartrending melancholy on her face. She was wearing a gray skirt and a white blouse and her lips were very pale.

"Unforgettable . . . that broadcast of yours," murmured Gad.

"The Old Man wrote it," said Ilana.

"But your voice . . ."

"That's the Old Man's creation too," said Ilana, sinking exhausted into a chair. And after a moment of complete silence she added: "Today I saw him crying. I have an idea that he cries more often than we know."

The lucky fellow, I thought to myself. At least he can cry. When a man weeps he knows that one day he will stop.

Joab gave us the latest news of Tel Aviv, of its atmosphere of anxiety and watchful waiting. People were afraid of mass reprisals, and all the newspapers had appealed to the Old Man to call off John Dawson's execution. The name of John Dawson rather than that of David ben Moshe was on everyone's lips.

"That's why the Old Man was crying," said Gad, brushing a stubborn lock of hair back from his forehead. "The Jews are not yet free of their persecution reflex. They haven't the guts to strike back."

"In London the Cabinet is in session," Joab went on. "In New York the Zionists are holding a huge demonstration in Madison Square Garden. The UN is deeply concerned."

"I hope David knows," said Ilana. Her face had paled to a bronze hue.

"No doubt the hangman will tell him," said Gad.

I understood the bitterness in his voice. David was a childhood friend and they had entered the Movement together. Gad had told me this only after David's arrest, for it would have been unsafe before. The less any one of us knew about his comrades the better; this is one of the basic principles of any underground organization.

Gad had been present when David was wounded; in fact, he was in command of the operation. It was supposed to be what we called a "soft job," but the courageous stupidity of a sentry had spoiled it. His was the fault if David was to be hanged on the morrow. Although wounded and in convulsions he had continued to crawl along the ground with a bullet in his belly and even to shoot off his gun. The mischief that a courageous, diehard fool can do!

IT WAS NIGHT. An army truck came to a halt at the entrance of the red-capped paratroopers' camp near Gedera, in the south. In it were a major and three soldiers.

"We've come to get some arms," the major said to the sentry. "A terrorist attack is supposed to take place this evening."

"Those goddamned terrorists," the sentry mumbled from under his mustache, handing back the major's identification papers.

"Very good, Major," he said, opening the gate. "You can come in."

"Thanks," said the Major. "Where are the stores?"

"Straight ahead and then two left turns."

The car drove through, followed these directions, and stopped in front of a stone building.

"Here we are," said the major.

They got out, and a sergeant saluted the major and opened the door. The major returned his salute and handed him an order with a colonel's signature at the bottom, an order to consign to the bearer five tommy guns, twenty rifles, twenty revolvers, and the necessary ammunition.

"We're expecting a terrorist attack," the major explained condescendingly.

"Goddamned terrorists," muttered the sergeant.

"We've no time to lose," the major added. "Can you hurry?"

"Of course, sir," said the sergeant. "I quite understand."

He pointed out the arms and ammunition to the three soldiers, who silently and quickly loaded them onto the truck. In a very few minutes it was all done.

"I'll just keep this order, sir," said the sergeant as the visitors started to go away.

"Right you are, Sergeant," said the major, climbing into the truck.

The sentry was just about to open the gate when in his sentry box the telephone rang. With a hasty apology he went to answer. The major and his men waited impatiently.

"Sorry, sir," said the sentry as he emerged from the box. "The sergeant wants to see you. He says the order you brought him is not satisfactory."

The major got down from the truck.

"I'll clear it up with him on the telephone," he said.

As the sentry turned around to reenter the box the major brought his fist down on the back of his neck. The sentry fell noiselessly to the ground. Gad went over to the gate, opened it, and signaled to the driver to go through. Just then the sentry came to and started shooting. Dan put a bullet into his belly while Gad jumped onto the truck and called out:

"Let's go! And hurry!"

The wounded sentry continued to shoot and one of his bullets punctured a tire. Gad retained his self-possession and decided that the tire must be changed.

"David and Dan, keep us covered," he said in a quiet, assured voice.

David and Dan grabbed two of the recently received tommy guns and stood by.

By now the whole camp was alerted. Orders rang out and gunfire followed. Every second was precious. Covered by David and Dan, Gad changed the tire. But the paratroopers were drawing near. Gad knew that the important thing was to make off with the weapons.

"David and Dan," he said, "stay where you are. We're leaving. See if you can hold them back for three minutes longer while we get away. After that you can make a dash for it. Try to get to Gedera, where friends will give you shelter. You know where to find them."

"Yes, I know," said David, continuing to shoot. "Go on, and hurry!"

The arms and ammunition were saved, but David and Dan had to pay. Dan was killed and David wounded. All on account of a stubbornly courageous sentry with a bullet in his belly!

"HE WAS A WONDERFUL FELLOW, David," said Ilana. Already she spoke of him as if he belonged to the past.

"I hope the hangman knows it," retorted Gad.

I understood his bitterness; indeed I envied it. He was losing a friend, and it hurt. But when you lose a friend every day it doesn't hurt so much. And I'd lost plenty of friends in my time; sometimes I thought of myself as a living graveyard. That was the real reason I followed Gad to Palestine and became a terrorist: I had no more friends to lose.

"They say that the hangman always wears a mask," said Joab, who had been standing silently in front of the kitchen door. "I wonder if it's true."

"I think it is," I said. "The hangman wears a mask. You can't see anything but his eyes."

Ilana went over to Gad, stroked his hair, and said in a sad voice:

"Don't torture yourself, Gad. This is war."

DURING THE HOUR that followed nobody said a word. They were all thinking of David ben Moshe. David was not alone in his death cell; his friends were with him. All except me. I did not think of David except when they pronounced his name. When they were silent my thoughts went out to someone else, to a man I did not yet know, any more than I knew David, but whom I was fated to know. My David ben Moshe had the name and face of an Englishman, Captain John Dawson.

We sat around the table and Ilana served us some steaming tea. For some time we sipped it without speaking. We looked into the golden liquid in our cups as if we were searching in it for the next step after our silence and the meaning of the events which had brought it about. Then, in order to kill time, we spoke of our memories, of such of them that centered on death.

"Death saved my life," Joab began.

He had a young, innocent, tormented face; dark, confused eyes, and hair as white as that of an old man. He wore a perpetually sleepy expression and yawned from one end of the day to the other.

"A neighbor who was against us because of his pacifist convictions reported me to the police," he went on. "I took shelter in an insane asylum whose superintendent was an old school friend. I stayed there for two weeks, until the police found my traces. 'Is he here?' they asked the superintendent. 'Yes,' he admitted. 'He's here; he's a very sick man.' 'What's the matter with him?' they asked. 'He imagines he's dead,' the superintendent told them. But they insisted on seeing me. I was brought to the superintendent's office, where two police officials assigned to the antiterrorist campaign were waiting. They spoke to me but I did not answer. They asked me questions but I pretended not to hear. Even so, they were not convinced that I was crazy. Overriding the superintendent's protest, they took me away and submitted me to forty-eight hours of interrogation. I played dead, and played it successfully. I refused to eat or drink; when they slapped my hands and face I did not react. Dead men feel no pain and so they do not cry. After forty-eight hours I was taken back to the asylum."

As I listened to Joab various thoughts floated to the surface of my mind. I remembered hearing some of my comrades refer to Joab as the Madman.

"Funny, isn't it?" he said. "Death actually saved my life."

We kept silence for several minutes, as if to pay homage to death for saving his life and giving the name of Madman to a fellow with an innocent, tormented face.

"Several days later, when I left the asylum, I saw that my hair had turned white," Joab concluded.

"That's one of death's little jokes," I put in. "Death loves to change the color of people's hair. Death has no hair; it has only eyes. God, on the other hand, has no eyes at all."

"God saved me from death," said Gideon.

We called Gideon the Saint. First because he *was* a saint, and second because he looked like one. He was a husky, inarticulate fellow some twenty years old, who took pains to make himself inconspicuous and was always mumbling prayers. He wore a beard and side curls, went nowhere without a prayer book in his pocket. His father was a rabbi, and when he learned that his son meant to become a terrorist he gave him his blessing. There are times, his father said, when words and prayers are not enough. The God of grace is also the God of war. And war is not a matter of mere words.

"God saved me from death," Gideon repeated. "His eyes saved me. I too was arrested and tortured. They pulled my beard, lit matches under my fingernails, and spat in my face, all in order to make me confess that I had taken part in an attempt against the life of the High Commissioner. But in spite of the pain I did not talk. More than once I was tempted to cry out, but I kept quiet because I felt that God's eyes were upon me. God is looking at me, I said to myself, and I must not disappoint Him. My torturers never stopped shouting, but I kept my thoughts on God and on His eyes, which are drawn to human pain. For lack of evidence they finally had to set me free. If I had admitted my guilt I should be dead."

"And then," I put in, "God would have closed His eyes."

Ilana refilled our cups.

"What about you, Ilana?" I asked. "What saved your life?"

"A cold in the head," she replied.

I burst out laughing, but no one else joined in. My laugh was raucous and artificial.

"A cold in the head?" I repeated.

"Yes," said Ilana, quite seriously. "The English have no description of me; they know only my voice. One day they hauled in a whole group of women, myself among them. At the police station a sound engineer compared each one of our voices to that of the mysterious announcer of the Voice of Freedom. Thanks to the fact that I had a heavy cold I was quickly eliminated and four other women were detained for further questioning."

Once more I was tempted to laugh, but the others were glum and silent. A cold, I thought to myself. And in this case it turned out to have more practical use than either faith or courage. Next we all looked at Gad, who was almost crushing his teacup between his fingers.

"I owe my life to three Englishmen," he said. With his head almost on his right shoulder and his eyes fixed on the cup, he seemed to be addressing the rapidly cooling tea. "It was very early in the game," he went on. "For reasons that no longer matter the Old Man had ordered three hostages taken. They were all sergeants, and I was assigned to kill one of them, any one; the choice was up to me. I was young then, about the age of Elisha, and suffered great mental agony from having this unwanted role thrust upon me. I was willing to play the executioner, but not the judge. Unfortunately, during the night I lost contact with the Old Man and could not explain my reluctance. The sentence had to be carried out at dawn, and how was I to choose the victim? Finally I had an idea. I went down to the cellar and told the three sergeants that the choice was up to them. If you don't make it, I said, then all three of you will be shot. They decided to draw lots, and when dawn came I put a bullet in the unlucky fellow's neck."

Involuntarily I looked at Gad's hands and face, the familiar hands and face of my friend, who had put a bullet in the neck of a fellow human being and now talked coldly, almost indifferently, about it. Was the sergeant's face gazing up at him from his cup of golden cool tea?

"What if the sergeants had refused to settle it among themselves?" I asked. "What then?"

Gad squeezed the cup harder than ever, almost as if he were trying to break it.

"I think I'd have killed myself instead," he said in a flat voice. And after a moment of heavy silence he added: "I tell you I was young and very weak."

All eyes turned toward me, in expectation of my story. I gulped down a mouthful of bitter tea and wiped the perspiration off my forehead.

"I owe my life to a laugh," I said. "It was during one winter at Buchenwald. We were clothed in rags and hundreds of people died of cold every day. In the morning we had to leave our barracks and wait outside in the snow for as long as two hours until they had been cleaned. One day I felt so sick that I was sure the exposure would kill me, and so I stayed behind, in hiding. Quite naturally I was discovered and the cleaning squad dragged me before one of the many assistant barracks leaders. Without stopping to question me he caught hold of my throat and said dispassionately: 'I'm going to choke you.' His powerful hands closed in on my throat and in my enfeebled condition I did not even try to put up a fight. Very well, I said to myself; it's all over. I felt the blood gather in my head and my head swell to several times its normal size, so that I must have looked like a caricature, a miserable clown. I was sure from one minute to the next that it would burst into a thousand shreds like a child's toy balloon. At this moment the assistant leader took a good look at me and found the sight so comical that he released his grip and burst out laughing. He laughed so long that he forgot his intention to kill. And that's how I got out of it unharmed. It's funny, isn't it, that I should owe my life to an assassin's sense of humor?"

I expected my listeners to scrutinize my head to see if it had really returned to its normal size, but they did nothing of the sort. They continued to stare into their stone-cold tea. In the next few minutes nobody opened his mouth. We had no more desire to call up the past or to listen to our fellows tell their troubled life stories. We sat in restless silence around the table. Every one of us, I am sure, was asking himself to what he *really* owed his life. Gideon was the first to speak.

"We ought to take the Englishman something to eat," he said.

Yes, I said to myself, Gideon is sad too. He's thinking of John Dawson. He must be; it's inevitable.

"I don't imagine he's hungry," I said aloud. "You can't expect a man condemned to die to have an appetite." And to myself I added: "Or a man condemned to kill, either."

There must have been a strange tone in my voice, for the others raised their heads and I felt the puzzled quality of their penetrating stares.

"No," I said stubbornly; "a man condemned to die can't be hungry."

They did not stir, but sat petrified as the seconds dragged interminably by.

"The condemned man's traditional last meal is a joke," I said loudly, "a joke in the worst possible taste, an insult to the corpse that he is about to be. What does a man care if he dies with an empty stomach?"

The expression of astonishment lingered in Gad's eyes, but Ilana looked at me with compassion and Gideon with friendliness. Joab did not look at me at all. His eyes were lowered, but perhaps that was his way of looking out of them.

"He doesn't know," remarked Gideon.

"He doesn't know what?" I asked, without any conscious reason for raising my voice. Perhaps I wanted to hear myself shout, to arouse my anger and see it reflected in the motionless shadows in the mirror and on the wall. Or perhaps out of sheer weakness. I felt powerless to change anything, least of all myself, in spite of the fact that I wanted to introduce a transformation into the room, to reorder the whole of creation. I would have made the Saint into a madman, have given John Dawson's name to Gad and his fate to David. But I knew there was nothing I could do. To have such power I should have had to take the place of death, not just of the individual death of John Dawson, the English captain who had no more appetite than I.

"What doesn't he know?" I repeated stridently.

"He doesn't know he's going to die," said Gideon in a sorrow-fully dreamy voice.

"His stomach knows," I retorted. "A man about to die listens only to his stomach. He pays no attention to his heart or to his past, or to yours for that matter. He doesn't even hear the voice of the storm. He listens to his stomach and his stomach tells him that he is going to die and that he isn't hungry."

I had talked too fast and too loud and I was left panting. I should have liked to run away, but my friends' stares transfixed me. Death sealed off every exit, and everywhere there were eyes.

"I'm going down to the cellar," said Gideon. "I'll ask him if he wants something to eat."

"Don't ask him anything," I said. "Simply tell him that tomor-row, when the sun rises above the bloodred horizon, he, John Dawson, will say good-bye to life, good-bye to his stomach. Tell him that he's going to die."

Gideon got up, with his eyes still on me, and started toward the kitchen and the entrance to the cellar. At the door he paused.

"I'll tell him," he said, with a quickly fading smile. Then he turned on his heels and I heard him going down the stairs.

I was grateful for his consent. He and not I would warn John

Dawson of his approaching end. I could never have done it. It's easier to kill a man than to break the news that he is going to die.

"Midnight," said Joab.

Midnight, I reflected, the hour when the dead rise out of their graves and come to say their prayers in the synagogue, the hour when God Himself weeps over the destruction of the Temple, the hour when a man should be able to plumb the depths of his being and to discover the Temple in ruins. A God that weeps and dead men that pray.

"Poor boy!" murmured Ilana.

She did not look at me, but her tears scrutinized my face. Her tears rather than her eyes caressed me.

"Don't say that, Ilana. Don't call me 'poor boy.' "

There were tears in her eyes, or rather there were tears in the place of her eyes, tears which with every passing second grew heavier and more opaque and threatened to overflow . . . I was afraid that suddenly the worst would happen: the dusky Ilana would no longer be there; she would have drowned in her tears. I wanted to touch her arm and say *Don't cry*. Say what you like, but don't cry.

But she wasn't crying. It takes eyes to cry, and she had no eyes, only tears where her eyes should have been.

"Poor boy!" she repeated.

Then what I had foreseen came true. Ilana disappeared, and Catherine was there instead. I wondered why Catherine had come, but her apparition did not particularly surprise me. She liked the opposite sex, and particularly she liked little boys who were thinking of death. She liked to speak of love to little boys, and since men going to their death are little boys she liked to speak to them of love. For this reason her presence in the magical room—magical because it transcended the differences, the boundary lines between the victim and the executioner, between the present and the past—was not surprising.

I had met Catherine in Paris in 1945, when I had just come from Buchenwald, that other magical spot, where the living were transformed into dead and their future into darkness. I was weakened and half starved. One of the many rescue committees sent me to a camp where a hundred boys and girls were spending their summer vacation. The camp was in Normandy, where the early morning breeze rustled the same way it did in Palestine.

Because I knew no French I could not communicate with the other boys and girls. I ate and sunbathed with them, but I had no way of talking. Catherine was the only person who seemed to know any German and occasionally we exchanged a few words. Sometimes she came up to me at the dining-room table and asked me whether I had slept well, enjoyed my meal, or had a good time during the day.

She was twenty-six or -seven years old; small, frail, and almost transparent, with silky blond, sunlit hair and blue, dreamy eyes which never cried. Her face was thin but saved from being bony by the delicacy of the features. She was the first woman I had seen from nearby. Before this—that is, before the war—I did not look at women. On my way to school or the synagogue I walked close to the walls, with my eyes cast down on the ground. I knew that women existed, and why, but I did not appreciate the fact that they had a body, breasts, legs, hands, and lips whose touch sets a man's heart to beating. Catherine revealed this to me.

The camp was at the edge of a wood, and after supper I went walking there all by myself, talking to the murmuring breeze and watching the sky turn a deeper and deeper blue. I liked to be alone.

One evening Catherine asked if she might go with me, and I

was too timid to say anything but yes. For half an hour, an hour, we walked in complete silence. At first I found the silence embarrassing, then to my surprise I began to enjoy it. The silence of two people is deeper than the silence of one. Involuntarily I began to talk.

"Look how the sky is opening up," I said.

She threw back her head and looked above her. Just as I had said, the sky was opening up. Slowly at first, as if swept by an invisible wind, the stars drew away from the zenith, some moving to the right, others to the left, until the center of the sky was an empty space, dazzlingly blue and gradually acquiring depth and outline.

"Look hard," I said. "There's nothing there."

From behind me Catherine looked up and said not a word.

"That's enough," I said; "let's go on walking."

As we walked on I told her the legend of the open sky. When I was a child the old master told me that there were nights when the sky opened up in order to make way for the prayers of unhappy children. On one such night a little boy whose father was dying said to God: "Father, I am too small to know how to pray. But I ask you to heal my sick father." God did what the boy asked, but the boy himself was turned into a prayer and carried up into heaven. From that day on, the master told me, God has from time to time shown Himself to us in the face of a child.

"That is why I like to look at the sky at this particular moment," I told Catherine. "I hope to see the child. But you are a witness to the truth. There's nothing there. The child is only a story."

It was then for the first time during the evening that Catherine spoke.

"Poor boy!" she exclaimed. "Poor boy!"

She's thinking of the boy in the story, I said to myself. And I loved her for her compassion.

After this Catherine often went walking with me. She questioned me about my childhood and my more recent past, but I did not always answer. One evening she asked me why I kept apart from the other boys and girls in the camp.

"Because they speak a language I can't understand," I told her.

"Some of the girls know German," she said.

"But I have nothing to say to them."

"You don't have to say anything," she said slowly, with a smile. "All you have to do is love them."

I didn't see what she was driving at and said so. Her smile widened and she began to speak to me of love. She spoke easily and well. Love is this and love is that; man is born to love; he is only alive when he is in the presence of a woman he loves or should love. I told her that I knew nothing of love, that I didn't know it existed or had a right to exist.

"I'll prove it to you," she said.

The next evening, as she walked at my left side over the leaf-covered path, she took hold of my arm. At first I thought she needed my support, but actually it was because she wanted to make me feel the warmth of her body. Then she claimed to be tired and said it would be pleasant to sit down on the grass under a tree. Once we had sat down she began to stroke my face and hair. Then she kissed me several times; first her lips touched mine and then her tongue burned the inside of my mouth. For several nights running we returned to the same place, and she spoke to me of love and desire and the mysteries of the heart. She took my hand and guided it over her breasts and thighs, and I realized that women had breasts and thighs and hands that could set a man's heart to beating and turn his blood to fire.

Then came the last evening. The month of vacation was over and I was to go back to Paris the next day. As soon as we had finished supper we went to sit for the last time under the tree. I felt sad and lonely, and Catherine held my hand in hers without speaking. The night was fair and calm. At intervals, like a warm breath, the wind played over our faces. It must have been one or two o'clock in the morning when Catherine broke the silence, turned her melancholy face toward me, and said:

"Now we're going to make love."

These words made me tremble. I was going to make love for the first time. Before her there had been no woman upon earth. I didn't know what to say or do; I was afraid of saying the wrong thing or making some inappropriate gesture. Awkwardly I waited for her to take the initiative. With a suddenly serious look on her face she began to get undressed. She took off her blouse and in the starlight I saw her ivory-white breasts. Then she took off the rest of her clothes and was completely naked before me.

"Take off your shirt," she ordered.

I was paralyzed; there was iron in my throat and lead in my veins; my arms and hands would not obey me. I could only look at her from head to foot and follow the rise and fall of her breasts. I was hypnotized by the call of her outstretched, naked body.

"Take off your shirt," she repeated.

Then, as I did not move, she began to undress me. Deliberately she took off my shirt and shorts. Then she lay back on the grass and said:

"Take me."

I got down on my knees. I stared at her for a long time and then I covered her body with kisses. Absently and without saying a word she stroked my hair.

"Catherine," I said, "first there is something I must tell you."

Her face took on a blank and anguished expression, and there was anguish in the rustle of the breeze among the trees.

"No, no!" she cried. "Don't tell me anything. Take me, but don't talk."

Heedless of her objection I went on:

"First, Catherine, I must tell you . . ."

Her lips twisted with pain, and there was pain in the rustle of the breeze.

"No, no, no!" she implored. "Don't tell me. Be quiet. Take me quickly, but don't talk."

"What I have to tell you is this," I insisted: "You've won the game. I love you, Catherine . . . I love you."

She burst into sobs and repeated over and over again:

"Poor boy! You poor boy!"

I picked up my shirt and shorts and ran away. Now I understood. She was referring not to the little boy in the sky but to me. She had spoken to me of love because she knew that I was the little boy who had been turned into a prayer and carried up into heaven. She knew that I had died and come back to earth, dead. This was why she had spoken to me of love and wanted to make love with me. I saw it all quite clearly. She liked making love with little boys who were going to die; she enjoyed the company of those who were obsessed with death. No wonder that her presence this night in Palestine was not surprising.

"Poor boy!" said Ilana, in a very quiet voice, for the last time. And a deep sigh escaped from her breast, which made her tears free to flow, to flow on and on until the end of time.

SUDDENLY I became aware that the room was stuffy, so stuffy that I was almost stifled.

No wonder. The room was small, far too small to receive so many visitors at one time. Ever since midnight the visitors had been pouring in. Among them were people I had known, people I had hated, admired, forgotten. As I let my eyes wander about the room I realized that all of those who had contributed to my formation, to the formation of my permanent identity, were there. Some of them were familiar, but I could not pin a label upon them; they were names without faces or faces without names. And yet I knew that at some point my life had crossed theirs.

My father was there, of course, and my mother, and the beggar. And the grizzled master. The English soldiers of the convoy we had ambushed at Gedera were there also. And around them friends and brothers and comrades, some of them out of my childhood, others that I had seen live and suffer, hope and curse at Buchenwald and Auschwitz. Alongside my father there was a boy who looked strangely like myself as I had been before the concentration camps, before the war, before everything. My father smiled at him, and the child picked up the smile and sent it to me over the multitude of heads which separated us.

Now I understood why the room was so stuffy. It was too small to hold so many people at a time. I forced a passage through the crowd until I came to the little boy and thanked him for the smile. I wanted to ask him what all these people were doing in the room, but on second thought I saw that this would be discourteous toward my father. Since he was present I should address my question to him.

"Father, why are all these people here?"

My mother stood beside him, looking very pale, and her lips tirelessly murmured: "Poor little boy, poor little boy! . . ."

"Father," I repeated, "answer me. What are you all doing here?"

His large eyes, in which I had so often seen the sky open up, were looking at me, but he did not reply. I turned around and found myself face-to-face with the rabbi, whose beard was more grizzled than ever.

"Master," I said, "what has brought all these people here tonight?"

Behind me I heard my mother whisper, "Poor little boy, my poor little boy."

"Well, Master," I repeated, "answer me, I implore you."

But he did not answer either; indeed, he seemed not even to have heard my question, and his silence made me afraid. As I had known him before, he was always present in my hour of need. Then his silence had been reassuring. Now I tried to look into his eyes, but they were two globes of fire, two suns that burned my face. I turned away and went from one visitor to another, seeking an answer to my question, but my presence struck them dumb.

Finally I came to the beggar, who stood head and shoulders above them all. And he spoke to me, quite spontaneously.

"This is a night of many faces," he said.

I was sad and tired.

"Yes," I said wearily, "this is a night of many faces, and I should like to know the reason why. If you are the one I think you are, enlighten and comfort me. Tell me the meaning of these looks, this muteness, these presences. Tell me, I beseech you, for I can endure them no longer."

He took my arm, gently pressed it, and said:

"Do you see that little boy over there?" and he pointed to the boy who looked like myself as I had been.

"Yes, I see him," I replied.

"He will answer all your questions," said the beggar. "Go talk to him."

Now I was quite sure that he was not a beggar. Once more I elbowed my way through the crowd of ghosts and arrived, panting with exhaustion, at the young boy's side.

"Tell me," I said beseechingly, "what you are doing here? And all the others?"

He opened his eyes wide in astonishment.

"Don't you know?" he asked.

I confessed that I did not know.

"Tomorrow a man is to die, isn't he?"

"Yes," I said, "at dawn tomorrow."

"And you are to kill him, aren't you?"

"Yes, that's true; I have been charged with his execution."

"And you don't understand, do you?"

"No."

"But it's all quite simple," he exclaimed. "We are here to be present at the execution. We want to see you carry it out. We want to see you turn into a murderer. That's natural enough, isn't it?"

"How is it natural? Of what concern is the killing of John Dawson to you?"

"You are the sum total of all that we have been," said the youngster who looked like my former self. "In a way we are the ones to execute John Dawson. Because you can't do it without us. Now do you see?"

I was beginning to understand. An act so absolute as that of killing involves not only the killer but, as well, those who have formed him. In murdering a man I was making them murderers.

"Well," said the boy, "do you see?"

"Yes, I see," I said.

"Poor boy, poor boy!" murmured my mother, whose lips were now as gray as the old master's hair.

"HE'S HUNGRY," said Gideon's voice unexpectedly.

I had not heard him come back up the stairs. Saints have a disconcertingly noiseless way. They walk, laugh, eat, and pray, all without making a sound.

"Impossible," I protested.

He can't be hungry, I was thinking. He's going to die, and a man who's going to die can't be hungry.

"He said so himself," Gideon insisted, with a shade of emotion in his voice.

Everyone was staring at me. Ilana had stopped crying, Joab was no longer examining his nails, and Gad looked weary. All the ghosts too seemed to be expecting something of me, a sign perhaps, or a cry.

"Does he know?" I asked Gideon.

"Yes, he knows." And after a moment he added: "I told him."

"How did he react?"

It was important for me to know the man's reaction. Was the

news a shock? Had he stayed calm, or protested his innocence?

"He smiled," said Gideon. "He said that he already knew. His stomach had told him."

"And he said he was hungry?"

Gideon hid his twitching hands behind his back.

"Yes, that's what he said. He said he was hungry and he had a right to a good last meal."

Gad laughed, but the tone of his laugh was hollow.

"Typically English," he remarked. "The stiff upper lip."

His remark hung over our heads in midair; no one opened up to receive it. My father shot me a hard glance, as if to say *A man is going to die, and he's hungry.*

"Might as well admit it," said Gad. "The English have iron digestions."

No one paid any attention to this remark either. I felt a sudden stab of pain in my stomach. I had not eaten all day. Ilana got up and went into the kitchen.

"I'll fix him something to eat," she declared.

I heard her moving about, slicing a loaf of bread, opening the icebox, starting to make coffee. In a few minutes she came back with a cup of coffee in one hand and a plate in the other.

"This is all I can find," she said. "A cheese sandwich and some black coffee. There's no sugar . . . Not much of a meal, but it's the best I can do." And after several seconds of silence she asked: "Who's going to take it down?"

The boy standing beside my father stared hard at me. His stare had a voice, which said:

"Go on. Take him something to eat. He's hungry, you know."

"No," I responded. "Not I. I don't want to see him. Above all, I don't want to see him eat. I want to think of him, later on, as a man who never ate."

I wanted to add that I had cramps in my stomach, but I realized that this was unimportant. Instead I said: "I don't want to be alone with him. Not now."

"We'll go with you," said the little boy. "It's wrong to hold back food from a man who's hungry. You know that."

Yes, I knew. I had always given food to the hungry. You, beggar, you remember. Didn't I offer you bread? But tonight is different. Tonight I can't do it.

"That's true," said the little boy, picking up the train of my reflections. "Tonight is different, and you are different also, or at least you're going to be. But that has nothing to do with the fact that a man's hungry and must have something to eat."

"But he's going to die tomorrow," I protested. "What's it matter whether he dies with a full stomach or an empty one?"

"For the time being he's alive," the child said sententiously. My father nodded in acquiescence, and all the others followed his example. "He's alive and hungry, and you refuse to give him anything to eat?"

All these heads, nodding like the tops of black trees, made me shudder. I wanted to close my eyes but I was ashamed. I couldn't close my eyes in the presence of my father.

"Very well," I said resignedly. "I accept. I'll take him something to eat." As if obeying the baton of an invisible conductor the nodding heads were still. "I'll take him something to eat," I repeated. "But first tell me something, little boy. Are the dead hungry too?"

He looked surprised.

"What—you don't know?" he exclaimed. "Of course they are."

"And should we give them something to eat?"

"How can you ask? Of course you should give them something to eat. Only it's difficult . . ."

"Difficult . . . difficult . . . difficult . . ." the ghosts echoed together.

The boy looked at me and smiled.

"I'll tell you a secret," he whispered. "You know that at midnight the dead leave their graves, don't you?"

I told him that I knew; I had been told.

"Have you been told that they go from the graveyard to the synagogue?"

Yes, I had been told that also.

"Well, it's true," said the little boy. Then, after a silence which accentuated what was to follow, he went on in a voice so still that if it had not been inside myself I could never have heard it: "Yes, it's true. They gather every night in the synagogue. But not for the purpose you imagine. They come not to pray but to eat—"

Everything in the room—walls, chairs, heads—began to whirl around me, dancing in a preestablished rhythm, without stirring the air or setting foot on the ground. I was the center of a multitude of circles. I wanted to close my eyes and stop up my ears, but my father was there, and my mother, and the master and the beggar and the boy. With all those who had formed me around me, I had no right to stop up my ears and close my eyes.

"Give me those things," I said to Ilana. "I'll take them to him."

The dancers stopped in their tracks, as if I were the conductor and my words his baton. I stepped toward Ilana, still standing at the kitchen door. Suddenly Gad rushed forward and reached her side before me.

"I'll do it," he said.

Almost brutally he snatched the cup and plate from Ilana's hands and went precipitately down the stairs.

Joab looked at his watch. "It's after two."

"Is that all?" asked Ilana. "It's a long night, the longest I've ever lived through."

"Yes, it's long," Joab agreed.

Ilana bit her lips. "There are moments when I think it will never end, that it will last indefinitely. It's like the rain. Here the rain, like everything else, suggests permanence and eternity. I say to myself: It's raining today and it's going to rain tomorrow and the next day, the next week and the next century. Now I say to myself: There's night now and there will be night tomorrow, and the day, the week, the century after."

She paused abruptly, took a handkerchief from the cuff of her blouse, and wiped her perspiring forehead.

"I wonder why it's so stuffy in here," she said, "particularly this late at night."

"It will be cooler early tomorrow," promised Joab.

"I hope so," said Ilana. "What time does the sun rise?"

"Around five o'clock."

"And what time is it now?"

"Twenty past two," said Joab, looking again at his watch.

"Aren't you hot, Elisha?" Ilana asked me.

"Yes, I am," I answered.

Ilana went back to her place at the table. I walked over to the window and looked out. The city seemed faraway and unreal. Deep in sleep, it spawned anxious dreams, hopeful dreams, dreams which would proliferate other dreams on the morrow. And these dreams in their turn would engender new heroes, who would live through the night and prepare to die at dawn, to die and to give death.

"Yes, I'm hot, Ilana," I said. "I'm stifling."

I DON'T KNOW how long I stood, sweating, beside the open window, before a warm, vibrant, reassuring hand was laid on my shoulder. It was Ilana.

"What are you thinking?" she said.

"I'm thinking of the night," I told her. "Always the same thing—"

"And of John Dawson?"

"Yes, of John Dawson."

Somewhere in the city a light shone in a window and then went out. No doubt a man had looked at his watch or a mother had gone to find out whether her child was smiling in his sleep.

"You didn't want to see him, though," said Ilana.

"I don't want to see him."

One day, I was thinking, my son will say: "All of a sudden you look sad. What's wrong?" "It's because in my eyes there is a picture of an English captain called John Dawson, just as he appeared to me at the moment of his death . . ." Perhaps I ought to put a mask on his face; a mask is more easily killed and forgotten.

"Are you afraid?" asked Ilana.

"Yes."

Being afraid, I ought to have told her, is nothing. Fear is only a color, a backdrop, a landscape. That isn't the problem. The fear of either the victim or the executioner is unimportant. What matters is the fact that each of them is playing a role which has been imposed upon him. The two roles are the extremities of the estate of man. The tragic thing is the imposition.

"You, Elisha, *you* are afraid?"

I knew why she had asked. You, Elisha, who lived through Auschwitz and Buchenwald? You who any number of times saw God die? You are afraid?

"I *am* afraid, though, Ilana," I repeated.

She knew quite well that fear was not in fact the real theme. Like death, it is only a backdrop, a bit of local color.

"What makes you afraid?"

Her warm, living hand was still on my shoulder; her breasts brushed me and I could feel her breath on my neck. Her blouse was wet with perspiration and her face distraught. She doesn't understand, I thought to myself.

"I'm afraid he'll make me laugh," I said. "You see, Ilana, he's quite capable of swelling up his head and letting it burst into a thousand shreds, just in order to make me laugh. That's what makes me afraid."

But still she did not understand. She took the handkerchief from her cuff and wiped my neck and temples. Then she kissed my forehead lightly and said:

"You torture yourself too much, Elisha. Hostages aren't clowns. There's nothing so funny about them."

Poor Ilana! Her voice was as pure as truth, as sad as purity. But she did not understand. She was distracted by the externals and did not see what lay behind them.

"You may be right," I said in resignation. "We make *them* laugh. They laugh when they're dead."

She stroked my face and neck and hair, and I could still feel the pressure of her breasts against my body. Then she began to talk, in a sad but clear voice, as if she were talking to a sick child.

"You torture yourself too much, my dear," she said several times in succession. At least she no longer called me "poor boy," and I was grateful. "You mustn't do it. You're young and intelligent, and you've suffered quite enough already. Soon it will all be over. The English will get out and we shall come back to the surface and lead a simple, normal life. You'll get married and have children. You'll tell them stories and make them laugh. You'll be happy because they're happy, and they *will* be happy, I promise you. How could they be otherwise with a father like you? You'll have forgotten this night, this room, me, and everything else—"

As she said "everything else" she traced a sweeping semicircle with her hand. I was reminded of my mother. She talked in the same moving voice and used almost the same words in the same places. I was very fond of my mother. Every evening, until I was nine or ten years old, she put me to sleep with lullabies or stories. There is a goat beside your bed, she used to tell me, a goat of gold. Everywhere you go in life the goat will guide and protect you. Even when you are grown up and very rich, when you know everything a man can know and possess all that he should possess, the goat will still be near you.

"You talk as if you were my mother, Ilana," I said.

My mother too had a harmonious voice, even more harmonious than Ilana's. Like the voice of God it had the power to dispel chaos and to impart a vision of the future which might have been mine, with the goat to guide me, the goat I had lost on the way to Buchenwald.

"You're suffering," said Ilana. "That's what it means when a man speaks of his mother."

"No, Ilana," I said. "At this moment she's the one to suffer."

Ilana's caresses became lighter, more remote. She was beginning to understand. A shadow fell across her face. For some time she was silent, then she joined me in looking at the hand night held out to us through the window.

"War is like night," she said. "It covers everything."

Yes, she was beginning to understand. I hardly felt the pressure of her fingers on my neck.

"We say that ours is a holy war," she went on, "that we're struggling against something and for something, against the English and for an independent Palestine. That's what we say. But these are words; as such they serve only to give meaning to our actions. And our actions, seen in their true and primitive light, have the odor and color of blood. This is war, we say; we must kill. There are those, like you, who kill with their hands, and others—like me—who kill with their voices. Each to his own. And what else can we do? War has a code, and if you deny this you deny its whole purpose and hand the enemy victory on a silver platter. That we can't afford. We need victory, victory in war, in order to survive, in order to remain afloat on the surface of time."

She did not raise her voice. It seemed as if she were chanting a lullaby, telling a bedtime story. There was neither passion nor despair nor even concern in her intonation.

All things considered, she was quite right. We were at war; we had an ideal, a purpose—and also an enemy who stood between us and its attainment. The enemy must be eliminated. And how? By any and all means at our command. There were all sorts of means, but they were unimportant and soon forgotten. The purpose, the end, this was all that would last. Ilana was probably correct in saying that one day I should forget this night. But the dead never forget; they would remember. In their eyes I should be forever branded a killer. There are not a thousand ways of being a killer; either a man is one or he isn't. He can't say I'll kill only ten or only twenty-six men; I'll kill for only five minutes or a single day. He who has killed one man alone is a killer for life. He may choose another occupation, hide himself under another identity, but the executioner or at least the executioner's mask will be always with him. There lies the problem: in the influence of the backdrop of the play upon the actor. War had made me an executioner, and an executioner I would remain even after the backdrop had changed, when I was acting in another play upon a different stage.

"I don't want to be a killer," I said, sliding rapidly over the word as I ejected it.

"Who does?" said Ilana.

She was still stroking my neck, but somehow I had the impression that it was not really *my* neck, *my* hair her fingers were caressing. The noblest woman in the world would hesitate to touch the skin of a killer, of a man who would have the label of killer his whole life long.

I cast a rapid glance behind me to see if the others were still there. Gideon and Joab were dozing, with their heads pillowed on their arms, on the table. Gideon seemed, even in his sleep, to be praying. Gad was still in the cellar and I wondered why he had stayed there so long. As for the ghosts, they followed the conversation but, to my surprise, took no part in it. Ilana was silent.

"What are you thinking?" I murmured.

She did not reply and after a few minutes I posed the question again. Still there was no answer. We were both silent. And the crowd behind me, the crowd of petrified silences, whose shadows absorbed the light and turned it into something sad, funereal, hostile, was silent as well. The sum of these silences filled me with fear. Their silences were different from mine; they were hard, cold, immobile, lifeless, incapable of change.

As a child I had been afraid of the dead and of the graveyard, their shadowy kingdom. The silence with which they surrounded themselves provoked my terror. I knew that now, at my back, in serried ranks as if to protect themselves from the cold, they were sitting in judgment upon me. In their frozen world the dead have nothing to do but judge, and because they have no sense of past or future they judge without pity. They condemn not with words or gestures but with their very existence.

At my back they were sitting in judgment upon me; I felt their silences judging mine. I wanted to turn around but the mere idea filled me with fear. Soon Gad will come up from the cellar, I said to myself, and later it will be my turn to go down. Dawn will come, and this crowd will melt into the light of day. For the present I shall stay beside Ilana, at the window, with my back to them.

A minute later I changed my mind. My father and mother, the master and the beggar were all there. I could not insult them indefinitely by turning my back; I must look at them face-to-face. Cautiously I wheeled around. There were two sorts of light in the room: one white, around the sleeping Gideon and Joab, the other black, enveloping the ghosts.

I left Ilana lost in thought, perhaps in regret, at the window, and began to walk about the room, pausing every now and then before a familiar face, a familiar sorrow. I knew that these faces, these sorrows, were sitting in judgment upon me. They were dead and they were hungry. When the dead are hungry they judge the living without pity. They do not wait until an action has been achieved, a crime committed. They judge in advance.

Only when I perceived the silence of the boy, a silence eloquent in his eyes, did I decide to speak. He had a look of anxiety which made him seem older, more mature. I shall speak up, I said to myself. They have no right to condemn the little boy.

As I approached my father I saw the sorrow on his face. My father had stolen away a minute before the Angel of Death came to take him; in cheating the Angel he had taken with him the human sorrow which he endured while he was alive.

"Father," I said, "don't judge me. Judge God. He created the universe and made justice stem from injustices. He brought it about that a people should attain happiness through tears, that the freedom of a nation, like that of a man, should be a monument built upon a pile, a foundation of dead bodies . . ."

I stood in front of him, not knowing what to do with my head, my eyes, my hands. I wanted to transfer the lifeblood of my body into my voice. At moments I fancied I had done so. I talked for a long time, telling him things that doubtless he already knew, since he had taught them to me. If I repeated them it was only in order to prove to him that I had not forgotten.

"Don't judge me, Father," I implored him, trembling with despair. "You must judge God. He is the first cause, the prime mover; He conceived men and things the way they are. You are dead, father, and only the dead may judge God."

But he did not react. The sorrow written upon his emaciated, unshaven face became even more human than before. I left him and went over to my mother, who was standing at his right side. But my pain was too great for me to address her. I thought I heard her murmur: "Poor boy, poor boy!" and tears came to my eyes. Finally I said that I wasn't a murderer, that she had not given birth to a murderer but to a soldier, to a fighter for freedom, to an idealist who had sacrificed his peace of mind—a possession more precious than life itself—to his people, to his people's right to the light of day, to joy, to the laughter of children. In a halting, feverishly sobbing voice, this was all that I could find to say.

When she too failed to react I left her and went to my old master, of all those present the least changed by death. Alive, he had been very much the same as now; we used to say that he was not of this world, and now this was literally true.

"I haven't betrayed you," I said, as if the deed were already done. "If I were to refuse to obey orders I should betray my living friends. And the living have more rights over us than the dead. You told me that yourself. *Therefore choose life*, it is written in the Scriptures. I have espoused the cause of the living, and that is no betrayal."

Beside him stood Yerachmiel, my friend and comrade and brother. Yerachmiel was the son of a coachman, with the hands of a laborer and the soul of a saint. We two were the master's favorite pupils; every evening he studied with us the secrets of the Kabbala. I did not know that Yerachmiel too was dead. I realized it only at the moment when I saw him in the crowd, at the master's side—or rather a respectful step behind him.

"Yerachmiel my brother," I said, ". . . remember . . . ?"

Together we had spun impossible dreams. According to the

Kabbala, if a man's soul is sufficiently pure and his love deep enough he can bring the Messiah to earth. Yerachmiel and I decided to try. Of course we were aware of the danger: No one can force God's hand with impunity. Men older, wiser, and more mature than ourselves had tried in vain to wrest the Messiah from the chains of the future; failing in their purpose, they had lost their faith, their reason, and even their lives. Yerachmiel and I knew all this, but we were resolved to carry out our plan regardless of the obstacles that lay in wait along the way. We promised to stick to each other, whatever might happen. If one of us were to die, the other would carry on. And so we made preparations for a voyage in depth. We purified our souls and bodies, fasting by day and praying by night. In order to cleanse our mouths and their utterances we spoke as little as possible and on the Sabbath we spoke not at all.

Perhaps our attempt might have been successful. But war broke out and we were driven away from our homes. The last time I had seen Yerachmiel he was one of a long column of marching Jews deported to Germany. A week later I was sent to Germany myself. Yerachmiel was in one camp, I in another. Often I wondered whether he had continued his efforts alone. Now I knew: he had continued, and he was dead.

"Yerachmiel," I said; "Yerachmiel my brother, remember . . ."

Something about him had changed: his hands. Now they were the hands of a saint.

"We too," I said, "my comrades in the Movement and I, are trying to force God's hand. You who are dead should help us, not hinder . . ."

But Yerachmiel and his hands were silent. And somewhere in the universe of time the Messiah was silent as well. I left him and went over to the little boy I used to be.

"Are you too judging me?" I asked. "You of all people have

the least right to do that. You're lucky; you died young. If you'd gone on living you'd be in my place."

Then the boy spoke. His voice was filled with echoes of disquiet and longing.

"I'm not judging you," he said. "We're not here to sit in judgment. We're here simply because you're here. We're present wherever you go; we are what you do. When you raise your eyes to heaven we share in their sight; when you pat the head of a hungry child a thousand hands are laid on his head; when you give bread to a beggar we give him that taste of paradise which only the poor can savor. Why are we silent? Because silence is not only our dwelling place but our very being as well. We *are* silence. And your silence is us. You carry us with you. Occasionally you may see us, but most of the time we are invisible to you. When you see us you imagine that we are sitting in judgment upon you. You are wrong. Your silence is your judge."

Suddenly the beggar's arm brushed against mine. I turned and saw him behind me. I knew that he was not the Angel of Death but the prophet Elijah.

"I hear Gad's footsteps," he said. "He's coming up the stairs."

"I HEAR Gad's footsteps," said Ilana, touching my arm. "He's coming up the stairs."

Slowly and with a blank look on his face Gad came into the room. Ilana ran toward him and kissed his lips, but gently he pushed her away.

"You stayed down there so long," she said. "What kept you?"

A cruel, sad smile crossed Gad's face.

"Nothing," he said. "I was watching him eat."

"He ate?" I asked in surprise. "You mean to say he was able to eat?"

"Yes, he ate," said Gad. "And with a good appetite too."

I could not understand.

"What?" I exclaimed. "You mean to say he was hungry?"

"I didn't say he was hungry," Gad retorted. "I said he ate with a good appetite."

"So he wasn't hungry," I insisted.

Gad's face darkened.

"No, he wasn't hungry."

"Then why did he eat?"

"I don't know," said Gad nervously. "Probably to show me that he can eat even if he's not hungry."

Ilana scrutinized his face. She tried to catch his eye, but Gad was staring into space.

"What did you do after that?" she asked uneasily.

"After what?" said Gad brusquely.

"After he'd finished eating."

Gad shrugged his shoulders.

"Nothing," he said.

"What do you mean, *nothing?*"

"Nothing. He told me stories."

Ilana shook his arm.

"Stories? What kind of stories?"

Gad sighed in resignation.

"Just stories," he repeated, obviously tired of answering questions he considered grotesque.

I wanted to ask if he had laughed, if the hostage had got a laugh out of him. But I refrained. The answer could only have been absurd.

Gad's reappearance had roused Gideon and Joab from their sleep. With haggard faces they looked around the room, as if to assure themselves they weren't dreaming. Stifling a yawn, Joab asked Gad for the time.

"Four o'clock," said Gad, consulting his watch.

"So late? I'd never have thought it."

Gad beckoned to me to come closer.

"Soon it will be day," he observed.

"I know."

"You know what you have to do?"

"Yes, I know."

He took a revolver out of his pocket and handed it to me. I hesitated.

"Take it," said Gad.

The revolver was black and nearly new. I was afraid to even touch it, for in it lay all the whole difference between what I was and what I was going to be.

"What are you waiting for?" asked Gad impatiently. "Take it."

I held out my hand and took it. I examined it for a long time as if I did not know what purpose it could possibly serve. Finally I slipped it into my trouser pocket.

"I'd like to ask you a question," I said to Gad.

"Go ahead."

"Did he make you laugh?"

Gad stared at me coldly, as if he had not understood my question or the necessity for it. His brow was furrowed with preoccupation.

"John Dawson," I said. "Did he make you laugh?"

Gad's eyes stared through me; I felt them going through my head and coming out the other side. He must have been wondering what was going on in my mind, why I harped on this unimportant question, why I didn't seem to be suffering or to be masking my suffering or lack of suffering.

"No," he said at last, "he didn't make me laugh."

His own mask cracked imperceptibly. All his efforts were bent upon controlling the expression of his eyes, but he had neglected his mouth, and it was there that the crack showed. His upper lip betrayed bitterness and anger.

"How did you do it?" I asked in mock admiration. "Weren't his stories funny?"

Gad made a strange noise, not unlike a laugh. The silence that followed accentuated the sadness which an invisible hand had traced upon his lips.

"Oh, they were funny all right, very funny. But they didn't make me laugh."

He took a cigarette out of his shirt pocket, lit it, drew a few puffs, and then, without waiting for me to ask anything more, went on:

"I was thinking of David, that's all."

I'll think of David too, I reflected. He'll protect me. John Dawson may try to make me laugh, but I won't do it. David will come to my rescue.

"It's getting late," said Joab, stifling another yawn.

The night was still looking in on us. But quite obviously it was getting ready to go away. I came to a sudden decision.

"I'm going down," I said.

"So soon?" said Gad, in a tone revealing either emotion or mere surprise. "You've got plenty of time. As much as an hour . . ."

I said that I wanted to go down before the time was up, to see the fellow, and talk, and get to know him. It was cowardly, I said, to kill a complete stranger. It was like war, where you don't shoot at men but into the night, and the wounded night emits cries of pain which are almost human. You shoot into the darkness, and you never know whether any of the enemy was killed, or which one. To execute a stranger would be the same thing. If I were to see him only as he died I should feel as if I had shot at a dead man.

This was the reason I gave for my decision. I'm not sure it was exact. Looking back, it seems to me that I was moved by curiosity. I had never seen a hostage before. I wanted to see a hostage who was doomed to die and who told funny stories. Curiosity or bravado? Perhaps a little of both . . .

"Do you want me to go with you?" asked Gad. A lock of hair had fallen over his forehead, but he did not push it back.

"No, Gad," I said. "I want to be alone with him."

Gad smiled. He was a commander, proud of his subaltern and expressing his pride in a smile. He laid his hand affectionately on my shoulder.

"Do you want someone to go with you?" asked the beggar.

"No," I repeated. "I'd rather be alone."

His eyes were immeasurably kind.

"You can't do it without them," he said, nodding his head in the direction of the crowd behind us.

"They can come later," I conceded.

The beggar took my head in his hands and looked into my eyes. His look was so powerful that for a moment I doubted my identity. I am that look, I said to myself. What else could I be? The beggar has many looks, and I am one of them. But his expression radiated kindness, and I knew that he could not regard kindly his own look. That was how my identity came back to me.

"Very well," he said; "they'll come later."

Now the boy, looking over the shadowy heads and bodies between us, offered to go with me. "Later," I said. My answer made him sad, but I could only repeat: "Later. I want to be alone with him."

"Good," said the child. "We'll come later."

I let my look wander over the room, hoping to leave it there and pick it up when I returned.

Ilana was talking to Gad, but he did not listen. Joab was yawning. Gideon rubbed his forehead as if he had a headache.

In an hour everything will be different, I reflected. I shan't see it the same way. The table, the chairs, the walls, the window, they will all have changed. Only the dead—my father and mother, the master and Yerachmiel—will be the same, for we all of us change together, in the same way, doing the same things.

I patted my pocket to make sure the revolver was still there. It was; indeed, I had the strange impression that it was alive, that its life was part of mine, that it had the same present and future destiny as myself. I was its destiny and it was mine. In an hour it too will have changed, I reflected.

"It's late," said Joab, stretching.

With my eyes I bade farewell to the room, to Ilana, to Gideon and his prayers, to Joab and his confused expression, to the table, the window, the walls, and the night. Then I went hurriedly into the kitchen as if I were going to my own execution. As I went down the stairs my steps slackened and became heavy.

J OHN DAWSON was a handsome man. In spite of his unshaven face, tousled hair, and rumpled shirt, there was something distinguished about him.

He seemed to be in his forties—a professional soldier, no doubt—with penetrating eyes, a resolute chin, thin lips, a broad forehead, and slender hands.

When I pushed open the door I found him lying on a camp bed, staring up at the ceiling. The bed was the only piece of furniture in the narrow white cell. Thanks to an ingenious system of ventilation we had installed, the windowless cell was less stuffy than the open room above.

When he became aware of my presence John Dawson showed neither surprise nor fear. He did not get up but simply raised himself into a sitting position. He scrutinized me at length without saying a word, as if measuring the density of my silence. His stare enveloped my whole being and I wondered if he saw that I was a mass of eyes.

"What time is it?" he asked abruptly.

In an uncertain voice I answered that it was after four. He

frowned, as if in an effort to grasp the hidden meaning of my words.

"When is sunrise?" he said.

"In an hour," I answered. And I added, without knowing why: "Approximately."

We stared at each other for a long interval, and suddenly I realized that time was not moving at its normal, regular pace. In an hour I shall kill him, I thought. And yet I didn't really believe it. This hour which separates me from murder will be longer than a lifetime. It will belong, always, to the distant future; it will never be one with the past.

There was something age-old in our situation. We were alone not only in the cell but in the world as well, he seated, I standing, the victim and the executioner. We were the first—or the last—men of creation; certainly we were alone. And God? He was present, somewhere. Perhaps He was incarnate in the liking with which John Dawson inspired me. The lack of hate between executioner and victim, perhaps this is God.

We were alone in the narrow white cell, he sitting on the bed and I standing before him, staring at each other. I wished I could see myself through his eyes. Perhaps he was wishing he could see himself through mine. I felt neither hate nor anger nor pity; I liked him, that was all. I liked the way he scowled when he was thinking, the way he looked down at his nails when he was trying to formulate his thoughts. Under other circumstances he might have been my friend.

"Are you the one?" he asked abruptly.

How had he guessed it? Perhaps by his sense of smell. Death has an odor and I had brought it in with me. Or perhaps as soon as I came through the door he had seen that I had neither arms nor legs nor shoulders, that I was all eyes.

"Yes," I said.

I felt quite calm. The step before the last is the hard one; the last step brings clearheadedness and assurance.

"What's your name?" he asked.

This question disturbed me. Is every condemned man bound to ask it? Why does he want to know the name of his executioner? In order to take it with him to the next world? For what purpose? Perhaps I shouldn't have told him, but I could refuse nothing to a man condemned to die.

"Elisha," I said.

"Very musical," he observed.

"It's the name of a prophet," I explained. "Elisha was a disciple of Elijah. He restored life to a little boy by lying upon him and breathing into his mouth."

"You're doing the opposite," he said with a smile.

There was no trace of anger or hate in his voice. Probably he too felt clearheaded and assured.

"How old are you?" he asked with aroused interest.

Eighteen, I told him. For some reason I added: "Nearly nineteen."

He raised his head and there was pity on his thin, suddenly sharpened face. He stared at me for several seconds, then sadly nodded his head.

"I'm sorry for you," he said.

I felt his pity go through me. I knew that it would permeate me completely, that the next day I should be sorry for myself.

"Tell me a story," I said. "A funny one, if you can."

I felt my body grow heavy. The next day it would be heavier still, I reflected. The next day it would be weighed down by my life and his death. "I'm the last man you'll see before you die," I went on. "Try to make him laugh."

Once more I was enveloped by his look of pity. I wondered if everyone condemned to die looked at the last man he saw in the same way, if every victim pitied his executioner.

"I'm sorry for you," John Dawson repeated.

By dint of an enormous effort I managed to smile.

"That's no funny story," I remarked.

He smiled at me in return. Which of our two smiles was the sadder?

"Are you sure it isn't funny?"

No, I wasn't so sure. Perhaps there *was* something funny about it. The seated victim, the standing executioner—smiling, and understanding each other better than if they were childhood friends. Such are the workings of time. The veneer of conventional attitudes was wiped off; every word and look and gesture was naked truth instead of just one of its facets. There was harmony between us; my smile answered his; his pity was mine. No human being would ever understand me as he understood me at this hour. Yet I knew that this was solely on account of the roles that were imposed upon us. This was what made it a funny story.

"Sit down," said John Dawson, making room for me to his left on the bed.

I sat down. Only then did I realize that he was a whole head taller than I. And his legs were longer than mine, which did not even touch the ground.

"I have a son your age," he began, "but he's not at all like you. He's fair-haired, strong, and healthy. He likes to eat, drink, go to the pictures, laugh, sing, and go out with the girls. He has none of your anxiety, your unhappiness."

And he went on to tell me more about this son who was "studying at Cambridge." Every sentence was a tongue of flame which burned my body. With my right hand I patted the revolver in my pocket. The revolver too was incandescent, and burned my fingers.

I mustn't listen to him, I told myself. He's my enemy, and the enemy has no story. I must think of something else. That's why I wanted to see him, in order to think of something else while he was talking. Something else . . . but what? Of Ilana? Of Gad? Yes, I should think of Gad, who was thinking of David. I should think of our hero, David ben Moshe, who . . .

I shut my eyes to see David better, but to no purpose, because I had never met him. A name isn't enough, I thought. One must have a face, a voice, a body, and pin the name of David ben Moshe upon them. Better think of a face, a voice, a body that I actually knew. Gad? No, it was difficult to imagine Gad as a man condemned to die. Condemned to die . . . that was it. Why hadn't I thought of it before? John Dawson was condemned to die; why shouldn't I baptize him David ben Moshe? For the next five minutes you are David ben Moshe . . . in the raw, cold, white light of the death cell of the prison at Acre. There is a knock at the door, and the rabbi comes in to read the Psalms with you and hear you say the *Vidui*, that terrible confession in which you admit your responsibility not only for the sins you have committed, whether by word, deed, or thought, but also for those you may have caused others to commit. The rabbi gives you the traditional blessing: "The Lord bless you and keep you . . ." and exhorts you to have no fear. You answer that you are unafraid, that if you had a chance you would do the same thing all over. The rabbi smiles and says that everyone on the outside is proud of you. He is so deeply moved that he has to make a visible effort to hold back his tears; finally the effort is too much for him and he sobs aloud. But you, David, do not cry. You have tender feelings for the rabbi because he is the last man (the executioner and his assistants don't count) you will see before you die. Because he is sobbing you try to comfort him. "Don't cry," you say, "I'm not afraid. You don't need to be sorry for me."

"I'm sorry for you," said John Dawson. "*You* worry me, not my son."

He put his feet down on the floor. He was so tall that when he stood up he had to bend over in order not to bump his head against the ceiling. He put his hands in the pockets of his rumpled khaki trousers and began to pace up and down the cell: five steps in one direction, five in the other.

"That I admit is funny," I observed.

He did not seem to hear, but went on pacing from wall to wall. I looked at my watch; it was twenty past four. Suddenly he stopped in front of me and asked for a cigarette. I had a package of Players in my pocket and wanted to give them to him. But he refused to take the whole package, saying quite calmly that obviously he didn't have time to smoke them all.

Then he said with sudden impatience:

"Have you a pencil and paper?"

I tore several pages out of my notebook and handed them to him, with a pencil.

"Just a short note which I'd like to have sent to my son," he declared. "I'll put down the address."

I handed him the notebook to use as a pad. He laid the notebook on the bed and leaned over to write from a standing position. For several minutes the silence was broken only by the sound of the pencil running over the paper.

I looked down in fascination at his smooth-skinned hands with their long, slender, aristocratic fingers. With hands like those, I thought, it's easy to get along. There's no need to bow, smile, talk, pay compliments, or bring flowers. A pair of such hands do the whole job. Rodin would have liked to sculpt them . . .

The thought of Rodin made me think of Stefan, a German I

had known at Buchenwald. He had been a sculptor before the war, but when I met him the Nazis had cut off his right hand.

In Berlin, during the first years after Hitler came to power, Stefan and some of his friends organized an embryonic resistance group which the Gestapo uncovered shortly after its founding. Stefan was arrested, questioned, and subjected to torture. Give us names, they told him, and we will set you free. They beat and starved him, but he would not talk. Day after day and night after night they prevented him from sleeping, but still he did not give in. Finally he was haled before the Berlin chief of the Gestapo, a timid, mild man, who in a soft-spoken, fatherly manner advised him to stop being foolishly stubborn. The sculptor heard him out in stony silence. "Come on," said the chief. "Give us just one name, as a sign of goodwill." Still Stefan would not speak. "Too bad," said the chief. "You're obliging me to hurt you."

At a sign from the chief two SS men led the prisoner into what looked like an operating room, with a dentist's chair installed near the window. Beside it, on a table with a white oilcloth cover, was an orderly array of surgical instruments. They shut the window, tied Stefan onto the chair, and lit cigarettes. The mild-mannered chief came into the room, wearing a white doctor's jacket.

"Don't be afraid," he said, "I used to be a surgeon."

He puttered around with the instruments and then sat down in front of the prisoner's chair.

"Give me your right hand," he said. Studying it at close range, he added: "I'm told you're a sculptor. You have nothing to say? Well, I know it. I can tell from your hands. A man's hands tell a lot about him. Take mine, for instance. You'd never take them for a surgeon's hands, would you? The truth is that I never wanted to be a doctor. I wanted to be a painter or a musician. I never became one, but I still have the hands of an artist. Look at them."

"I looked at them, with fascination," Stefan told me. "He had the most beautiful, the most angelic hands I have ever seen. You would have sworn that they belonged to a sensitive, unworldly man."

"As a sculptor you need your hands," the Gestapo chief went on. "Unfortunately *we* don't need them," and so saying he cut off a finger.

The next day he cut off a second finger, and the day after that a third. Five days, five fingers. All five fingers of the right hand were gone.

"Don't worry," the chief assured him. "From a medical point of view, everything is in good order. There's no danger of infection."

"I saw him five times," Stefan told me. (For some inexplicable reason he was not killed but simply sent to a concentration camp.) "Every day for five days I saw him from very nearby. And every time I could not take my eyes off those hands of his, the most beautifully shaped hands I had ever seen . . ."

John Dawson finished his note and held it out to me, but I hardly saw it. My attention was taken by his proud, smooth-skinned, frail hands.

"Are you an artist?" I asked him.

He shook his head.

"You've never painted or played a musical instrument, or at least wanted to do so?"

He scrutinized me in silence and then said dryly:

"No."

"Then perhaps you studied medicine."

"I never studied medicine," he said, almost angrily.

"Too bad."

"Too bad? Why?"

"Look at your hands. They're the hands of a surgeon. The kind of hands it takes to cut off fingers."

Deliberately he laid the sheets of paper on the bed.

"Is that a funny story?" he asked.

"Yes, very funny. The fellow who told it to me thought so. He used to laugh over it until he cried."

John Dawson shook his head and said in an infinitely sad voice:

"You hate me, don't you?"

I didn't hate him at all, but I wanted to hate him. That would have made it all very easy. Hate—like faith or love or war—justifies everything.

"Elisha, why did you kill John Dawson?"

"He was my enemy."

"John Dawson? Your enemy? You'll have to explain that better."

"Very well. John Dawson was an Englishman. The English were enemies of the Jews in Palestine. So he was my enemy."

"But Elisha, I still don't understand why you killed him. Were you his only enemy?"

"No, but I had orders. You know what that means."

"And did the orders make him your only enemy? Speak up, Elisha. Why did you kill John Dawson?"

If I had alleged hate, all these questions would have been spared me. Why did I kill John Dawson? Because I hated him, that's all. The absolute quality of hate explains any human action even if it throws something inhuman around it.

I certainly wanted to hate him. That was partly why I had come to engage him in conversation before I killed him. It was absurd reasoning on my part, but the fact is that while we were talking I hoped to find in him, or in myself, something that would give rise to hate.

A man hates his enemy because he hates his own hate. He says to himself: This fellow, my enemy, has made me capable of hate. I hate him not because he's my enemy, not because he hates me, but because he arouses me to hate.

John Dawson has made me a murderer, I said to myself. He has made me the murderer of John Dawson. He deserves my hate. Were it not for him, I might still be a murderer, but I wouldn't be the murderer of John Dawson.

Yes, I had come down to the cellar to feed my hate. It seemed easy enough. Armies and governments the world over have a definite technique for provoking hate. By speeches and films and other kinds of propaganda they create an image of the enemy in which he is the incarnation of evil, the symbol of suffering, the fountainhead of the cruelty and injustice of all times. The technique is infallible, I told myself, and I shall turn it upon my victim.

I did try to draw upon it. All enemies are equal, I said. Each one is responsible for the crimes committed by the others. They have different faces, but they all have the same hands, the hands that cut my friends' tongues and fingers.

As I went down the stairs I was sure that I would meet the man who had condemned David ben Moshe to death, the man who had killed my parents, the man who had come between me and the man I had wanted to become, and who was now ready to kill the man in me. I felt quite certain that I would hate him.

The sight of his uniform added fuel to my flames. There is nothing like a uniform for whipping up hate. When I saw his slender hands I said to myself: Stefan will carve out my hate for them. Again, when he bent his head to write the farewell note to his son, the son "studying at Cambridge," who liked to "laugh and go out with the girls," I thought: David is writing a last letter too, probably to the Old Man, before he puts his head in the hangman's noose. And when he talked, my heart went out to David, who had no one to talk to, except the rabbi. You can't talk to a rabbi, for he is too concerned with relaying your last words to God. You can confess your sins, recite the Psalms or the prayers for the dead, receive his consolation or console him, but you can't talk, not really.

I thought of David whom I had never met and would never know. Because he was not the first of us to be hanged we knew exactly when and how he would die. At about five o'clock in the morning the cell door would open and the prison director would say: Get ready, David ben Moshe; the time has come. "The time has come," this is the ritual phrase, as if this and no other time had any significance. David would cast a look around the cell and the rabbi would say: "Come, my son." They would go out, leaving the cell door open behind them (for some reason no one ever remembers to close it) and start down the long passageway leading to the execution chamber. As the man of the hour, conscious of the fact that the others were there solely on his account, David would walk in the center of the group. He would walk with his head held high—all our heroes held their heads high—and a strange smile on his lips. On either side of the passageway a hundred eyes and ears would wait for him to go by, and the first of the prisoners to perceive his approach would intone "Hatikva," the song of hope. As the group advanced the song would grow louder, more human, more powerful, until its sound rivaled that of the footsteps . . .

When John Dawson spoke of his son I heard David's footsteps and the rising song. With his words John Dawson was trying to cover up the footsteps, to erase the sight of David walking down the passageway and the strange smile on his lips, to drown out the despairing sound of "Hatikva," the song of hope.

I wanted to hate him. Hate would have made everything so simple . . . Why did you kill John Dawson? I killed him because I hated him. I hated him because David ben Moshe hated him, and David ben Moshe hated him because he talked while he, David, was going down the somber passageway at whose far end he must meet his death.

"You hate me, Elisha, don't you?" John Dawson asked. There was a look of overflowing tenderness in his eyes.

"I'm trying to hate you," I answered.

"Why must you try to hate me, Elisha?"

He spoke in a warm, slightly sad voice, remarkable for the absence of curiosity.

Why? I wondered. What a question! Without hate, everything that my comrades and I were doing would be done in vain. Without hate we could not hope to obtain victory. Why do I try to hate you, John Dawson? Because my people have never known how to hate. Their tragedy, throughout the centuries, has stemmed from their inability to hate those who have humiliated and from time to time exterminated them. Now our only chance lies in hating you, in learning the necessity and the art of hate. Otherwise, John Dawson, our future will only be an extension of the past, and the Messiah will wait indefinitely for his deliverance.

"Why must you try to hate me?" John Dawson asked again.

"In order to give my action a meaning which may somehow transcend it."

Once more he slowly shook his head.

"I'm sorry for you," he repeated.

I looked at my watch. Ten minutes to five. Ten minutes to go. In ten minutes I should commit the most important and conclusive act of my life. I got up from the bed.

"Get ready, John Dawson," I said.

"Has the time come?" he asked.

"Very nearly," I answered.

He rose and leaned his head against the wall, probably in order to collect his thoughts or to pray or something of the kind.

Eight minutes to five. Eight minutes to go. I took the revolver out of my pocket. What should I do if he tried to take it from me? There was no chance of his escaping. The house was well guarded and there was no way of getting out of the cellar except through the kitchen. Gad, Gideon, Joab, and Ilana were on guard upstairs, and John Dawson knew it.

Six minutes to five. Six minutes to go. Suddenly I felt quite clearheaded. There was an unexpected light in the cell; the boundaries were drawn, the roles well defined. The time of doubt and questioning and uncertainty was over. I was a hand holding a revolver; I was the revolver that held my hand.

Five minutes to five. Five minutes to go.

"Have no fear, my son," the rabbi said to David ben Moshe. "God is with you."

"Don't worry, I'm a surgeon," said the mild-mannered Gestapo chief to Stefan.

"The note," John Dawson said, turning around. "You'll send it to my boy, won't you?"

He was standing against the wall; he was the wall. Three minutes to five. Three minutes to go.

"God is with you," said the rabbi. He was crying, but now David did not see him.

"The note. You won't forget, will you?" John Dawson insisted.

"I'll send it," I promised, and for some reason I added: "I'll mail it today."

"Thank you," said John Dawson.

David is entering the chamber from which he will not come out alive. The hangman is waiting for him. He is all eyes. David mounts the scaffold. The hangman asks him whether he wants his eyes banded. Firmly David answers no. A Jewish fighter dies with his eyes open. He wants to look death in the face.

Two minutes to five. I took a handkerchief out of my pocket, but John Dawson ordered me to put it back. An Englishman dies with his eyes open. He wants to look death in the face.

Sixty seconds before five o'clock. One minute to go.

Noiselessly the cell door opened and the dead trooped in, filling us with their silence. The narrow cell had become almost unbearably stuffy.

The beggar touched my shoulder and said:

"Day is at hand."

And the boy who looked the way I used to look said, with an uneasy expression on his face:

"This is the first time—" His voice trailed off, and then, as if remembering that he had left the sentence suspended, he picked it up: "the first time I've seen an execution."

My father and mother were there too, and the grizzled master, and Yerachmiel. Their silence stared at me.

David stiffened and began to sing "Hatikva."

John Dawson smiled, with his head against the wall and his body as erect as if he were saluting a general.

"Why are you smiling?" I asked.

"You must never ask a man who is looking at you the reason for his smile," said the beggar.

"I'm smiling," said John Dawson, "because all of a sudden it has occurred to me that I don't know why I am dying." And after a moment of silence he added: "Do you?"

"You see?" said the beggar. "I told you that was no question to ask a man who is about to die."

Twenty seconds. This minute was more than sixty seconds long.

"Don't smile," I said to John Dawson. What I meant was: "I can't shoot a man who is smiling."

Ten seconds.

"I want to tell you a story," he said, "a funny story."

I raised my right arm.

Five seconds.

"Elisha—"

Two seconds. He was still smiling.

"Too bad," said the little boy. "I'd like to have heard his story."

One second.

"Elisha—" said the hostage.

I fired. When he pronounced my name he was already dead; the bullet had gone through his heart. A dead man, whose lips were still warm, had pronounced my name: *Elisha*.

He sank very slowly to the ground, as if he had slipped from the top of the wall. His body remained in a sitting position, with the head bowed down between the knees, as if he were still waiting to be killed. I stayed for a few moments beside him. There was a pain in my head and my body was growing heavy. The shot had left me deaf and dumb. That's it, I said to myself. It's done. I've killed. I've killed Elisha.

The ghosts began to leave the cell, taking John Dawson with them. The little boy walked at his side as if to guide him. I seemed to hear my mother say: "Poor boy! Poor boy!"

Then with heavy footsteps I walked up the stairs leading to the kitchen. I walked into the room, but it was not the same. The ghosts were gone. Joab was no longer yawning. Gideon was looking down at his nails and praying for the repose of the dead. Ilana lifted a sad countenance upon me; Gad lit a cigarette. They were silent, but their silence was different from the silence which all night long had weighed upon mine. On the horizon the sun was rising.

I went to the window. The city was still asleep. Somewhere a child woke up and began to cry. I wished that a dog would bark, but there was no dog anywhere nearby.

The night lifted, leaving behind it a grayish light the color of stagnant water. Soon there was only a tattered fragment of darkness, hanging in midair, the other side of the window. Fear caught my throat. The tattered fragment of darkness had a face. Looking at it, I understood the reason for my fear. The face was my own.

Day

TRANSLATED FROM THE FRENCH BY

ANNE BORCHARDT

For Paul Braunstein

I was once more struck by the truth of the ancient saying: Man's heart is a ditch full of blood. The loved ones who have died throw themselves down on the bank of this ditch to drink the blood and so come to life again; the dearer they are to you, the more of your blood they drink.

—NIKOS KAZANTZAKIS, *Zorba the Greek*

Preface

 D AY* IS MY SECOND NOVEL and third book. In a concrete sense, it is the sequel to *Dawn*. Do the two stories bring the same character to life? You might say that each can be found in the other.

This novel deals with a number of obvious themes, but its true subject remains unspoken: Having survived the cruelest of wars, how does one go on in a hostile or indifferent world?

Stripped of everything resembling a normal existence, having lost everything except his memory, my hero suffers from an inability to count on the future, to become attached to another person, thus to hope.

One evening, crossing Times Square in Manhattan, he is hit by a taxi. In his hospital bed he spends weeks battling the pain from his multiple injuries.

Battling death? Life too.

*Le Jour (*Day*) was titled *The Accident* when it was first published in English.

Wavering between these two callings, each as brutal as the other, he lives through old fears and memories again.

He struggles to understand why fate has spared *him* and not so many others. Was it to know happiness? His happiness will never be complete. To know love? He will never be sure of being worthy of love. A part of him is still back there, on the other side, where the dead deny the living the right to leave them behind.

His recovery will be a road into exile, a journey in which the touch of the woman he loves will matter less than the image of his grandmother buried under a mountain of ashes.

After night comes day, inviting the dead to seek an open heart in which to find rest, an emissary who may become an ally, a friend.

This is the novel's theme. Set within the background of what is so poorly called the Holocaust, the novel does not deal directly with the event. As I have said elsewhere, I feel unable to tell the story of this event, much less imagine it. A novel about Auschwitz is not a novel—or else it is not about Auschwitz.

That said, certain episodes here are true—that is, taken from life. The accident actually happened to me. I didn't see the taxi coming. The possibility of a suicidal impulse was invented for the sake of the story.

In fact, the question has haunted me for a long time: Does life have meaning after Auschwitz? In a universe cursed because it is guilty, is hope still possible? For a young survivor whose knowledge of life and death surpasses that of his elders, wouldn't suicide be as great a temptation as love or faith?

MANY YEARS AGO, long after publishing this short narrative, I read somewhere (I think it was in a book by Michael Elkins) about the tragedy of children and adolescents who had emerged from hiding in forests and underground shelters at the time of the Liberation, who soon fell ill from exhaustion or malnutrition.

Transported to various hospitals, they baffled doctors with their refusal to be fed, choosing instead to let themselves slip into death.

This was their simple and heartrending way of launching their own accusation at a so-called civilized society that had allowed people to stand by idly and betray the very humanity of mankind by remaining indifferent.

The suicides of these children, like the murders of their parents, will never be forgiven.

—ELIE WIESEL

THE ACCIDENT occurred on an evening in July, right in the heart of New York, as Kathleen and I were crossing the street to go to see the movie *The Brothers Karamazov*. The heat was heavy, suffocating: it penetrated your bones, your veins, your lungs. It was difficult to speak, even to breathe. Everything was covered with an enormous, wet sheet of air. The heat stuck to your skin, like a curse.

People walked clumsily, looking haggard, their mouths dry like the mouths of old men watching the decay of their existence; old men hoping to take leave of their own beings so as not to go mad. Their bodies filled them with disgust.

I was tired. I had just finished my work: a five-hundred-word cable. Five hundred words to say nothing. To cover up another empty day. It was one of those quiet and monotonous Sundays that leave no mark on time. Washington: nothing. United Nations: nothing. New York: nothing. Even Hollywood said: nothing. The movie stars had deserted the news.

It wasn't easy to use five hundred words to say that there was nothing to say. After two hours of hard work, I was exhausted.

"What shall we do now?" Kathleen asked.

"Whatever you like," I answered.

We were on the corner of Forty-fifth Street, right in front of the Sheraton-Astor. I felt stunned, heavy, a thick fog in my head. The slightest gesture was like trying to lift a planet. There was lead in my arms, in my legs.

To my right I could see the human whirlwind on Times Square. People go there as they go to the sea: neither to fight boredom nor the anguish of a room filled with blighted dreams, but to feel less alone, or more alone.

The world turned in slow motion under the weight of the heat. The picture seemed unreal. Beneath the colorful neon carnival, people went back and forth, laughing, singing, shouting, insulting one another, all of this with an exasperating slowness.

Three sailors had come out of the hotel. When they saw Kathleen they stopped short and, in unison, gave a long admiring whistle.

"Let's go," Kathleen said, pulling me by the arm. She was obviously annoyed.

"What do you have against them?" I asked. "They think you're beautiful."

"I don't like them to whistle like that."

I said, in a professorial tone, "It's their way of looking at a woman: they see her with their mouths and not with their eyes. Sailors keep their eyes for the sea: when they are on land, they leave their eyes behind as tokens of love."

The three admirers had already been gone for quite some time.

"And you?" Kathleen asked. "How do you look at me?"

She liked to relate everything to us. We were always the center of her universe. For her, other mortals lived only to be used as comparisons.

"I? I don't look at you," I answered, slightly annoyed. There was a silence. I was biting my tongue. "But I love you. You know that."

"You love me, but you don't look at me?" she asked gloomily. "Thanks for the compliment."

"You don't understand," I went right on. "One doesn't necessarily exclude the other. You can love God, but you can't look at Him."

She seemed satisfied with this comparison. I would have to practice lying.

"Whom do you look at when you love God?" she asked after a moment of silence.

"Yourself. If man could contemplate the face of God, he would stop loving him. God needs love; he does not need understanding."

"And you?"

For Kathleen, even God was not so much a subject for discussion as a way to bring the conversation back to us.

"I too," I lied. "I too, I need your love."

We were still in the same spot. Why hadn't we moved? I don't know. Perhaps we were waiting for the accident.

I'll have to learn to lie, I kept thinking. Even for the short time I have left. To lie well. Without blushing. Until then I had been lying much too badly. I was awkward, my face would betray me and I would start blushing.

"What are we waiting for?" Kathleen was getting impatient.

"Nothing," I said.

I was lying without knowing it: we were waiting for the accident.

"You still aren't hungry?"

"No," I answered.

"But you haven't eaten anything all day," she said reproachfully.

"No."

Kathleen sighed.

"How long do you think you can hold out? You're slowly killing yourself . . ."

There was a small restaurant nearby. We went in. All right, I told myself. I'll also have to learn to eat. And to love. You can learn anything.

Ten or twelve people, sitting on high red stools, were eating silently at the counter. Kathleen now found herself in the cross fire of their stares. She was beautiful. Her face, especially around the lips, showed the first signs of a fear that was waiting for a chance to turn into live suffering. I would have liked to tell her once more that I loved her.

We ordered two hamburgers and two glasses of grapefruit juice.

"Eat," Kathleen said, and she looked up at me pleadingly.

I cut off a piece and lifted it to my mouth. The smell of blood turned my stomach. I felt like throwing up. Once I had seen a man eating with great appetite a slice of meat without bread. Starving, I watched him for a long time. As if hypnotized, I followed the motion of his fingers and jaws. I was hoping that if he saw me there, in front of him, he would throw me a piece. He didn't look up. The next day he was hanged by those who shared his barracks: he had been eating human flesh. To defend himself he had screamed, "I didn't do any harm: he was already dead . . ." When I saw his body swinging in the latrine, I wondered, What if he had seen me?

"Eat," Kathleen said.

I swallowed some juice.

"I'm not hungry," I said with an effort.

A few hours later the doctors told Kathleen, "He's lucky. He'll suffer less because his stomach is empty. He won't vomit so much."

"Let's go," I told Kathleen as I turned to leave.

I could feel it: another minute there and I'd faint.

I paid for the hamburgers and we left. Times Square hadn't changed. False lights, artificial shadows. The same anonymous crowd twisting and untwisting. In the bars and in the stores, the same rock 'n' roll tunes hitting away at your temples with thousands of invisible little hammers. The neon signs still announced that to drink this or that was good for your health, for happiness, for the peace of the world, of the soul, and of I don't know what else.

"Where would you like to go?" Kathleen inquired.

She pretended not to have noticed how pale I was. Who knows, I thought. She too perhaps will learn how to lie.

"Far," I answered. "Very far."

"I'll go with you," she declared.

The sadness and bitterness of her voice filled me with pity. Kathleen has changed, I told myself. She, who believed in defiance, in fighting, in hatred, had now chosen to submit. She, who refused to follow any call that didn't come from herself, now recognized defeat. I knew that our suffering changes us. But I didn't know that it could also destroy others.

"Of course," I said. "I won't go without you."

I was thinking: to go far away, where the roads leading to simplicity are known not merely to a select group, but to all; where love, laughter, songs, and prayers carry with them neither anger nor shame; where I can think about myself without anguish, without contempt; where the wine, Kathleen, is pure and not mixed with the spit of corpses; where the dead live in cemeteries and not in the hearts and memories of men.

"Well?" Kathleen asked, pursuing her idea. "Where shall we go? We can't stand here all night."

"Let's go to the movies," I said.

It was still the best place. We wouldn't be alone. We would think about something else. We would be somewhere else.

Kathleen agreed. She would have preferred to go back to my place or to hers, but she understood my objection: it would be too hot, while the movie would be air-conditioned. I came to the conclusion that it wasn't so hard to lie.

"What shall we see?"

Kathleen looked around her, at the theaters that surrounded Times Square. Then she exclaimed excitedly, "*The Brothers Karamazov*! Let's see *The Brothers Karamazov*."

It was playing on the other side of the square. We would have to cross two avenues. An ocean of cars and noises separated us from the movie.

"I'd rather see some other picture," I said. "I like Dostoyevski too much."

Kathleen insisted: it was a good, great, extraordinary movie. Yul Brynner as Dmitri. It was a picture one had to see.

"I'd rather see an ordinary mystery," I said. "Something without philosophy, without metaphysics. It's too hot for intellectual exercises. Look, *Murder in Rio* is playing on this side. Let's go to that. I'd love to know how they commit murders in Brazil."

Kathleen was stubborn. Once again, she wanted to test our love. If Dostoyevski won, I loved her; otherwise I didn't. I glanced at her. Still the fear around her lips, the fear that was going to become suffering. Kathleen was beautiful when she suffered; her eyes were deeper, her voice warmer, fuller; her dark beauty was simpler and more human. Her suffering had a quality of saintliness. It was her way of offering herself. I couldn't see Kathleen suffer without telling her I loved her, as if love was the negation of evil. I had to stop her suffering.

"You really care that much?" I asked her. "You're really that anxious to see the good brothers Karamazov mistreated?"

Apparently she was. It was Yul Brynner or our love.

"In that case, let's go."

A triumphant smile, which lasted only a second, lit up her face. Her fingers gripped my arm as if to say: now I believe in what is happening to us.

We took three or four steps, to the edge of the sidewalk. We had to wait a little. Wait for the red light to become green, for the flow of cars to stop, for the policeman who was directing traffic to raise his hand, for the cabdriver, unaware of the role he was going to play in a moment, to reach the appointed spot. We had to wait for the director's cue.

I turned around. The clock in the TWA window said 10:25.

"Come on," Kathleen decided, pulling me by the arm. "It's green."

We started to cross the street. Kathleen was walking faster than I. She was on my right, a few inches ahead of me at most. The brothers Karamazov weren't very far away anymore, but I didn't see them that night.

What did I hear first? The grotesque screeching of brakes or the shrill scream of a woman? I no longer remember.

WHEN I CAME TO, for a fraction of a second, I was lying on my back in the middle of the street. In a tarnished mirror a multitude of heads were bending over me. There were heads everywhere. Right, left, above, and even underneath. All of them alike. The same wide-open eyes reflecting fright and curiosity. The same lips whispering the same incomprehensible words.

An elderly man seemed to be saying something to me. I think it was not to move. He had close-cropped hair and a mustache. Kathleen no longer had the beautiful black hair that she was so proud of. Disfigured, her face had lost its youth. Her eyes, as if in the presence of death, had grown larger, and, incredibly enough, she had grown a mustache.

A dream, I told myself. Just a dream that I'll forget when I wake up. Otherwise, why should I be here, on the pavement? Why would these people be around me as if I were going to die? And why would Kathleen suddenly have a mustache?

Noises, coming from all directions, bounced against a curtain of fog they weren't able to penetrate. I couldn't make out anything that was being said. I would have liked to tell them not to talk, because I couldn't hear them. I was dreaming, while they were not. But I was unable to utter the slightest sound. The dream had made me deaf and mute.

A poem by Dylan Thomas—always the same one—kept coming back to me, about not going gently into the night, but to "rage, rage, against the dying of the light."

Scream? Deaf-mutes don't scream. They go gently into the night, lightly, timidly. They don't scream against the dying of the light. They can't: their mouths are full of blood.

It's useless to scream when your mouth is filled with blood: people see the blood but cannot hear you scream. That's why I was silent. And also because I was dreaming of a summer night when my body was frozen. The heat was sickening, the faces bent over me streaming with sweat—sweat falling in rhythmical drops—and yet I was dreaming that I was so cold I was dying. How can one cry out against a dream? How can one scream against the dying of the light, against life that grows cold, against blood flowing out?

IT WAS ONLY LATER, much later, when I was already out of danger, that Kathleen told me about the circumstances surrounding the accident.

A speeding cab approaching from the left had caught me, dragging me several yards. Kathleen had suddenly heard the screeching of brakes and a woman's shrill scream.

She barely had time to turn around before a crowd was already surrounding me. She didn't know at first that I was the man lying at the spectators' feet.

Then, having a strong feeling that it was I, she pushed her way through and saw me: crushed with pain, curled up, my head between my knees.

And the people were talking, talking endlessly . . .

"He's dead," one of them said.

"No, he's not. Look, he's moving."

Preceded by the sound of sirens, the ambulance arrived within twenty minutes. During that time I showed few signs of life. I didn't cry, I didn't moan, I didn't say anything.

In the ambulance I came to several times for a few seconds. During these brief moments I gave Kathleen astonishingly precise instructions about things I wanted her to do for me: inform the paper; call one of my friends and ask him to replace me temporarily; cancel various appointments; pay the rent, the phone bill, the laundry. Having handed her the last of these immediate problems, I closed my eyes and didn't open them again for five days.

Kathleen also told me this: the first hospital to which the ambulance took me refused to let me in. There wasn't any room. All the beds were taken. At least that's what they said. But Kathleen thought it was just a pretext. The doctors, after one glance at me, had decided there was no hope. It was better to be rid of a dying man as fast as possible.

The ambulance drove on to New York Hospital. Here, it seemed, they weren't afraid of the dying. The doctor on duty, a composed and sympathetic-looking young resident, immediately took care of me while trying to make a diagnosis.

"Well, Doctor?" Kathleen had asked.

Through some miracle she hadn't been sent out of the emergency room while Dr. Paul Russel was taking care of me.

"At first sight it looks rather bad," the young doctor answered.

And he explained in a professional tone, "All the bones on the left side of his body are broken; internal hemorrhage; brain concussion. I can't tell about his eyes yet, whether they'll be affected or not. The same for his brain: let's hope it hasn't been damaged."

Kathleen tried not to cry.

"What can be done, Doctor?"

"Pray."

"Is it that serious?"

"Very serious."

The young doctor, whose voice was as restrained as an old man's, looked at her for a moment, then asked, "Who are you? His wife?"

On the verge of hysteria, Kathleen just shook her head to say no.

"His fiancée?"

"No," she whispered.

"His girlfriend?"

"Yes."

After hesitating a moment, he had asked her softly, "Do you love him?"

"Yes," Kathleen whispered.

"In that case, there are good reasons not to lose hope. Love is worth as much as prayer. Sometimes more."

Then Kathleen burst into tears.

AFTER THREE DAYS of consulting and waiting, the doctors decided that it was worth trying surgery after all. In any case I didn't have much to lose. On the other hand, with luck, if all went well . . .

The operation lasted a long time. More than five hours. Two surgeons had to take turns. My pulse fell dangerously low, I was almost given up for dead. With blood transfusions, shots, and oxygen, they brought me back to life.

Finally the surgeons decided to limit the operation to the hip. The ankle, the ribs, and the other small fractures could wait. The vital thing for the time being was to stop the bleeding, sew together the torn arteries, and close the incision.

I was brought back to my room and for two days swung between life and death. Dr. Russel, who was devotedly taking care of me, was still pessimistic about the final result. My fever was too high and I was losing too much blood.

On the fifth day I at last regained consciousness.

I'll always remember: I opened my eyes and had to close them right away because I was blinded by the whiteness of the room. A few minutes went by before I could open them again and locate myself in time and space.

On both sides of my bed there were bottles of plasma hanging from the wall. I couldn't move my arms: two big needles were fastened to them with surgical tape. Everything was ready for an emergency transfusion.

I tried to move my legs: my body no longer obeyed me. I felt a sudden fear of being paralyzed. I made a superhuman effort to shout, to call a nurse, a doctor, a human being, to ask for the truth. But I was too weak. The sounds stuck in my throat. Maybe I've lost my voice too, I thought.

I felt alone, abandoned. Deep inside I discovered a regret: I would have preferred to die.

An hour later, Dr. Russel came into the room and told me I was going to live. My legs were not going to be amputated. I couldn't move them because they were in a cast that covered my whole body. Only my head, my arms, my toes, were visible.

"You've come back from very far," the young doctor said.

I didn't answer. I still felt regret at having come back from so far.

"You must thank God," he went on.

I looked at him more carefully. As he sat on the edge of my bed, his fingers intertwined, his eyes were filled with an intense curiosity.

"How does one thank God?" I asked him.

My voice was only a whisper. But I was able to speak. This filled me with such joy that tears came to my eyes. That I was still alive had left me indifferent, or nearly so. But the knowledge that I could still speak filled me with an emotion that I couldn't hide.

The doctor had a wrinkled baby face. He was blond. His light blue eyes showed a great deal of goodness. He was looking at me very attentively. But this didn't bother me. I was too weak.

"How does one thank God?" I repeated.

I would have liked to add: Why thank him? I had not been able to understand for a long time what in the world God had done to deserve man.

The doctor continued to look at me closely, very closely. A strange gleam—perhaps a strange shadow—was in his eyes.

Suddenly my heart jumped. Frightened, I thought: he knows something.

"Are you cold?" he asked, still looking at me.

"Yes," I answered, worried. "I'm cold."

My body was trembling.

"It's your fever," he explained.

Usually they take your pulse. Or else they touch your forehead with the back of their hand. He did nothing. He knew.

"We'll try to fight the fever," he went on sententiously. "We'll give you shots. Many shots. Penicillin. Every hour. Day and night. The enemy now is fever."

He stopped talking and looked at me for a long time before going on. He seemed to be looking for a sign, an indication, a solution to a problem whose particulars I couldn't guess.

"We're afraid of infection," he continued. "If the fever goes up, you're lost."

"And the enemy will be victorious," I said in a tone of voice that intended irony. "You see, Doctor, what people say is true: man carries his fiercest enemy within himself. Hell isn't others. It's ourselves. Hell is the burning fever that makes you feel cold."

An indefinable bond had grown between us. We were speaking the mature language of men who are in direct contact with death. I tried to put on a smile but, being too cold, I could only manage a grin. That's one reason why I don't like winter: smiles become abstract.

Dr. Russel got up.

"I'll send the nurse. It's time for a shot."

He was touching his lips with his fingers, as if to think better, and then added, "When you feel better, we'll have a lot to talk about."

Again I had the uncomfortable impression that he knew—or at least that he suspected—something.

I closed my eyes. Suddenly I became conscious of the pain that was torturing me. I had not realized it before. And yet the suffering was there. It was the air I was breathing, the words forming in my brain, the cast that covered my body like a flaming skin. How had I managed to remain unaware of it until then? Perhaps I had been too absorbed in the conversation with the doctor. Did he know I was suffering, suffering horribly? Did he know I was cold? Did he know that the suffering was burning my flesh and that at the same time I was shaking with an unbearable cold, as if I were being plunged first into a furnace and then into an icy tub? Apparently he did. He knew. Paul Russel was a perceptive doctor. He could see me biting my lips furiously.

"You're in pain," he stated.

He was standing motionless at the foot of my bed. I was ashamed that my teeth were chattering in his presence.

"It's normal," he went on without waiting for an answer. "You're covered with wounds. Your body is rebelling. Pain is your body's way of protesting. But I told you: suffering is not the enemy, the fever is. If it goes up you are lost."

Death. I was thinking: He thinks that death is my enemy. He's mistaken. Death is not my enemy. If he doesn't know that, he knows nothing. Or at least he doesn't know everything. He has seen me come back to life, but he doesn't know what I think of life and death. Or could he possibly know and not show it? Doubt, like the insistent buzz of a bee inside me, was putting my nerves on edge.

I could feel the fever, as it spread, seize me by the hair, which seemed like a burning torch. The fever was throwing me from one world into another, up and down, very high up and very far down, as if it meant to teach me the cold of high places and the heat of abysses.

"Would you like a sedative?" the doctor inquired.

I shook my head. No, I didn't want any. I didn't need any. I wasn't afraid.

I heard his steps moving toward the door, which must have been somewhere behind me. Let him go, I thought. I'm not afraid of being alone, of walking the distance between life and death. No, I don't need him. I'm not afraid. Let him go!

He opened the door, hesitated before closing it. He stopped. Was he going to come back?

"Incidentally," he said softly, so softly I could hardly hear him. "Incidentally, I nearly forgot to tell you . . . Kathleen . . . she's an extremely charming young woman. Extremely charming . . ."

With that he quietly left the room. Now I was alone. Alone as only a paralyzed and suffering man can be. Soon the nurse would come, with her penicillin, to fight the enemy. It was maddening: to fight the enemy with an injection, with the help of a nurse. It was laughable. But I didn't laugh. The muscles in my face were motionless, frozen.

The nurse was going to come soon. That's what the young doctor had said, the doctor whose calm voice was like an old man's, having just discovered that human goodness carries its own reward. What else had he told me? Something about Kathleen. Yes: he had mentioned her name. Charming young woman. No. Not that. He had said something else: extremely charming. Yes: that's it. That's what he had said: Kathleen is a charming young woman. I remembered perfectly: extremely charming.

Kathleen . . . Where could she be now? In what world? In the one above or the one below? I hope she won't come. I hope she won't appear in this room. I don't want her to see me like this. I hope she won't come with the nurse. I hope she won't become a nurse. And that she won't give me penicillin. I don't want her help in my fight against the enemy. She's a charming girl, extremely charming, but she doesn't understand. She doesn't understand that death is not the enemy. That would be too easy. She doesn't understand. She has too much faith in the power, in the omnipotence of love. Love me and you'll be protected. Love each other and all will be well: suffering will leave man's earth forever. Who said that? Christ probably. He also believed too much in love. As for me, love or death. I didn't care. I was able to laugh when I thought about either. Now too, I could burst out laughing. Yes, but the muscles in my face didn't obey me. I was too cold.

It had been cold on the day—no, the evening—that evening when I met Kathleen for the first time.

A WINTER EVENING. Outside, a wind sharp enough to cut through walls and trees.

"Come along," Shimon Yanai told me. "I'd like you to meet Halina."

"Let me listen to the wind," I answered (I wasn't in a talkative mood). "The wind has more to say than your Halina. The sound of the wind carries the regrets and prayers of dead souls. Dead souls have more to say than living ones."

Shimon Yanai—the most beautiful mustache in Palestine, not to say in the whole Middle East—wasn't paying any attention to what I was saying.

"Come," he said, his hands in his pockets. "Halina is waiting for us."

I gave in. I thought: perhaps Halina is a dead soul too.

We were standing in the lobby during an intermission at the ballet in Paris, the Roland Petit Company or the Marquis de Cuevas, I no longer remember.

"Halina must be an attractive woman," I said as we crossed the lobby to get to the bar.

"What makes you think that?" asked Shimon Yanai, who seemed amused.

"The way you're dressed tonight. You look like a bum."

I liked to tease him. Shimon was in his forties, tall, bushy hair, blue and dreamy eyes. He never wanted to be taken seriously. "You spend hours in front of the mirror mussing your hair, spoiling the knot in your tie, rumpling your trousers," I would often tell him, ironically but with affection. There was something pathetic about his love for the Bohemian.

I knew him well because he came to Paris often and gave me tips for the newspaper. He liked to be with journalists. He needed them. He was the Paris representative of the Hebrew Resistance Movement—the state of Israel hadn't been born yet—and he didn't hesitate to admit that the press could be helpful to him.

Halina was waiting for us at the bar, a glass in her hand. She was thirtyish. Thin, narrow face, pale, with the eternally frightened look of a woman fighting with her past.

We shook hands.

"I thought you'd be older." She was smiling awkwardly.

"I am," I said. "At times I am as old as the wind."

Halina laughed. She didn't really know how to laugh. When she laughed, she could break your heart. Her laughter was as haunting as a dead soul.

"I'm serious," she said. "I read your articles. They are written by a man who has come to the end of his life, to the end of his hopes."

"That is a sign of youth," I answered. "The young today don't believe that someday they'll be old: they are convinced they'll die young. Old men are the real youngsters of our generation. They at least can brag about having had what we do not have: a slice of life called youth."

The young woman's face became still paler. "What you are saying is dreadful."

I burst out laughing, but my laughter must have sounded forced: I didn't feel like laughing. Not any more than like talking.

"Don't listen to me," I said. "Shimon will tell you: my words are never serious. I am playing, that's all. Playing at frightening you. But you mustn't pay any attention. What I'm saying is just wind."

I was going to leave them—on the usual pretext of an urgent phone call to make—when I noticed a worried look in Halina's eyes.

"Shimon!" she exclaimed without raising her voice. "Look who is here: Kathleen!"

Shimon looked where she was pointing and for a second— only a second—his face clouded over. His cheeks darkened, as if from a painful memory.

"Go and ask her to join us," Halina said.

"But she's not alone . . ."

"Just for a minute! She'll come."

She did come. And that's when it all started.

Actually I could easily have left while Shimon was talking to her at the other end of the lobby. My phone call was just as urgent then as it had been before. I didn't at all feel like staying. At first glance it looked like the classic situation. Three characters: Shimon, Halina, Kathleen. Halina loves Shimon, who doesn't love her; Shimon loves Kathleen, who does not love him; Kathleen loves . . . I didn't know whom she loved and cared less. I was thinking: they make one another suffer, in a tightly closed circle. Better not to have anything to do with it, not even as a witness. I'd never been interested in sterile suffering. Other people's suffering only attracts me to the extent that it allows man to become conscious of his strength and of his weakness, in a climate that favors rebellion. The loves of Halina and Shimon allowed nothing of the kind.

"I have to go," I told Halina.

She looked at me but didn't hear; she was watching Shimon and Kathleen at the end of the lobby.

"I have to go," I said again.

She seemed to come out of a dream, surprised to see me next to her. "Please stay," she asked in a humble, almost humiliated tone of voice. Then she added, either to convince me or to stress her indifference, "You're going to meet Kathleen. She is an extraordinary girl. You'll see."

It had become useless to resist: Kathleen and Shimon were there.

"Hello, Halina," Kathleen said in French with a strong American accent.

"Hello, Kathleen," Halina answered, barely hiding a certain nervousness. "Let me introduce a friend . . ."

Without a gesture, without a move, without saying a word, Kathleen and I looked at each other for a long time, as if to establish a direct contact. She had a long, symmetrical face, uncommonly beautiful and touching. Her nose turned up slightly, accentuating her sensuous lips. Her almond-shaped eyes were filled with a dark, secret fire: an inactive volcano. With her, there could be real communication. All of a sudden I understood why Halina's laughter wasn't more carefree.

"You already know each other?" Halina asked with her awkward smile. "You look at each other as if you knew each other."

Shimon was silent. He was looking at Kathleen.

"Yes," I answered.

"What?" Halina exclaimed, not quite believing it. "You've already met?"

"No," I answered. "But we already know each other."

An imperceptible quiver went through Shimon's mustache. The situation was becoming unpleasantly tense when a warning bell suddenly rang. The intermission was over. The lobby began to empty.

"Shall we see you after the show?" Halina asked.

"I'm afraid not," Kathleen answered. "Someone is waiting for me."

"And you?" Halina looked at me, her big eyes filled with a cold sadness.

"No," I answered. "I have to make a phone call. It's urgent."

Halina and Shimon went off. We were alone, Kathleen and I.

"Do you speak English?" she asked me in English, as if in a hurry.

"I do."

"Wait for me," she said.

She walked quickly to the man who was waiting at the other end of the lobby, said a few words to him. I still had a chance to leave. But why run away? And where to? The desert is the same everywhere. Souls die in it. And sometimes they play at killing the souls that are not yet dead.

When Kathleen came back a few seconds later, I saw a fleeting expression of defiance and decision on her face, as if she had just completed the most important act of her life. The man she had just left and humiliated remained completely motionless and stiff, as if struck by a curse.

Inside, the curtain had gone up.

"Let's leave," Kathleen said in English.

I felt like asking endless questions, but decided to keep them for later.

"All right," I said. "Let's leave."

We left the lobby hurriedly. The man stayed behind alone. For a long time after I was afraid to go back to that theater. I was afraid of finding him there, on the very spot where we had left him.

We went down the stairs, got our coats, and went out into the street, where the wind whipped us angrily. The air was clear and pure, as it is on the peaks of snowy mountains.

We began to walk. It was cold. We were advancing slowly, as if to prove that we were strong and that the cold had no power over us.

Kathleen hadn't taken my arm and I hadn't taken hers. She didn't look at me and I didn't look at her. Either of us would have gone on walking at the same pace if the other had stopped suddenly to think, or to pray.

After walking silently along the Seine for an hour or two, we crossed the Pont du Châtelet, and then, when we reached the middle of the Pont Saint-Michel, I stopped to look at the river. Kathleen took two more steps and stopped too.

The Seine, reflecting the sky and the lampposts, now showed us its mysterious winter face, its quiet cloudiness, where any life is extinguished, where any light dies. I looked down and thought that someday I too would die.

Kathleen came closer and was about to say something. With a motion of my head, I stopped her.

"Don't talk," I told her after a while.

I was still thinking about death and didn't want her to talk to me. It is only in silence, leaning over a river in winter, that one can really think about death.

One day I had asked my grandmother, "How should one keep from being cold in a grave in the winter?"

My grandmother was a simple, pious woman who saw God everywhere, even in evil, even in punishment, even in injustice. No event would ever find her short of prayers. Her skin was like white desert sand. On her head she wore an enormous black shawl which she never seemed able to part with.

"He who doesn't forget God isn't cold in his grave," she said.

"What keeps him warm?" I insisted.

Her thin voice had become like a whisper: it was a secret. "God Himself." A kind smile lit up her face all the way to the shawl that covered half her forehead. She smiled like that every time I asked her a question with an obvious answer.

"Does that mean that God is in the grave, with the men and the women that are buried?"

"Yes," my grandmother assured me. "It is He who keeps them warm."

I remember that then a strange sadness came upon me. I felt pity for God. I thought: He is more unhappy than man, who dies only once, who is buried in only one grave.

"Grandma, tell me, does God die too?"

"No, God is immortal."

Her answer came as a blow. I felt like crying. God was buried alive! I would have preferred to reverse the roles, to think that God is mortal and man not. To think that, when man acts as if he were dying, it is God who is covered with earth.

Kathleen touched my arm. I jumped.

"Don't touch me," I told her. I was thinking of my grandmother and you cannot truly remember a dead grandmother if you aren't alone, if a girl with black hair—black like my grandmother's shawl—touches your arm.

Suddenly it occurred to me that my grandmother's smile had a meaning that the future was to reveal: she knew that my question did not concern her, that she would not know the cold of a grave. Her body had not been buried but entrusted to the wind that had blown it in all directions. And it was her body—my grandmother's white and black body—that whipped my face, as if to punish me for having forgotten. No, Grandmother! No! I haven't forgotten. Every time I'm cold, I think of you, I think only of you.

"Come on," Kathleen said. "Let's go. I'm getting cold."

We started walking again. The wind cut our faces, but we went on. We didn't walk faster. Finally we stopped on Boulevard Saint-Germain, opposite the Deux-Magots.

"Here we are," she said.

"This is where you live?"

"Yes. Do you want to come up?"

I had to fight against myself not to say no. I wanted to stay with her too much, to talk to her, to touch her hair, to see her fall asleep. But I was afraid of being disappointed.

"Come," Kathleen insisted.

She opened the heavy door and we walked up one flight to her apartment.

I was cold. And I was thinking of my grandmother, whose face was white like the transparent desert sand, and whose shawl was as black as the dense night of cemeteries.

W HO ARE YOU?"
        I could hardly hear my own voice. Thousands of
        needles were injecting fire into my blood. I was
thirsty. I felt hot. My throat was dry. My veins were about to
burst. And yet the cold hadn't left me. My body, shaken by convulsions, trembled like a tree in a storm, like leaves in the wind,
like the wind in the sea, like the sea in the head of a madman,
of a drunkard, of a dying man.

"Who are you?" I asked again, while my teeth chattered. I
could feel there was someone in the room.

"The nurse," said an unknown voice.

"Water," I said. "I'm thirsty. I'm burning. Please give me
some water."

"You mustn't drink," the voice said. "You'll feel bad. If you
drink, you'll throw up."

Against my will, I began to cry silently.

"There, now," the nurse said. "I'm going to moisten your
face."

She wiped my forehead and then my lips with a wet towel which caught fire as it touched my skin.

"What time is it?" I asked.

"Six o'clock."

"At night?"

"Yes."

I thought: when Dr. Russel came to see me, it was well before noon. Six penicillin shots, I hadn't even noticed.

"Are you in pain?" the nurse asked.

"I'm thirsty."

"It's the fever that's making you thirsty."

"Do I still have a high fever?"

"Yes."

"How high?"

"High."

"I want to know."

"I'm not allowed to tell you. That's the rule."

The door opened. Someone came in. Whispers.

"Well, my friend? What have you got to say?"

Dr. Russel was trying to be casual.

"I'm thirsty, Doctor."

"The enemy refuses to retreat," he said. "It's up to you to hold out."

"He'll win, Doctor. He doesn't suffer from thirst."

I thought: Grandmother would have understood. It was hot in the airless, waterless chambers. It was hot in the room where her livid body was crushed by other livid bodies. Like me, she must have opened her mouth to drink air, to drink water. But there was no water where she was, there was no air. She was only drinking death, as you drink water or air, mouth open, eyes closed, fingers clenched.

Suddenly I felt a strange need to speak out loud. To tell the story of Grandmother's life and death, to describe her black shawl that used to frighten me until I was reassured by her kind, simple expression. Grandmother was my refuge. Every time my father scolded me, she would intervene: fathers are like that, she'd explain smilingly. They get angry over nothing.

One day my father slapped me. I had stolen some money from the store cash register in order to give it to a classmate. A sickly, poor little boy. They called him Haïm the orphan. I always felt ill at ease in his presence. I knew I was happier than he was and this made me feel guilty. Guilty that my parents were alive. That's why I stole the money. But when my father asked me, trying to find out what I had done with it, I didn't tell him. After all, I couldn't tell my father that I felt guilty because he was alive! He slapped my face and I ran to Grandmother. I could tell her the whole truth. She didn't scold me. Sitting in the middle of the room, she lifted me onto her lap and began to sob. Her tears fell on my head, which she was holding against her bosom, and I discovered to my surprise that a grandmother's tears are so hot that they burn everything in their path.

"She's there," the doctor said. "She's outside. In the hallway. Do you want her to come in?"

With the strength that came from my fear, I screamed, "No! I don't, I don't."

I thought he was talking about my grandmother. I didn't want to see her. I knew she had died—of thirst, maybe—and I was afraid she wouldn't be as I remembered her. I was afraid she wouldn't have the black shawl on her head, nor those burning tears in her eyes, nor that clear, calm expression that could make you forget you were cold.

"You should see her," the doctor said softly.

"No! Not now!"

My tears left scars on my cheeks, on my lips, on my chin.

From time to time, they even managed to slip under the cast. Why was I crying? I had no idea. I think it was because of Grandmother. She used to cry very often. She would cry when she was happy and also when she was unhappy. When she was neither happy nor unhappy, she would cry because she could no longer feel the things that bring about happiness and unhappiness. I wanted to prove to her that I had inherited her tears, which, as it is written, open all doors.

"It's up to you," the doctor said. "Kathleen can come back tomorrow."

Kathleen! What did she have to do with this? How did she meet Grandmother? Had she also died?

"Kathleen?" I said, letting my head fall back. "Where is she?"

"Outside," the doctor said, somewhat surprised. "In the hallway."

"Bring her in."

The door opened and light footsteps came toward my bed. Again I made a desperate effort to open my eyes, but my eyelids felt sewn together.

"How are you, Kathleen?" I asked in a barely audible voice.

"Fine."

"You see: I am Dmitri Karamazov's most recent victim."

Kathleen forced a little laugh.

"You were right. It's a bad movie."

"Better to die than to see it."

Kathleen's laugh sounded false.

"You're exaggerating . . ."

Whispers. The doctor was speaking to her very softly.

"I have to leave you," Kathleen said, sounding very sorry.

"Be careful crossing the street."

She leaned over to kiss me. An old fear took hold of me.

"You mustn't kiss me, Kathleen!"

She pulled back her head abruptly. For a moment there was silence in the room. Then I felt her hand on my forehead. I was going to tell her to take it away quickly and not to run the risk of catching fire, but she had already taken it away.

Kathleen tiptoed out of the room, followed by the doctor. The nurse stayed with me. I would really have liked to know what she looked like: old or young, beautiful or sullen, blond or brunette . . . But I still couldn't move my eyelids. All my efforts to open them came to nothing. At one point I told myself that willpower wasn't enough, that I had to use both my hands. But they were tied to the sides of the bed and the big needles were still there.

"I'm going to give you two shots," the nurse announced in a voice from which I could guess nothing.

"Two? Why two?"

"First penicillin. And the second to help you fall asleep."

"You don't have a third one against thirst?" I had a hard time breathing. My lungs were going to burst: empty kettles forgotten on the fire.

"You'll sleep. You won't be thirsty."

"I won't dream that I'm thirsty?"

The nurse lifted the covers. "I'll give you a shot against dreams."

She's nice, I thought. Her heart is made of gold. She suffers when I suffer. She's quiet when I'm thirsty. She's quiet when I sleep. She's quiet when I dream. She is probably young, beautiful, beaming, attractive. She has a serious face, laughing eyes. She has a sensual mouth, made for kissing, not for talking. Just like Grandmother's eyes, which she used not for looking, not for wondering, but simply for crying.

First shot. Nothing. I didn't feel it. Second shot, this one in the arm. Still nothing. I had so much pain that I couldn't even feel the injection.

The nurse fixed the covers, put the needles in a metal box, moved a chair, and turned a switch.

"I'm putting out the light," she said. "You'll go to sleep soon."

All at once I got the idea that she too would want to kiss me before leaving. Just a little meaningless kiss on the forehead or on the cheek and maybe even on the eyelids. They do that in hospitals. A good nurse kisses her patients when she says good night. Not on the mouth. On the forehead, on the cheeks. It reassures them. A patient thinks he is less ill if a woman wants to kiss him. He doesn't know that a nurse's mouth isn't made for speaking, or even for crying, but for keeping quiet and for kissing patients so they can fall asleep without fear, without fear of the dark.

Again, I was completely covered with perspiration.

"You mustn't kiss me," I whispered.

The nurse laughed in a friendly way.

"Of course not. It makes you thirsty."

Then she left the room. And I waited to fall asleep.

"TELL ME a little about yourself," Kathleen said.

We were sitting in her room, where it was pleasantly warm. We were listening to a Gregorian chant, which swelled inside us. The words and the music contained a peace that no storm could have disturbed.

On a small table, our two cups were still half full. The coffee had become cold. The semidarkness made me keep my eyes closed. The feeling of exhaustion that had been weighing me down at the beginning of the evening had completely disappeared. My nerves tense, I was conscious that time, as it passed through me, was carrying a part of me along with it.

"Tell me," Kathleen said. "I want to know you."

Her legs folded under her, she was sitting on my right on the beige couch. A dream was floating in the air, looking for a place on which to settle.

"I don't feel like it," I answered. "I don't feel like talking about myself."

To talk about myself, really talk about myself, I would have had to tell the story of my grandmother. I didn't feel like expressing it in words: Grandmother could only be expressed in prayers.

After the war, when I arrived in Paris, I had often, very often, been urged to tell. I refused. I told myself that the dead didn't need us to be heard. They are less bashful than I. Shame has no hold on them, while I was bashful and ashamed. That's the way it is: shame tortures not the executioners but their victims. The greatest shame is to have been chosen by destiny. Man prefers to blame himself for all possible sins and crimes rather than come to the conclusion that God is capable of the most flagrant injustice. I still blush every time I think of the way God makes fun of human beings, His favorite toys.

Once I asked my teacher, Kalman the Kabbalist, the following question: For what purpose did God create man? I understand that man needs God. But what need of man has God?

My teacher closed his eyes and a thousand wounds, petrified arteries traveled by terror-stricken truths, drew a tangled labyrinth on his forehead. After a few minutes of contemplation, his lips formed a delicate, very distant smile.

"The Holy Books teach us," he said, "that if man were conscious of his power, he would lose his faith or his reason. For man carries within him a role which transcends him. God needs him to be ONE. The Messiah, called to liberate man, can only be liberated by him. We know that not only man and the universe will be freed, but also the one who established their laws and their relations. It follows that man—who is nothing but a handful of earth—is capable of reuniting time and its source, and of giving back to God his own image."

At the time I was too young to understand the meaning of my teacher's words. The idea that God's existence could be bound to mine had filled me with a miserable pride as well as a deep pity.

A few years later I saw just, pious men walking to their death, singing, "We are going to break, with our fire, the chains of the

Messiah in exile." That's when the symbolic implication of what my teacher had said struck me. Yes, God needs man. Condemned to eternal solitude, He made man only to use him as a toy, to amuse Himself. That's what philosophers and poets have refused to admit: in the beginning there was neither the Word nor Love, but laughter, the roaring, eternal laughter whose echoes are more deceitful than the mirages of the desert.

"I want to know you," Kathleen said.

Her face had darkened. The dream, finding no place to settle, had dissolved. I thought: it could have entered her wide-open eyes. But dreams never enter from outside.

"You might end up hating me," I told her.

She drew her legs under her still more. Her whole body contracted, became smaller, as if it had wanted to follow the dream and disappear altogether.

"I'll take a chance," she answered.

She'll hate me, I thought. It is unavoidable. What happened will happen again. The same causes bring about the same effects, the same hatreds. Repetition is a decisive factor in the tragic aspect of our condition.

I don't know the name of the first man who openly cried out his hatred to me, nor who he was. He represented all the nameless and faceless people who live in the universe of dead souls.

I was on a French ship sailing to South America. It was my first encounter with the sea. Most of the time I was on deck, studying the waves, which, untiringly, dug graves only to fill them again. As a child I had searched for God because I imagined him great and powerful, immense and infinite. The sea gave me such an image. Now I understood Narcissus: He hadn't fallen into the fountain. He had jumped into it. At one point my desire to be one with the sea became so strong that I nearly jumped overboard.

I had nothing to lose, nothing to regret. I wasn't bound to the world of men. All I had cared for had been dispersed by smoke. The little house with its cracked walls, where children and old men came humming to pray or study in the melancholy light of candles, was nothing but ruins. My teacher, who had been the first to teach me that life is a mystery, that beyond words there is silence, my teacher, whose head was always hanging as if he didn't dare face heaven—my teacher had long since been reduced to ashes. And my little sister, who made fun of me because I never played with her, because I was too serious, much too serious, my little sister no longer played.

It was a stranger who, unknowingly, unwittingly, had prevented me from giving up that night. As I stood at the rail he had come up behind me, I don't know from where, and had started talking to me. He was an Englishman.

"Beautiful night," he said, leaning against the railing on my right, nearly touching me.

"Very beautiful," I answered coldly.

I thought: beautiful night for saying good-bye to cheaters, to the constants that become uncertainties, to ideals which imply treason, to the world where there is no longer room for what is human, to history that leads to the destruction of the soul instead of broadening its powers!

The stranger wasn't intimidated by my ill humor. He continued. "The sky is so close to the sea that it is difficult to tell which is reflected in the other, which one needs the other, which one is dominating the other."

"That's true," I again answered coldly.

He stopped for a moment. I could see his profile: thin, sharp, noble.

"If the two were at war," he went on, "I'd be on the side of the sea. The sky only inspires painters. Not musicians. While the sea . . . Don't you feel that the sea comes close to man through its music?"

"Perhaps," I answered with hostility.

Again he stopped, as if wondering whether he shouldn't leave me alone. He decided to stay.

"Cigarette?" he asked, holding out his pack.

"No thanks. I don't feel like smoking."

He lit his cigarette and threw the match overboard: a shooting star swallowed up by darkness.

"They're dancing inside," he said. "Why don't you join them?"

"I don't feel like dancing."

"You prefer to be alone with the sea, don't you?"

His voice had suddenly changed. It had become more personal, less anonymous. I wasn't aware that a man could change his voice as he would change a mask.

"Yes, I prefer to remain alone with the sea," I answered nastily, stressing the word "alone."

He took a few puffs on his cigarette.

"The sea. What does it make you think of?"

I hesitated. The fact that he was shrouded in darkness, that I didn't know him, that I probably wouldn't even recognize him the next day in the dining room, worked in his favor. To talk to a stranger is like talking to stars: it doesn't commit you.

"The sea," I said, "makes me think of death."

I had the impression that he smiled.

"I knew it."

"How did you know?" I asked, disconcerted.

"The sea has a power of attraction. I am fifty and have been traveling for thirty years. I know all the seas in the world. I know. One mustn't look at the waves for too long. Especially at night. Especially alone."

He told me about his first trip. His wife was with him. They had just gotten married. One night he left his wife, who was sleeping, and went up on deck to get some air. There he became aware of the terrible power of the sea over those who see in it their transformed silhouette. He was happy and young; and yet he felt a nearly irresistible need to jump, to be carried away by the living waves whose roar, more than anything else, evokes eternity, peace, the infinite.

"I'm telling you," he repeated very softly. "One mustn't look at the sea for too long. Not alone, and not at night."

Then I too started telling him things about myself. Knowing that he had thought about death and was attracted by its secret, I felt closer to him. I told him what I had never told anyone. My childhood, my mystic dreams, my religious passions, my memories of German concentration camps, my belief that I was now just a messenger of the dead among the living . . .

I talked for hours. He listened, leaning heavily on the railing, without interrupting me, without moving, without taking his eyes off a shadow that followed the ship. From time to time he would light a cigarette and, even when I stopped in the middle of a thought or a sentence, he said nothing.

Sometimes I left a sentence unfinished, jumped from one episode to another, or described a character in a word without mentioning the event with which he was connected. The stranger didn't ask for explanations. At times I spoke very softly, so softly that it was impossible that he heard a word of what I was saying; but he remained motionless and silent. He seemed not to dare exist outside of silence.

Only toward the end of the night did he recover his speech. His voice, a streak of shade, was hoarse. The voice of a man who, alone in the night, looks at the sea, looks at his own death.

"You must know this," he finally said. "I think I'm going to hate you."

Emotion made me gasp. I felt like shaking his hand to thank him. Few people would have had the courage to accompany me lucidly to the end.

The stranger threw his head back as if to make sure that the sky was still there. Suddenly he started hammering the railing with his clenched fist. And in a restrained, deep voice he repeated the same words over and over, "I'm going to hate you . . . I'm going to hate you . . ."

Then he turned his back to me and walked off.

A fringe of white light was brightening the horizon. The sea was quiet, the ship was dozing. The stars had started to disappear. It was daybreak.

I stayed on deck all day. I came back to the same place the following night. The stranger never joined me again.

"I'LL TAKE A CHANCE," Kathleen said.

I got up and took a few steps around the room to stretch my legs. I stopped at the window and looked out. The sidewalk across the street was covered with snow. A strange anguish came over me. Cold sweat covered my forehead. Once again the night would lift its burden and it would be day. I was afraid of the day. At night, I find all faces familiar, every noise sounds like something already heard. During the day, I only run into strangers.

"Do you know what Shimon Yanai told me about you?" Kathleen asked.

"I have no idea."

What could he have told her? What does he know about me? Nothing. He doesn't know that when I get carried away by a sun-

set, my heart fills with such nostalgia for Sighet, the little town of
my childhood, it begins to pound so hard, so fast, that a week later
I still haven't caught my breath; he doesn't know that I'm more
moved by a Hasidic melody, which brings men back to his origins,
than by Bach, Beethoven, and Mozart together; he couldn't know
that when I look at a woman, it is always the image of my grandmother that I see.

"Shimon Yanai thinks you're a saint," Kathleen said.

My answer was a loud, unrestrained laugh.

"Shimon Yanai says that you suffered a lot. Only saints suffer
a lot."

I couldn't stop laughing. I turned toward Kathleen, toward her
eyes, not made for seeing, nor for crying, but for speaking and
perhaps for making people laugh. She was hiding her chin in the
neck of her sweater, concealing her lips, which were trembling.

"Me, a saint? What a joke . . ."

"Why are you laughing?"

"I'm laughing," I answered, still shaking, "I'm laughing because I'm not a saint. Saints don't laugh. Saints are dead. My
grandmother was a saint: she's dead. My teacher was a saint: he's
dead. But me, look at me, I'm alive. And I'm laughing. I'm alive
and I'm laughing because I'm not a saint . . ."

At first I had had a hard time getting used to the idea that
I was alive. I thought of myself as dead. I couldn't eat, read, cry: I
saw myself dead. I thought I was dead and that in a dream I imagined myself alive. I knew I no longer existed, that my real self had
stayed *there*, that my present self had nothing in common with the
other, the real one. I was like the skin shed by a snake.

Then one day, in the street, an old woman asked me to come
up to her room. She was so old, so dried out, that I couldn't hold
back my laughter. The old woman grew pale and I thought she
was going to collapse at my feet.

"Haven't you any pity?" she said in a choked voice.

Then, all of a sudden, reality struck me: I was alive, laughing, making fun of unhappy old women, I was able to humiliate and hurt old women who, like saints, spit on their own bodies.

"Where does suffering lead to?" Kathleen asked tensely. "Not to saintliness?"

"No!" I shouted.

That stopped my laughter. I was getting angry. I walked away from the window and stood in front of her; she was sitting on the floor now, her arms around her knees and her head resting on her arms.

"Those who say that are false prophets," I said.

I had to make an effort not to scream, not to wake up the whole house, and the dead who were waiting outside in the wind and the snow flurries. I went on:

"Suffering brings out the lowest, the most cowardly in man. There is a phase of suffering you reach beyond which you become a brute: beyond it you sell your soul—and worse, the souls of your friends—for a piece of bread, for some warmth, for a moment of oblivion, of sleep. Saints are those who die before the end of the story. The others, those who live out their destiny, no longer dare look at themselves in the mirror, afraid they may see their inner image: a monster laughing at unhappy women and at saints who are dead . . ."

Kathleen listened, in a daze, her eyes wide open. As I spoke, her back bent over even more. Her pale lips whispered the same sentence tirelessly: "Go on! I want to know more. Go on!"

Then I fell on my knees, took her head in my hands, and, looking straight into her eyes, I told her the story of my grandmother, then the story of my little sister, and of my father, and of my mother; in very simple words, I described to her how man can become a grave for the unburied dead.

I kept talking. In every detail, I described the screams and the nightmares that haunt me at night. And Kathleen, very pale, her eyes red, continued to beg:

"More! Go on! More!"

She was saying "more" in the eager voice of a woman who wants her pleasure to last, who asks the man she loves not to stop, not to leave her, not to disappoint her, not to abandon her halfway between ecstasy and nothing. "More . . . More . . ."

I kept looking at her and holding her. I wanted to get rid of all the filth that was in me and graft it onto her pupils and her lips, which were so pure, so innocent, so beautiful.

I bared my soul. My most contemptible thoughts and desires, my most painful betrayals, my vaguest lies, I tore them from inside me and placed them in front of her, like an impure offering, so she could see them and smell their stench.

But Kathleen was drinking in every one of my words as if she wanted to punish herself for not having suffered before. From time to time she insisted in the same eager voice that sounded so much like the old prostitute's, "More . . . More . . ."

Finally I stopped, exhausted. I stretched out on the carpet and closed my eyes.

We didn't talk for a long time: an hour, perhaps two. I was out of breath. I was wet with perspiration, my shirt stuck to my body. Kathleen didn't stir. Outside, the night softly moved on.

Suddenly we heard the noise of the milkman's truck, coming from the street. The truck stopped near the door.

Kathleen took a deep breath and said, "I feel like going down and kissing the milkman."

I didn't answer. I didn't have the strength.

"I would like to kiss him," Kathleen said, "just to thank him. To thank him for being alive."

I was silent.

"You're not saying anything." She sounded surprised. "You're not laughing?"

And as I still didn't say anything, she began to stroke my hair, then her fingers explored the outlines of my face. I liked the way she caressed me.

"I like you to touch me," I told her, my eyes still closed. After hesitating, I added, "You see, it's the best proof that I'm not a saint. Saints in that respect are like the dead: they don't know desire."

Kathleen's voice became lighter and sounded more provocative. "And you desire me?"

"Yes."

I again felt like laughing: a saint, me? What a wonderful joke! Me, a saint! Does a saint feel this desire for a woman's body? Does he feel this need to take her into his arms, cover her with kisses, to bite her flesh, to possess her breath, her life, her breasts? No, a saint would not be willing to make love to a woman, with his dead grandmother watching, wearing her black shawl that seems to hold the nights and days of the universe.

I sat down. And I said angrily, "I'm not a saint!"

"No?" Kathleen asked without being able to smile.

"No," I repeated.

I opened my eyes and noticed that she was really suffering. She was biting her lips; there was despair in her face.

"I'll prove to you that I'm not a saint," I muttered angrily.

Without a word I started to undress her. She didn't resist. When she was naked, she sat down again as before. Her head resting on her knees, she looked at me in anguish as I too undressed. Now there were two lines around her mouth. I could see fear in her eyes. I was pleased; she was afraid of me, and that was good. Those who, like me, have left their souls in hell, are here only to frighten others by being their mirrors.

"I am going to take you," I told her in a harsh, almost hostile voice. "But I don't love you."

I thought: She must know. I'm not a saint at all. I'll make love without any commitments. A saint commits his whole being with every act.

She undid her hair, which fell to her shoulders. Her breast rose and fell irregularly.

"What if I fall in love with you?" she asked with studied naïveté.

"Small chance! You'll hate me rather."

Her face became a little sadder, a little more distressed. "I'm afraid you're right."

Somewhere, above the city, there was a hint of dawn in the foggy world.

"Look at me," I said.

"I'm looking at you."

"What do you see?"

"A saint," she answered.

I laughed again. There we were, both naked, and one of us was a saint? It was grotesque! I took her brutally, trying to hurt her. She bit her lips and didn't cry out. We stayed together until late that afternoon.

Without saying another word.

Without exchanging a kiss.

S UDDENLY, the fever vanished. My name was taken off the
critical list. I still had pain, but my life was no longer in
danger. I was still given antibiotics, but less frequently.
Four shots a day. Then three, then two. Then none.

When I was allowed visitors, I had been in the hospital for
nearly a week and in a cast for three days.

"Your friends may come to see you today," the nurse said as
she washed me.

"Fine," I said.

"That's your only reaction? Aren't you pleased to be able to
see your friends?"

"I am. Very pleased."

"You've come a long way," she said.

"A very long way."

"You're not talkative."

"No."

I had discovered one advantage in being ill: you can remain
silent without having to apologize.

"After breakfast, I'll come and shave you," the nurse said.

"It won't be necessary," I answered.

"Not necessary?"

She seemed not to believe me: nothing that's done in a hospital is unnecessary!

"That's right. Unnecessary. I want to grow a beard."

She stared at me a moment, then gave her verdict.

"No. You need a shave. You look too ill this way."

"But I am ill."

"You are. But if I shave you you'll feel better."

And without giving me time to answer, she continued, "You'll feel like new."

She was young, dark, obstinate. Tall, buttoned up in her white uniform, she towered over me and not merely because she was standing up.

"All right," I said, to put an end to the discussion. "In that case, fine."

"Good! That's the boy!"

She was happy with her victory, her mouth wide open, showing her white teeth. Laughingly, she began to tell me all kinds of stories which seemed to have the following moral: death is afraid to attack those who make themselves look nice in the morning. The secret of immortality may well be to find the right shaving cream.

After helping me wash, she brought my breakfast.

"I'll feed you as if you were a baby. Aren't you ashamed to be a baby? At your age?"

She left and immediately returned with an electric razor.

"We want you to look nice. I want my baby to be nice!"

The razor made a tremendous noise. The nurse went on chattering. I wasn't listening to her. I was thinking about the night of the accident. The cab was speeding. I had no idea it would send me to the hospital.

"There you are," the nurse said, beaming. "Now you're nice."

"I know," I said. "Now I'm like a newborn baby!"

"Wait and I'll bring you a mirror!"

She had very large eyes, with black pupils, and the white around them was very white.

"I don't want it," I said.

"I'll bring it, you'll see."

"Listen," I said threateningly, "if you hand me a mirror I'll break it. A broken mirror brings seven years of unhappiness! Is that what you want? Seven years of unhappiness?"

For a second her eyes were still, wondering if I wasn't joking.

"It's true. Anybody will tell you: one should never break a mirror."

She was still laughing, but now her voice sounded more worried than before. She was wiping her hands on her white uniform.

"You're a bad boy," she said. "I don't like you."

"Too bad!" I answered. "I adore you!"

She muttered something to herself and left the room.

I was facing the window and could see the East River from my bed. A small boat was going by: a grayish spot on a blue background. A mirage.

Someone knocked at the door.

"Come in!"

Dr. Paul Russel, hands in his pockets, was back to resume our conversation where we had left off.

"Feeling better this morning?"

"Yes, Doctor. Much better."

"No more fever. The enemy is beaten."

"A beaten enemy, that's dangerous," I remarked. "He'll only think of vengeance."

The doctor became more serious. He took out a cigarette and offered it to me. I refused. He lit it for himself.

"Do you still have pain?"

"Yes."

"It will last a few weeks more. You're not afraid?"

"Of what?"

"Of suffering."

"No. I'm not afraid of suffering."

He looked me straight in the eye. "What are you afraid of, then?"

Again I had the impression that he was keeping something from me. Could he actually know? Had I talked in my sleep during the operation?

"I'm not afraid of anything," I answered, staring back at him.

There was a silence.

He went to the window and stayed there a few moments. There, I thought: the back of a man and the river no longer exists. Paradise is when nothing comes between the eye and the tree.

"You have a beautiful view," he said without turning.

"Very beautiful. The river is like me: it hardly moves."

"Sheer illusion! It is calm only on the surface. Go beneath the surface, you'll see how restless it is . . ." He turned suddenly. ". . . Just like you, as a matter of fact."

What does he know exactly? I wondered, somewhat worried. He speaks as if he knows. Is it possible that I betrayed myself?

"Every man is like the river," I said to shift the conversation toward abstractions. "Rivers flow toward the sea, which is never full. Men are swallowed up by death, which is never satiated."

He made a gesture of discouragement, as if to say, All right, you don't want to talk, you're dodging, it doesn't matter. I'll wait.

Slowly he moved toward the door, then stopped.

"I have a message for you. From Kathleen. She's coming to see you in the late afternoon."

"You saw her?"

"Yes. She's been coming every day. She's an extremely nice girl."

"Ex-treme-ly."

He was standing in the opening of the door. His voice seemed very close. The door must have been right next to my bed.

"She loves you," he said. His voice became hard, insistent. "And you? Do you love her?"

He stressed the "you." I was breathing faster. What does he know? I asked myself, tormented.

"Of course," I answered, trying to look calm. "Of course I love her."

Nothing stirred. There was complete silence. In the hallway, the foggy loudspeaker announced: "Dr. Braunstein, telephone . . . Dr. Braunstein, telephone . . ." Echoes from another world. In the room there was utter silence.

"Fine," Dr. Russel said. "I have to go. I'll see you tonight, or tomorrow."

Another boat was gliding by the window. Outside the air was sharp, alive. I thought: At this very moment, men are walking in the streets, without ties, in their shirtsleeves. They are reading, arguing, eating, drinking, stopping to avoid a car, to admire a woman, to look at windows. Outside, at this very moment, men are walking.

Toward the beginning of the afternoon, some of my colleagues showed up. They came together, gay and trying to make me feel equally gay.

They told me some gossip: who was doing what, who was saying what, who was unfaithful to whom. The latest word, the latest indiscretion, the latest story.

Then the conversation came back to the accident.

"You must admit you've been lucky: this could have been it," one of them said.

And another: "Or you could have lost a leg."

"Or even your mind."

"You're going to be rich," Sandor, a Hungarian, said. "I was hit by a car once myself. I got a thousand dollars from the insurance company. You were lucky it was a cab. Cabs always have a lot of insurance. You'll be rich, you'll see, you lucky bastard!"

I hurt everywhere. I couldn't move. I was practically paralyzed. But I was very lucky. I was going to be rich. I'd be able to travel, go to nightclubs, keep mistresses, be on top of the world: what luck! They just about said they envied me.

"I'd always been told that in America you find dollars in the street," I said. "So it's true: you just have to fall down to pick them up."

They laughed still more and I laughed with them. Once or twice the nurse came in to bring me something to drink and she also laughed with them.

"And you know this morning he didn't even want to shave!" she told them.

"He's rich," Sandor said. "Rich men can afford to be unshaven."

"You're funny," the nurse exclaimed, clapping her hands. "And did he tell you about the mirror?"

"No!" they all shouted together. "Tell us about the mirror!"

She told them that I had refused to look at myself in the mirror that morning.

"Rich men are afraid of mirrors," I said. "Mirrors have no respect for that which glitters. They're too familiar with it."

It was warm in the room, even warmer than in the cast. My friends were perspiring. The nurse was wiping her forehead with the back of her hand. When she left, Sandor winked.

"Not bad, hmm?"

"She must be something!" another added.

"Well, you won't get bored here, you can be sure of that much!"

"No, I won't get bored," I said.

We had been together for quite some time when Sandor remembered that there was a press conference at four.

"That's true, we'd forgotten."

They left in a hurry, taking their laughter with them into the hallway, into the street, and finally, where it assumes a historic function, into the United Nations building.

IT WAS NEARLY SEVEN when Kathleen arrived. She seemed paler than usual, and gayer, also more exuberant. It was as if she were living the happiest moments of her life. What a beautiful view! Look, the river! And such a nice room! So big, so clean! You're looking great!

It's weird, I thought. A hospital room is the gayest place on earth. Everybody turns into an actor. Even the patients. You put on new attitudes, new makeup, new joys.

Kathleen kept talking. Even though she didn't like people who talk without saying anything, she was doing precisely that now. Why is she afraid of silence? I wondered, as I grew more tense. Is it possible she knows something too? She is in a position to know. She was there at the time of the accident. A little ahead. She may have turned around.

I would have liked to steer the conversation to that subject, but I couldn't stop the flow of her words. She kept talking and talking. Isak is replacing you on the paper. In the office, the phone keeps ringing: all kinds of people asking how you are. And you know, even the one—what's his name?—you know the one I mean, the fat one, the one who looks pregnant, you know, the one who's angry at you, even he called. Isak told me. And—

There was a knock on the door. A nurse—a new one, not the morning nurse—brought in my dinner. She was an old woman with glasses, haughtily indifferent. She offered to help me eat.

"Don't bother," Kathleen said. "I'll do it."

"Very well," the old nurse said. "As you wish."

I wasn't hungry. Kathleen kept insisting: some soup? Yes, yes. You have to. You've lost a lot of strength. Come on. Just one spoonful. Just one. One more. Do it for me. And one more. Fine. And now the rest. Let's see: a piece of meat. Ah! Does that look good!

I closed my eyes and tried not to hear. That was the only way. I suddenly felt like shouting. But I knew I shouldn't. Anyway what would have been the use?

Kathleen talked on and on.

". . . I also retained a lawyer. A very good one. He's going to sue the cab company. He'll be here tomorrow. He is very hopeful. He says you'll get a lot of money . . ."

When I was through eating, she took the tray and put it on the table. I could see as she busied herself how tired she was. Now I understood why she was talking so much: she was at the end of her strength. Behind her forced good humor was exhaustion. Seven days. It had been a week since the accident.

"Kathleen?" I called.

"Yes?"

"Come here. Sit down."

She obeyed and sat on the bed.

"What is it?" she asked, worried.

"I want to ask you something."

She frowned. "Yes?"

"I don't recognize you. You've changed. You talk a lot. Why?"

A shudder went through her eyelids, through her shoulders.

"So many things have happened in a week," she said, blushing slightly. "I want to tell you about them. Everything. Don't forget that I haven't talked to you in a week . . ."

She looked at me as if she had been beaten, and lowered her head. Then slowly, mechanically, she repeated several times in a low, tired, toneless voice, "I don't want to cry, I don't want to cry, I don't want to . . ."

Poor Kathleen, I thought. Poor Kathleen. I have changed her. Kathleen so proud, Kathleen whose will was stronger than others', Kathleen whose strength was pure and who was truly tough, Kathleen against whom men with character, strong-minded men, liked to pit themselves; now Kathleen didn't even have the strength to hold back her tears, her words.

I had transformed her. And she had wanted to change me! "You can't change a human being," I had told her in the beginning, once, a thousand times. "You can change someone's thoughts, someone's attitudes, someone's ties. You might even change someone's desires, but that's all." "That's enough for me," she had answered.

And the battle had started. She wanted to make me happy no matter what. To make me taste the pleasures of life. To make me forget the past. "Your past is dead. Dead and buried," she would say. And I would answer, "I am my past. If it's buried, I'm buried with it."

She was fighting stubbornly. "I'm strong," she would say. "I'll win." And I would answer, "You are strong. You are beautiful. You have all the qualities to conquer the living. But here you are fighting the dead. You cannot conquer the dead!" "We shall see."

"I don't want to cry," she said, her head down, as if under the weight of all the dead since creation.

I had said human beings don't change? I was wrong. They do.

The dead are all-powerful. That's what she refused to understand: that the dead are invincible. That through me she was fighting them.

The only child of very rich parents, she was determined and obstinate. Her arrogance was almost naïve. She wasn't accustomed to losing battles. She thought she could take the place of my fate.

Once I had asked her if she loved me. "No," she had answered heatedly. And it was true. She hadn't lied. The truly proud don't lie.

Our understanding had nothing to do with love. Not at first. Later, yes. But not at the beginning. What united us was exactly what kept us apart. She liked life and love; I only thought of life and love with a strong feeling of shame. We stayed together. She needed to fight and I was watching her. I watched her knocking against the cold, unchanging reality she had discovered first in my words, then in my silence.

We traveled a lot. The days were full, the hours dense. Time was once more an adventure. Whenever Kathleen watched a beautiful dawn, she knew how to make me share her enthusiasm; in the street she was the one to point out beautiful women; at home she taught me that the body is also a source of joy.

At first, at the very beginning, I avoided her kisses. We were living together but our mouths had never met. Something in me shrank from the touch of her lips. It was as if I were afraid that she would become different if I kissed her. Several times she had nearly asked me why, but she had been too proud. Then, little by little, I let myself go. Every kiss reopened an old wound. And I was aware that I was still capable of suffering. That I was still answering the calls of the past.

Our affair lasted a whole year. When we celebrated the first anniversary of our meeting—that's what we liked to call our affair—we both decided to separate. Since the experiment had foundered, there was no reason to draw it out.

That night neither one of us slept. Stretched out next to each other, frightened, in silence, we waited for daybreak. Just before dawn, she pulled me toward her and in the dark our bodies made love for the last time. An hour later, still silent, I got up, dressed, and left the room without saying good-bye, without even turning around.

Outside, the biting morning wind whipped the houses. The streets were still deserted. Somewhere a door creaked. A window lit up, lonely and pale. It was cold. My legs would have liked me to run. I managed to walk slowly, very slowly: I didn't want to give in to any weakness. My eyes were crying, probably because of the cold.

"I don't want to cry," Kathleen said.

She was shaking her lowered head.

Poor Kathleen, I thought. You too have been changed by the dead.

THE LAWYER came the next day. He wore glasses, was of medium height, and had the self-satisfied air of someone who knows the answer before he has even asked you the question.

He introduced himself: Mark Brown. "Call me Mark."

He sat down as if he were at home and took a large yellow pad out of his briefcase.

"I talked to your doctors," he said. "You were in very bad shape. That's very good."

"You're right, that's very good."

He understood the irony. "Of course I'm only speaking from the point of view of the lawsuit," he said, winking at me.

"So am I," I answered. "I hear you're going to make me rich."

"I have high hopes."

"Be careful. My enemies will never forgive me: I'm about to become a rich journalist!"

He laughed: "For once the law will be on the side of literature!"

He started asking me detailed questions: What exactly had happened on the night of the accident? Had I been alone? No. Who was with me? Kathleen. Yes, the young woman who had called him. Had we quarreled? No. Had we waited for the light to turn green before crossing the street? Yes. The cab had come from the left. Had I seen it approaching?

I took a little more time to answer this last question. Mark took off his glasses and as he wiped them he repeated, "Did you see it approaching?"

"No," I said.

He looked at me more sharply. "You seem to hesitate."

"I'm trying to relive the incident, to see it again."

Mark was intelligent, perceptive. To prepare a good case, he was determined to get lots of details which, on the surface, seemed to have no direct relation to the accident. Before working out his strategy he wanted to know everything. His questioning lasted several hours. He seemed satisfied.

"Not the shadow of a doubt," he decided. "The driver is guilty of negligence."

"I hope he won't have to suffer because of this!" I said. "I wouldn't want him to be punished. After all he didn't do it on purpose . . ."

"Don't worry," he reassured me, "he won't have to pay; it will be the insurance company. We have nothing against him, poor chap."

"You're sure, absolutely sure, that nothing will happen to him?"

Poor devil, I thought. It wasn't his fault. The day before, his wife had called and asked me to forgive him. She was calling on behalf of her husband. He was afraid. He was even afraid to ask me to forgive him.

"Absolutely sure," the lawyer said with a little, dry laugh. "You'll be richer and he won't be any poorer. So, there's nothing to worry about."

I couldn't hide a sigh of relief.

EVERY MORNING Dr. Russel came to chat. He had made it a habit to end his daily rounds with me. Often he would remain an hour or more. He would walk in without knocking, sit on the windowsill, his hands in the pockets of his white coat, his legs crossed, his eyes reflecting the changing colors of the river.

He spoke a lot about himself, his life in the army—he had been in the Korean War—his work, the pleasures and disappointments that came with it. Each prey torn away from death made him as happy as if he had won a universal victory. A defeat left dark rings under his eyes. I only had to look at him carefully to know whether the night before he had won or lost the battle. He considered death his personal enemy.

"What makes me despair," he often told me bitterly, "is that our weapons aren't equal. My victories can only be temporary. My defeats are final. Always."

One morning he seemed happier than usual. He gave up his favorite spot near the window and started walking up and down the room like a drunkard, talking to himself.

"You have been drinking, Doctor!" I teased him.

"Drinking!" he exclaimed. "Of course I haven't been drinking. I don't drink. Today I'm simply happy. Awfully happy. I won! Yes, this time I won . . ."

His victory tasted like wine. He couldn't stand still. To split up his happiness he would have liked to be simultaneously himself and someone else: witness and hero. He wanted to sing and to hear himself singing, to dance and to see himself dancing, to climb to the top of the highest mountain and to shout, to scream with all his strength, "I won! I conquered Death!"

The operation had been difficult, dangerous: a little twelve-year-old boy who had a very slim chance of surviving. Three doctors had given up hope. But he, Paul Russel, had decided to try the impossible.

"The kid will make it!" he thundered, his face glowing as if lit up by a sun inside him. "Do you understand? He's going to live! And yet all seemed lost! The infection had reached his leg and was poisoning his blood. I amputated the leg. The others were saying that it wouldn't do any good. That it was too late. That the game was lost. But I didn't hesitate. I started to act. For each breath, I had to fight with every weapon I had. But you see: I won! This time I really won!"

The joy of saving a human life, I thought. I have never experienced it. I didn't even know that it existed. To hold in your hands a boy's life is to take God's place. I had never dreamt of rising above the level of man. Man is not defined by what denies him, but by that which affirms him. This is found within, not across from him or next to him.

"You see," Paul Russel said in a different tone of voice, "the difference between you and me is this. Your relation with what surrounds you and with what marks the limits of your horizon develops in an indirect way. You only know the words, the skin, the appearances, the ideas, of life. There'll always be a curtain between you and your neighbor's life. You're not content to know man is alive; you also want to know what he is doing with his life. For me this is different. I am less severe with my fellow men. We have the same enemy and it has only one name: Death. Before it we are all equal. In its eyes no life has more weight than another. From that point of view, I am just like Death. What fascinates me in man is his capacity for living. Acts are just repetitions. If you had ever held a man's life in the palm of your hand, you too would come to prefer the immediate to the future, the concrete to the ideal, and life to the problems which it brings with it."

He stood at the window for a moment and stopped talking, just long enough to smile, before continuing an octave lower.

"Your life, my friend, I had it right there. In the palm of my hand."

He turned slowly, his hand held out. Little by little his face became as it usually was and his gestures became less abrupt.

"Do you believe in God, Doctor?"

My question took him by surprise. He stopped suddenly, wrinkling his forehead.

"Yes," he answered. "But not in the operating room. There I only count on myself."

His eyes looked deeper. He added, "On myself and on the patient. Or, if you prefer, on the life in the diseased flesh. Life wants to live. Life wants to go on. It is opposed to death. It fights. The patient is my ally. He fights on my side. Together we are stronger than the enemy. Take the boy last night. He didn't accept death. He helped me to win the battle. He was holding on, clinging. He was asleep, anesthetized, and yet he was taking part in the fight . . ."

Still motionless, he again stared at me intensely. There was an awkward silence. Once more I had the impression he knew, that he was speaking only to penetrate my secret. Now, I decided. Now or never. I had to put an end to any uncertainty.

"Doctor, I would like to ask you a question."

He nodded.

"What did I say during the operation?"

He thought a moment. "Nothing. You didn't say anything."

"Are you sure? Not even a word?"

"Not even a word."

I was relieved and couldn't help smiling.

"My turn now," the doctor said seriously. "I also have a question."

My smile froze. "Go ahead," I said.

I had to fight an urge to close my eyes. All of a sudden the room seemed too light. Anxiety took hold of my voice, my breath, my eyes.

The doctor lowered his head slightly, almost imperceptibly.

"Why don't you care about living?" he asked very softly.

For a moment everything shook. Even the light flickered and changed color. It was white, red, black. The blood was beating in my temples. My head was no longer my own.

"Don't deny it," the doctor went on, speaking still more softly. "Don't deny it. I know."

He knows. He knows. He knows. My throat was in an invisible vise. I was going to choke any moment.

Weakly I asked him who had told him: Kathleen?

"No. Not Kathleen. Nobody. Nobody told me. But I know it anyway. I guessed. During the operation. You never helped me. Not once. You abandoned me. I had to wage the fight alone, all alone. Worse. You were on the other side, against me, on the side of the enemy."

His voice became hard, painfully hard. "Answer me! Why don't you want to live? Why?"

I was calm again. He doesn't know, I thought. The little he is guessing is nothing. An impression. That's all. Nothing definite. Nothing worked out. And yet he is moving in the right direction. Only he's not going all the way.

"Answer me," he repeated. "Why? Why?"

He was becoming more and more insistent. His lower lip was shaking nervously. Was he aware of it? I thought: He's angry at me because I left him alone, because even now I escape him and have neither gratitude nor admiration for him. That's why he's angry. He guessed that I don't care about living, that deep inside me there is no desire left to go on. And that undermines the foundation of his philosophy and his system of values. Man, according to his book, must live and must fight for his life. He must help doctors and not fight them. I had fought him. He brought me back to life against my will. I had nearly joined my grandmother. I was actually on the threshold. Paul Russel stood behind me and prevented me from crossing. He was pulling me toward him. Alone against Grandmother and the others. And he had won. Another victory for him. A human life. I should shout with happiness and make the walls of the universe tremble. But instead I disturb him. That's what is distressing him.

Dr. Russel was making an obvious effort to restrain himself. He was still looking at me with anger, his cheeks purple, his lips trembling.

"I order you to answer me!"

A pitiless inquisitor, he had raised his voice. A cold anger made his hands rigid.

I thought: He is going to shout, to hit me. Who knows? He might be capable of strangling me, of sending me back to the battlefield. Dr. Russel is a human being, therefore capable of hatred, capable of losing control. He could easily put his hands around my neck and squeeze. That would be normal, logical on his part. I represent a danger to him. Anyone who rejects life is a threat to him and to everything he stands for in this world where life already counts for so little. In his eyes I am a cancer to be eliminated. What would become of humanity and of the laws of equilibrium if all men began to desire death?

I felt very calm, completely controlled. If I had searched further I might have discovered that my calm also hid the satisfaction, the strange joy—or was it simply humor?—that comes from the knowledge of one's own strength, of one's own solitude. I was telling myself: He doesn't know. And I alone can decide to tell him, to transform his future. At this very moment, I am his fate.

"Did I tell you the dream I had during the first operation I ever had?" I asked him smilingly in an amused tone of voice. "No? Shall I tell you? I was twelve. My mother had taken me to a clinic that belonged to my cousin, the surgeon Oscar Sreter, to have my tonsils removed. He had put me to sleep with ether. When I woke up, Oscar Sreter asked me, 'Are you crying because it hurts?' 'No,' I answered. 'I'm crying because I just saw God.' Strange dream. I had gone to heaven. God, sitting on his throne, was presiding over an assembly of angels. The distance which separated Him from me was infinite, but I could see Him as clearly as if He had been right next to me. God motioned to me and I started to walk forward. I walked several lifetimes, but the distance grew no shorter. Then two angels picked me up, and suddenly I found myself face-to-face with God. At last! I thought. Now I can ask Him the question that haunts all the wise men of Israel: What is the meaning of suffering? But, awed, I couldn't utter a sound. In the meantime other questions kept moving through my head: When will the hour of deliverance come? When will Good conquer Evil, thus allowing chaos to be forever dispelled? But my lips could only tremble and the words stuck in my throat. Then God talked to me. The silence had become so total, so pure, that my heart was ashamed of its beating. The silence was still as absolute, when I heard the words of God. With Him the word and the silence were not contradictory. God answered all my questions and many others. Then two angels took me by the arm again and brought me back. One of them told the other, 'He has become heavier,' and the other replied, 'He is carrying an important answer.' That is when I woke up. Dr. Sreter was leaning over me with a smile. I wanted to tell him that I had just heard the words of God, when I realized to my horror that I had forgotten them. I no longer knew what God had told me. My tears began to flow. 'Are you crying because it hurts?' the good Dr. Sreter asked me. 'It doesn't hurt,' I answered. 'I'm crying because I just saw God. He talked to me and I forgot what He said.' The doctor burst into a friendly laugh: 'If you want I can put you back to sleep, and you can ask Him to repeat . . .' I was crying and my cousin was laughing heartily . . . And you see, Doctor, this time, stretched out on your operating table, fast asleep, I didn't see God in my dream. He was no longer there."

Paul Russel had been listening attentively. Leaning forward, he seemed to be looking for a hidden meaning in every word. His face had changed.

"You haven't answered my question!" he remarked, still tense.

So he hadn't understood. An answer to his question? But this was an answer! Couldn't he see how the second operation was different from the first? It wasn't his fault. He couldn't understand. We were so different, so far from each other. His fingers touched life. Mine death. Without an intermediary, without partitions. Life, death, each as bare, as true as the other. The problem went beyond us. It was in an invisible sphere, on a faraway screen, between two powers for whom we were only ambassadors.

Standing in front of my bed, he filled the room with his presence. He was waiting. He suspected a secret that made him angry. That's what was throwing him off. We were both young, and above all we were alive. He looked at me steadily, stubbornly, to catch in me that which eluded him. In the same way primitive man must have watched the day disappear behind the mountain.

I felt like telling him: Go. Paul Russel, you are a straightforward and courageous man. Your duty is to leave me. Don't ask me to talk. Don't try to know. Neither who I am, nor who you are. I am a storyteller. My legends can only be told at dusk. Whoever listens questions his life. Go, Paul Russel. Go. The heroes of my legends are cruel and without pity. They are capable of strangling you. You want to know who I am, truly? I don't know myself. Sometimes I am Shmuel, the slaughterer. Look at me carefully. No, not at my face. At my hands.

THEY WERE ABOUT TEN in the bunker. Night after night they could hear the German police dogs looking through the ruins for Jews hiding out in their underground shelters. Shmuel and the others were living on practically no water or bread, on hardly any air. They were holding out. They knew that there, down below in their narrow jail, they were free; above, death was waiting for them. One night a disaster nearly occurred. It was Golda's fault. She had taken her child with her. A baby, a few months old. He began to cry, thus endangering the lives of all. Golda was trying to quiet him, to make him sleep. To no avail. That's when the others, including Golda herself, turned to Shmuel and told him: "Make him shut up. Take care of him, you whose job it is to slaughter chickens. You will be able to do it without making him suffer too much." And Shmuel gave in to reason: the baby's life in exchange for the lives of all. He had taken the child. In the dark his groping fingers felt for the neck. And there had been silence on earth and in heaven. There was only the sound of dogs barking in the distance.

A SLIGHT SMILE came to my lips. Shmuel too had been a doctor, I thought.

Motionless, Paul Russel was still waiting.

MOISHE is a smuggler. He too comes from Sighet. We were friends. Every morning at six, ever since we were eight years old, we met in the street and, lantern in hand, we walked to the *cheder*, where we found books bigger than we. Moishe wanted to become a rabbi. Today he is a smuggler and he is wanted by every police force in Europe. In the concentration camp he had seen a pious man exchange his whole week's bread rations for a prayer book. The pious man passed away less than a month later. Before dying he had kissed his precious book and murmured, "Book, how many human beings have you destroyed?" That day Moishe had decided to change the course of his existence. And that's how the human race gained a smuggler and lost a rabbi. And it isn't any the worse off for it.

YOU WANT TO KNOW who I am, Doctor? I am also Moishe the smuggler. But above all I am the one who saw his grandmother go to heaven. Like a flame, she chased away the sun and took its place. And this new sun which blinds instead of giving light forces me to walk with my head down. It weighs upon the future of man. It casts a gloom over the hearts and vision of generations to come.

If I had spoken to him out loud, he would have understood the tragic fate of those who came back, left over, living-dead. You must look at them carefully. Their appearance is deceptive. They are smugglers. They look like the others. They eat, they laugh, they love. They seek money, fame, love. Like the others. But it isn't true: they are playing, sometimes without even knowing it. Anyone who has seen what they have seen cannot be like the others, cannot laugh, love, pray, bargain, suffer, have fun, or forget.

Like the others. You have to watch them carefully when they pass by an innocent-looking smokestack, or when they lift a piece of bread to their mouths. Something in them shudders and makes you turn your eyes away. These people have been amputated; they haven't lost their legs or eyes but their will and their taste for life. The things they have seen will come to the surface again sooner or later. And then the world will be frightened and won't dare look these spiritual cripples in the eye.

If I had spoken out loud, Paul Russel would have understood why one shouldn't ask those who came back too many questions: they aren't normal human beings. A spring snapped inside them from the shock. Sooner or later the results must appear. But I didn't want him to understand. I didn't want him to lose his equilibrium; I didn't want him to see a truth which threatened to reveal itself at any moment.

I began to persuade him he was wrong so he would go away, so he would leave me alone. Of course I wanted to live. Obviously I wanted to live, create, do lasting things, help man make a step forward, contribute to the progress of humanity, its happiness, its fulfillment! I talked a long time, passionately, using complicated, grandiloquent words and abstract expressions on purpose. And since he still wasn't completely convinced, I threw in the argument to which he couldn't remain deaf: love. I love Kathleen. I love her with all my heart. And how can one love if at the same time one doesn't care about life, if one doesn't believe in life or in love?

The young doctor's face gradually assumed its usual expression. He had heard the words he wanted to hear. His philosophy wasn't threatened. Everything was in order again. Nothing like friendship between patients and doctors! Nothing is more sacred than life, or healthier, or greater, or more noble. To refuse life is a sin; it's stupid and mad. You have to accept life, cherish it, love it, fight for it as if it were a treasure, a woman, a secret happiness.

Now he was becoming friendly again. He offered me a cigarette, encouraging me to accept it. He was no longer tense. His lips had their normal color again. There was no more anger in his eyes.

"I'm glad," he said finally. "At the beginning I was afraid . . . I admit my mistake. I'm glad. Really."

I TOO. I was glad to have convinced him. Really.

Nothing easier. He only wanted to be deceived and I had played his game. I had recited a text he knew by heart. Love is a question mark, not an exclamation point. It can explain everything without calling on arguments whose strength as well as whose weakness is based on logic. A boy who is in love knows more about the universe and about creation than a scholar. Why do we have to die? Because I love you, my love. And why do parallel lines meet at infinity? What a question! It's only because I love you, my love.

And it works. For them, for the boy and for the girl, prisoners of a magic circle, the answer seems completely valid. In their eyes there is a direct relation between their adventure and the mysteries of the universe.

Yes, it was easy. I love Kathleen. Therefore life has a meaning, man isn't alone. Love is the very proof of God's existence.

Kathleen. In the end I managed to convince her also. True, this was more difficult. She knew me better and was on her guard. Unlike the young doctor, who was running away from uncertainties, she had a feeling for nuances. For her, Hamlet was just romantic and the question he asked himself was too simplistic. The problem is not: to be or not to be. But rather: to be and not to be. What it comes down to is that man lives while dying, that he represents death to the living, and that's where tragedy begins.

Why had she come back? She shouldn't have. I had even told her so. No. I hadn't told her. She was unhappy. This had surprised me so much that I had felt incapable of telling her not to reopen the parentheses.

She was suffering. Even on the telephone, her voice had betrayed her weariness. Five years had gone by since my silent departure. It had been bitingly cold that morning. Now it was fall. Five years! I had heard from Shimon Yanai that Kathleen had gone back to Boston and had married a man much older than she, and quite rich.

One afternoon, in the office. Up to my neck in work: the General Assembly of the United Nations was holding its annual session. Speeches, statements, accusations and counteraccusations, resolutions and counterresolutions. Judging from what was said on the speaker's platform, our planet was extremely ill.

The phone rang.

At the other end, in a whisper, a voice murmured, "It's Kathleen."

That's all she said and there was a long silence. I looked at the receiver I was holding in my hand and I had the impression it was alive. I thought: years ago, winter; now, fall.

"I would like to see you," Kathleen added.

Her voice had the sound of despair. Of nothingness.

"Where are you?" I asked her.

She mentioned a hotel.

"Wait for me," I said.

We hung up at the same time.

She was staying at one of the most expensive and most elegant places in New York. Her apartment was on the fifteenth floor. Quietly I pushed the half-open door. Kathleen was framed by the window. Her beautiful black hair fell to her shoulders. She was wearing a dark gray dress with a low-cut back. I was moved.

"Hello, Kathleen," I said as I walked in.

"Hello," she answered without turning.

I walked toward the open window. It looked on Central Park, the no-man's-land which at night, in this enormous city, shelters with equal kindness criminals and lovers. The trees were turning orange. It was humid and hot: the last heat wave before winter. Far below, thousands of cars drove into the foliage and disappeared. The sun grafted its golden rays onto the skyscrapers' windows.

"Help me," Kathleen said, her eyes fixed on the dead leaves that covered the park.

Furtively I looked at her left profile. From the curve of her neck I could see that she was still sensitive.

"You will help me, won't you?" she said.

"Of course," I answered.

Only then did she turn her face toward me, with a look of gratitude. She was still beautiful, but her beauty had lost its pride.

"I've suffered a lot," she said.

"Don't say anything," I answered. "Let me look at you."

I sat down in an armchair and she began to walk about the room. When she talked, a line of sadness appeared near her upper lip. From time to time her eyes had the hard expression that comes from humiliation. She was smoking more than she used to. I thought: Kathleen the proud, Kathleen the untamable, Kathleen the queen—here she is. A beaten woman. A drowning woman.

She sat in the armchair opposite me. She was breathing heavily.

"I want to talk," she said.

"Go ahead," I told her.

"I'm not ashamed to tell you that I want to talk."

"Go ahead," I told her.

"I am no longer ashamed to tell you that I suffered a lot."

"Go ahead, talk."

She was trying to live up to the image she still had of herself. She used to speak firmly and with harsh words. She never used to speak of her own suffering. Now she did. You just had to listen to her and look at her closely to realize that her beauty had lost its power and its mystery.

She spoke for a long time. Sometimes her eyes would cloud over. But she managed not to cry, and I was grateful.

She had gotten married. He loved her. She didn't love him. She did not even love the feeling she had inspired in him. She had agreed to marry him precisely because she did not care about him. What she wanted was to suffer, to pay. Finally her husband understood: Kathleen saw in him not a companion but a kind of judge. She didn't expect happiness from him, however limited, but punishment. That's why he also began to suffer. Their life became a torture chamber. Each was the tormentor and victim of the other. This went on for three years. Then, one day, her husband had had enough. He asked for a divorce. She came to New York. To rest, to find herself again, to see me.

"You'll help me, won't you?"

"Of course," I answered.

All she asked was to stay beside me. Her life was empty. She was hoping to climb up again. To start living again, intensely, as before. To be moved to tears by a transparent dusk, to laugh aloud in the theater, to protest against ugliness. All she wanted was to become once more what she had been.

I should have refused. I know. Kathleen—the one I had known—deserved more than my consent. To help her was to insult her, to humiliate her. But I accepted. She was unhappy and I was too weak, perhaps too cowardly, to say no to a woman who was hitting her head against a wall, even if this woman was Kathleen.

"Of course," I repeated. "I'll help you."

She moved forward, as if to throw herself into my arms, but held herself back. We looked at each other in silence for a long time.

WHO IS SARAH?"
I was speechless. Sitting on the edge of the bed, Kathleen watched me with a smile. Her eyes didn't accuse me, they just looked curious.

"You spoke her name the first day, when you were in a coma. You said nothing else. Sarah."

"Why did you wait until today to ask me?"

I had been in the hospital for four weeks.

"I was too curious. I wanted to prove to myself that I was able to wait."

"That's all I said?"

"That's all."

"You're sure?"

"I'm sure. The first few days I was never very far away. You said nothing else. You didn't unclench your teeth. But once or twice you spoke that name: Sarah."

An old suffering stirred somewhere. I didn't know exactly where.

"Sarah," I said distractedly.

Kathleen kept smiling. Her eyes showed no worry. But anguish was there, around her swollen mouth, waiting for a chance to invade her whole face, her whole being.

"Who is she?" she asked again.

"Sarah was my mother's name," I said.

The smile disappeared. Naked suffering was now mixed with the anguish. Kathleen was hardly breathing.

I told her: as a child I lived with the perpetual fear of forgetting my mother's name after I died. In school my teacher had told me: three days after your funeral, an angel will come and knock three times on your grave. He'll ask you your name. You will answer. "I am Eliezer, the son of Sarah." Woe if you forget! A dead soul, you will remain buried for all eternity. You won't be able to come before the tribunal to know if your place is in paradise or in hell with those who waited too long before repenting. You will be condemned to wander in the sphere of chaos where nothing exists, neither punishment nor pain, neither justice nor injustice, neither past nor future, neither hope nor despair. It is a serious thing to forget your mother's name. It is like forgetting your own origin. Remember: "Eliezer, the son of Sarah, the son of Sarah, Sarah, Sarah . . ."

"Sarah was my mother's name," I said. "I didn't forget it."

Kathleen's body twisted as if she were tied to an invisible stake. She was afraid not to suffer enough. But then she shouldn't have used the state I was in to interpret my silences, to gather names that I had kept secret. My mother's name was Sarah. I never talked about it. I loved her but I had never told her. I loved her with such violence that I had to seem hard toward her so she wouldn't guess. Yes. She is dead. She went to heaven at the side of my grandmother.

"Sarah," Kathleen said in a broken voice. "I like that name. It sounds like biblical times."

"My mother's name was Sarah," I said again. "She is dead."

Kathleen's face was twisted with pain. She looked like a sorceress who has lost her true face from having put on too many masks. A great fire burned around her. Suddenly she cried out and began to sob. My mother, I had never seen my mother cry.

SARAH.
It was also the name of a girl with blue eyes and golden hair whom I had met in Paris long before I knew Kathleen.

I was reading a newspaper in front of a café near Montparnasse. She was drinking lemonade at the table next to mine. She was trying to attract my attention and this made me blush. She noticed it and smiled.

Embarrassed, I didn't know what attitude to adopt. Where to hide my head, my hands, where to hide my confusion. Finally, unable to stand it anymore, I spoke to her.

"You know me?"

"No," she said, shaking her head.

"Do I know you?"

"I don't think so," she said teasingly.

I couldn't help stuttering. "Then . . . why? Why . . . why are you staring at me like that?"

She seemed about to shudder, to laugh, or to sigh. "Just like that," she answered.

While cursing my own bashfulness, I buried myself in the

newspaper, trying to forget the blond girl and to avoid her straightforward, innocent eyes and the sadness of her smile. The print danced before my eyes. The words didn't stay still long enough for me to catch them. I was going to call the waiter in order to pay and leave, when the girl with the strange smile began to talk to me.

"You're waiting for someone?"

"No," I said.

"I'm not either."

And as she said this, she came over to my table with her glass of lemonade.

"You're alone?" she asked me.

"No," I said, blushing still more.

"You don't feel alone?"

"Not at all."

"Really?"

She did not seem to believe me. And her smile was there, like a third presence, somewhere on her face. In her eyes? No. Her eyes were cold, frightened. On her lips? Not there either. They were sensuous, bitter, tired. Where was it then? There, between her forehead and her chin, but I couldn't tell exactly where.

"Really?" she repeated. "You don't feel alone?"

"No."

"How do you manage?"

I was losing face.

"I don't know," I blurted out. "I don't know. I read a lot."

She took a sip, raised her head, and began to laugh at me openly. I had noticed that in the meantime her real smile had vanished. Maybe she had swallowed it.

"Do you want to make love?" she asked in the same tone of voice.

"Now?" I exclaimed with surprise. "In the afternoon?"

In my mind, lovemaking was a thing of the night. To make love during the day seemed to me like getting undressed in the middle of the street.

"Right away," she answered. "Do you want to?"

"No," I said quickly.

"Why not?"

"I . . . I don't have any money."

She stared at me a minute with the mocking and forgiving attitude of someone who knows and forgives all.

"That doesn't matter," she said after a pause. "You'll pay me some other time."

I was ashamed. I was afraid. I was young, without any experience. I was afraid not to know what to do. And mostly, I was afraid of afterward: I would never be the same anymore.

"Well? You want to?"

A lock of hair was falling on her forehead. Again the smile appeared. Now I no longer knew if it was the first smile or the one it replaced, the true or the false one.

"Yes," I answered. "I want to."

I thought: this girl has, without knowing it, perhaps, the most elusive smile I have ever seen. I might be able to capture it while making love to her.

"Call the waiter," she said.

I called him. I paid for my coffee; she paid for her lemonade. We got up and began to walk. I felt awkward, ill at ease. Smaller than I, she walked on my right; her head only came a little above my shoulders. I didn't dare look at her.

She lived not far away. The hotel doorman seemed to be sleeping. The girl took her key and told me it was on the third floor. I followed her. From the back she looked less young.

When we got to the third floor, we turned right and went into her room. She told me to close the door. I closed it softly; I didn't want it to make any noise.

"Not like that," the girl said. "Lock it."

I turned the key. I was filled with a new kind of anxiety. I didn't talk, as I was sure my voice would tremble. Alone with a woman. Alone in a hotel room with a woman. With a prostitute. And soon we would make love. For I was sure of it: she was a prostitute. Otherwise she would have acted differently.

I was alone with her in her neat and clean room, most of which was painted gray. My first woman would be a prostitute. A prostitute whose strange smile was the smile of a saint.

She had drawn the shades, taken off her shoes, and was waiting. Standing near the bed, she was waiting. I felt very stupid, not knowing what to do. Get undressed? Just like that? I thought: first I should kiss her. In the movies the man always kisses the woman before making love to her. I stepped toward her, looked at her intensely, then harshly pulled her toward me and kissed her on the mouth for a long time. Instinctively I had closed my eyes. When I opened them I saw hers, and in them an animal-like terror. This made me draw back a step.

"What's the matter?" I asked her, my heart beating.

"Nothing," she answered; her voice came from another world. "Nothing. Come. Let's make love."

All of a sudden she brought her hand to her mouth. Her face became white as if all life had left it.

"What's the matter with you? Say something!"

She didn't answer. Her hand on her mouth, she was looking through me as if I were transparent. Her eyes were dry, like a blind child's.

"Have I offended you?" I asked.

She didn't hear me.

"Do you want me to leave you?"

She was far away, taking refuge where no stranger was allowed. I could only be present outside. I understood that by kissing her I had set in motion an unknown mechanism.

"Say something," I begged her.

My plea didn't reach her. She looked mad, possessed. Maybe I had only lived for this meeting, I thought. For this meeting with a prostitute who preserved within her a trace of innocence, like madmen who in the midst of their madness hold on to a trace of lucidity.

This lasted a few minutes. Then she seemed to wake up; her hand fell from her face. A tired and infinitely sad smile lit up her features.

"You must forgive me," she said softly. "I spoiled everything. Excuse me. It was stupid of me."

She began to undress, but I no longer felt like making love to her. Now I only wanted to understand.

"Wait," I told her. "Let's talk a little."

"You no longer want to make love?" she asked, worried.

"Later," I reassured her. "First let's talk a little."

"What would you like to talk about?"

"About you."

"What do you want to know?"

Mechanically she unhooked her skirt.

"Who are you?"

"A girl. A girl like many others."

"No," I protested. "You're not like the others."

She let her skirt fall to the floor. Now she was unbuttoning her blouse.

"How do you know?" she asked.

"Intuition probably," I answered awkwardly.

Now she was only wearing a black bra and panties. Slowly she stretched out on the bed. I sat down next to her.

"Who are you?" I asked again.

"I told you. A girl, a girl like many others."

Unconsciously I was stroking her hair.

"What is your name?"

"It doesn't matter."

"What is your name?"

"Sarah."

A familiar sadness took hold of me.

"Sarah," I said. "A beautiful name."

"I don't like it."

"Why not?"

"Sometimes it frightens me."

"I like it," I said. "It was my mother's name."

"Where is she?"

I was still stroking her hair. My heart felt heavy. Should I tell her? I couldn't pronounce such simple, such very simple words: "My mother is dead."

"My mother is dead," I said finally.

"Mine too."

Silence. I was thinking of my mother. If she saw me now . . . she would ask me:

Who is this girl?

My wife, I would say.

And what is her name?

Sarah, Mother.

Sarah?

Yes, Mother. Sarah.

Have you gone mad? Have you forgotten that I too am called Sarah?

No, Mother. I haven't forgotten.

Then, have you forgotten that a man has no right to marry a woman who bears his own mother's name? Have you forgotten that this brings bad luck? That a mother dies from this?

No, Mother. I haven't forgotten. But you can no longer die. You are already dead.

That's true . . . I am dead . . .

"Do you really want to know?"

Sarah's voice brought me back to earth. She was looking straight ahead, as if she were looking through walls, years, and memories, in order to reach the source, where the sky touches the earth, where life calls for love. Sarah put this question to me as if I, by myself, had created the universe.

"You really want to know who I am?"

Her voice had become hard, pitiless.

"Of course," I answered, hiding my fear.

"In that case . . ."

THERE ARE TIMES when I curse myself. I shouldn't have listened. I should have fled. To listen to a story under such circumstances is to play a part in it, to take sides, to say yes or no, to move one way or the other. From then on there is a before and an after. And even to forget becomes a cowardly acceptance.

I should have run away. Or put my hands over my ears. Or thought about something else. I should have screamed, or sung, or kissed her, kissed her on the mouth so she would have stopped talking. Made love to her. Told her that I loved her. Anything, just so she would have stopped talking. So she would have stopped talking.

I did nothing. I listened. Attentively. I was sitting on the edge of the bed, next to her half-undressed body, listening to her story. My clenched fingers were like a vise around my throat.

Now, every time I think of her, I curse myself, as I curse those who do not think of her, who did not think of her at the time of her undoing. Her inscrutable face was like a sick child's. She looked straight ahead without fear, piercing the walls as if she could see the chaos that preceded the creation of the world.

I think of her and I curse myself, as I curse history which has made us what we are: a source of malediction. History which deserves death, destruction. Whoever listens to Sarah and doesn't change, whoever enters Sarah's world and doesn't invent new gods and new religions, deserves death and destruction. Sarah alone had the right to decide what is good and what is evil, the right to differentiate what is true from what usurps the appearance of truth.

And I was sitting next to her half-naked body, and listening. Each word tightened the vise. I was going to strangle myself.

I should have left. Fast. Fast. I should have fled when she opened her mouth, as soon as I noticed the first sign.

I stayed. Something was holding me back. I wanted to suffer with her. To suffer the way she was suffering. I also felt that she was going to humiliate herself. Maybe that prevented me from leaving. I wanted to take part in her humiliation. I was hoping her humiliation would fall back on me too.

She spoke and I listened in silence. Sometimes I felt like screaming like an animal.

Sarah spoke in an even, monotonous voice, stopping only to let silence comment upon an image that words would have been too weak to evoke. Her story opened a secret floodgate within me.

I knew there had been Sarahs in the concentration camps. I had never met any, but I had heard of them. I didn't know their faces were those of sick children. I had no idea that someday I would kiss one of them on the mouth.

Twelve years old. She was twelve years old when, separated from her parents, she had been sent to a special barracks for the camp officers' pleasure. Her life had been spared because there are German officers who like little girls her age. Who like to make love to little girls her age.

Suddenly she turned her darkened eyes toward me: God was still in them. The God of chaos and impotence. The God who tortures twelve-year-old children.

"Did you ever sleep with a twelve-year-old woman?" she asked me.

Her voice was calm, composed, naked. I tried not to scream. I couldn't justify myself. It would have been too easy.

"But you have felt like it, haven't you?" she asked when she noticed I kept quiet. "All men feel like it."

My eyes burned from her stare. I was afraid to scream. I couldn't justify myself. Not to her. Especially not to her. She deserved better.

"Tell me," she went on in a somewhat softer voice. "Is that why you're not making love to me? Because I'm no longer twelve?"

The God of impotence made her eyes flame. Mine too. I thought: I am going to die. Whoever sees God must die. It is written in the Bible. I had never quite understood that: Why should God be allied with death? Why should He want to kill a man who succeeded in seeing Him? Now, everything became clear. God was ashamed. God likes to sleep with twelve-year-old girls. And He doesn't want us to know. Whoever sees it or guesses it must die so as not to divulge the secret. Death is only the guard who protects God, the doorkeeper of the immense brothel that we call the universe. I am going to die, I thought. And my fingers, clenched around my throat, kept pressing harder and harder, against my will.

Sarah decided to let me breathe a moment. She again looked straight ahead and went on talking as if I didn't exist or as if I alone existed, everywhere and always.

"He was drunk. A drunken pig. He was laughing. He stank of obscenity. Especially his laugh. 'It's my birthday today,' he said. 'I want a present. A special present!' He examined me from head to toe and snickered, 'You'll be my birthday present.' I didn't understand the meaning of his words. I was twelve. At that age you don't know yet that girls can be offered as birthday presents . . . I wasn't alone in the barracks. A dozen women stood around us. Bertha was white. So were the others. White. Like corpses. He alone, the drunkard, was red. His hands too, like the butcher's. And his laughter went from his mouth to his eyes. 'You'll be my birthday present, you!' he said. Bertha was biting her lips. She was my friend."

She was a beautiful and sad-looking woman. She carried her head like an Oriental princess. The night she arrived in the camp, she had lost her daughter who was about Sarah's age.

"She's too young, sir," she interceded. "She's only a child."

"If she's here it means she is no longer a child," he had answered, winking. "Otherwise, she would be you know where. Up there . . ."

His fat finger pointed to the ceiling.

"Bertha was my friend," Sarah said. "She didn't give up. She fought to the end. To save me she was ready to take my place. The others too for that matter."

Sarah was silent for a moment.

In the half-darkness of the barracks, Bertha tried to divert him. Without saying a word, she began to undress. The other women—brunettes, blondes, redheads—without consulting one another did the same. In a flash they were all naked like silent, motionless statues. Sarah thought it was a bad dream, a sick nightmare. Or that she had gone mad. An inhuman silence had come over the barracks, contrasting vividly with the tenseness on the women's faces. Outside, the sun was moving behind the horizon, spilling its rusty blood over the moving shadows. It seemed that if the scene went on something terrible would happen at any moment; something that would shatter the universe, change the course of time, unmask destiny, and allow man to see at last what awaits him beyond truth, beyond death.

That's when the drunkard caught the child by the arm and brutally pulled her outside the barracks. It was already dark. A reddish glow rose from the earth, filling the sky with the deep color of blood.

"The officer was intelligent," Sarah said. "Among all the naked women who were in the barracks he had chosen me, although I was dressed. Because I was twelve. Men like to make love to women who are twelve."

Again she turned her head toward me and the vise tightened around my throat with renewed vigor.

"You too," she said. "If I were twelve, you would have made love to me."

I couldn't listen to her anymore. I had reached the end of my strength, and I thought: One more word and I'll die. I'll die here, on this bed, where men come to sleep with a golden-haired girl and in fact don't know that they are making love to a twelve-year-old child.

For a brief moment I had the idea that perhaps I should take her right away. Abruptly. Without gestures, without useless words. To show her that one could fall still lower. That mud is everywhere and has no bottom. I got up slowly, took her hand, and kissed it gently. I wanted her to see. I wanted her to realize that I wanted her. That I desired her. That I too did not transcend the limits of my body. I placed my lips on her cold hand.

"That's all?" she asked me. "You don't want to do anything else?"

She laughed. She was trying to laugh like the other one, like the drunkard in the barracks. But she didn't succeed. She wasn't drunk. There was nothing obscene in her hands, or in her voice. She was as pure as one could be.

"I do," I answered shaken.

Bending over her, I kissed her on the mouth again. She didn't return my kiss. My lips were sealed on hers, my tongue was looking for hers. She remained passive, absent.

I straightened up and after a short hesitation I said very slowly, "I'll tell you what you are . . ."

She tried to talk but I didn't give her a chance.

". . . You are a saint. A saint: that's what you are."

A flash of surprise crossed her sick and childlike face. Her eyes looked clearer. More cruel.

"You are mad!" she said violently. "You are really mad!"

And, letting loose, she laughed again. She imitated someone laughing. But her eyes didn't laugh. Nor did her mouth.

"Me, a saint!" she said. "You are out of your mind. Didn't I tell you how old I was when I had my first man? How old I was when I embarked on my career?"

She stressed the word "career," looking defiant as she asked her question.

"Yes," I said. "You did tell me. Twelve. You were twelve."

She was laughing more and more. It's the drunkard, I thought. He hasn't left her yet.

"And in your opinion," she went on, "a woman who starts her career at twelve is a saint? Right?"

"Right," I said. "A saint."

I thought: Let her cry. Let her scream. Let her insult me. Anything would be better than this laugh which belongs to someone else, to a body without a soul, to a head without eyes. Anything would be better than this foreign and harmful laugh which turns her into a possessed soul.

"You're mad," Sarah said in a voice that tried to be gay and joyous. "The drunkard was only the first. After him came the others. All the others. I became the 'special present' of the barracks. The 'special present' that they all wanted to give themselves. I was more popular than all the other women combined. All the men loved me: the happy and the unhappy, the good and the bad, the old and the young, the gay and the taciturn. The timid and the depraved, the wolves and the pigs, the intellectuals and the butchers, all of them, do you hear? All came to me. And you think I am a saint. You are out of your mind, you poor man."

And she laughed even more. But the laugh had nothing to do with her. Her whole being brought to mind an ageless, nameless suffering. Her laugh sounded dry, inhuman: it wasn't hers, but God's or the drunkard's.

"You poor man!" she said. "I pity you! I would like to do something for you. Tell me, when is your birthday? I'll have a present for you. A special present . . ."

And her laugh settled in me. Someday I too will be possessed. Sarah, in her black underwear, one leg slightly bent, suddenly stopped laughing. I felt the final blow was coming. Instinctively I started moving back toward the door. That's where I heard her scream.

"You're mad!"

"Be quiet! For heaven's sake, be quiet!" I shouted.

I knew she would talk, that she would tell me something terrible, abominable, words that I would always hear whenever I tried to find happiness in a woman's body.

"Be still!" I begged.

"A saint, me?" she screamed like a madwoman. "I want you

to know this and remember it: Sometimes I felt pleasure with them . . . I hated myself afterward and even while it lasted, but my body sometimes loved them . . . And my body is me . . . Me, a saint? Do you know what I really am? I was telling you. I am—"

I had reached the limit. I couldn't take it anymore. I was going to throw up. Quickly I unlocked the door and opened it as fast as I could. I had to get out of that house at once. Second floor. First floor. Doorman. The street. Run. Fast. Run.

Only later, while running, did I notice that my fingers were still clutching my throat.

"SARAH," I said in a choked voice.

"Yes," Kathleen said. "It's your mother's name. I know."

"It's the name of a saint."

I spent days and weeks looking for Sarah. I went back to the café where I had met her. I asked in every hotel in the neighborhood. To no avail. Nobody seemed to have seen or known the golden-haired girl who bore my mother's name. The waiter who had served us did not remember. The hotel doormen all said they had never seen her. And yet I didn't give up hope. Sometimes I think I'm still looking for her. I would like to meet her, if only once. To do what I should have done that afternoon: make love to her.

"Your mother is dead," Kathleen said.

She wanted to hurt herself. Suffer openly. So I would see. So I would know that she was suffering with me, that we were bound together by suffering. She was able to hurt me just to show me that she too was unhappy.

"I know she is dead," I said. "But sometimes I refuse to admit it. Sometimes I think that mothers can't die."

It's true. I can't believe my mother is dead. Perhaps because I didn't see her dead. I saw her walking away with hundreds of people who were swallowed up by the night. If she had told me, "Good-bye, my son. I'm going to die," perhaps I could believe it more now.

Father is dead. I know that. I saw him pass away. I don't look for him among the people in the street. But sometimes I look for my mother. She's not dead. Not really. Here and there I see one of her features in some woman on the subway, on a bus, in a café. And these women, I love and hate them at the same time.

Kathleen. Tears were coming to her eyes. My mother didn't cry. At least not when other people were there. She only offered her tears to God.

Kathleen looked a little like my mother; she had her high forehead, and her chin had the same pure lines. But Kathleen wasn't dead. And she was crying.

I N THE BEGINNING she didn't cry. We were on the same level. We dealt with each other like equals. We were free. Each one free from himself and free from the other. When I didn't feel like keeping a date, I didn't. She did the same. And neither of us was angry or even hurt. When I didn't talk for a whole night, she didn't try to make me explain. The familiar question asked by lovers, "What are you thinking about?" didn't enter our conversations. Hardness had become our religion. Nothing was said that wasn't essential. We tried to convince each other that we could live, hope, and despair, alone. Each kiss could have been the last. At any moment the temple could have collapsed. The future didn't exist since it was useless. At night we made love silently, almost like our own witnesses. A stranger watching us in the street could easily have taken us for enemies. Rightly so, perhaps. True enemies aren't always the ones who hate each other.

I shouldn't have said I'd see her again in New York. I should have told her that it wasn't worthy of us to reopen the parentheses: air moving into it would make everything rot.

She had changed. Kathleen was no longer free. She only imitated the other. Her marriage had destroyed her inside. She had lost all interest in life. The days were all alike. People all said the same thing. Instead of listening to them, you could follow TV programs. Her husband's friends and colleagues bored her. Their wives got on her nerves; she saw herself sentenced to become one of them. Very soon.

In New York, we met every day. She came to my place. I went to her place. We went out a lot, to the theater, to concerts. We discussed literature, music, poetry. I tried to be nice. I was patient, kind, understanding. I treated her as if she were ill. The fight had been over for a long time. Now I was trying to help her get back on her feet.

We seldom evoked the past and only with caution, so as not to tarnish it. Sometimes as we listened to a passage from Bach, or noticed the shape of a cloud playing with the sun, we were seized by the same emotion. She would touch my hand and ask me, "Do you remember?"

And I would answer, "Yes, Kathleen. Of course. I remember."

Before, she would never have felt like proving to me that she remembered. On the contrary, we both would have felt ashamed to have fallen prey to the past, to an emotion from the past. I would have turned my head away. I would have talked about something else. Now we no longer struggled.

Then one day, she confessed . . .

We were drinking coffee in her room. On the radio Isaac Stern was playing the Beethoven violin concerto. We had heard it in Paris at the Salle Pleyel. I remembered that she had taken my hand and that I had pushed her away brusquely. If she would take my hand now, I thought, I wouldn't pull it away.

"Look at me," Kathleen said.

I looked at her. She had a tormented smile. She had the face of a woman who has been abandoned and is conscious of it. She was tapping on the cup with her long fingers.

"Yes," I told her. "I remember."

She put down the cup, got up, and knelt before me. There, without lowering her head, without blushing, in a firm voice—almost as she used to be—she told me, "I think I love you."

She was going to continue but I interrupted her. "Be quiet!" I told her harshly.

I didn't want to hear her say: I have loved you since the first time we met.

My harshness was not reflected on her face. But her smile had become a little deeper, a little more sickly.

"It isn't my fault," she apologized. "I tried. I struggled."

Beethoven, the Salle Pleyel, Stern, love. Love that makes everything complicated. While hate simplifies everything. Hatred puts accents on things and beings, and on what separates them. Love erases accents. I thought: here's another minute that will punctuate my existence.

"Are you sad?" Kathleen asked, distressed.

"No."

Poor Kathleen! She was no longer trying to imitate her other self. Her face was covered with anguish. Her eyes had become strangely small.

"You're going to leave me?"

Love and despair. They go together. One contains some trace of the other. I thought: She must have suffered a lot. It is my turn to try to repair the damage. I have to treat her as if she were ill. I know. To do this is to insult her other self. But the other self doesn't exist. No longer exists. And this one is broken.

"I'm not going to leave you," I answered in the voice of a faithful friend.

A tear slid down her cheek. "You pity me," Kathleen said.

"I don't pity you," I said eagerly.

I was lying. I would have to lie. A lot. She was ill. It is all right to lie to sick people. To her other self I would not have lied.

During the following weeks and months, Kathleen wasted away.

Having nothing to do—she neither felt like working nor needed to work—she spent her days in her room, at her window, or in front of a mirror, alone and unhappy, conscious of her solitude, of her unhappiness.

As before, we went on seeing each other every evening. Dinners, shows, concerts. Once I tried to reason with her: she was wrong to feel sorry for herself. It wasn't worthy of her or of me. She should find some work, be busy, fill up her days. She had to find an aim in life.

"An aim," she said, shrugging her shoulders. "An aim. What aim? The Salvation Army? Be a patron of starving artists? Go to India to help the lepers? An aim? Where would I look for it?"

That's when I had an idea. I told her that I loved her too.

She refused to believe it. She demanded proof. I proved it to her. All the incidents that in the past had shown that there was no love between us, now, all of a sudden, showed the contrary. "Why did you pull away your hand at the concert?" "I didn't want to betray myself." "Why didn't you ever tell me that you loved me?" "Because I loved you." "Why did you always look me right in the eyes?" "To discover my love mirrored in them."

For weeks she was on her guard. And so was I. I considered myself her nurse. Sometimes I toyed with the thought that perhaps she too was treating me like a sick person. Someday we would take off our masks. One of us would say: I was only playing. So was I, the other would answer. And there would be a bitter taste in our mouths. But then it was a pity this was only a game.

However, she wasn't playing. If you play you do not suffer. The part of us which observes us, which watches us play, does not suffer. Kathleen had suffered. In spite of my arguments, she wasn't convinced. She often cried while I was away. When we were together her good spirits were too forced.

I was no longer free. My freedom would have humiliated Kathleen, who had been without freedom for so long. I had invented an attitude toward her which I could no longer get rid of.

If only this had done some good! If only it had helped Kathleen! But she was still unhappy and her laugh was still without sincerity.

Kathleen was getting worse and worse. She began to drink. She was letting herself go.

I discussed this with her. "You have no right to act this way."

"Why not?" she would say, her eyes wide open with an expression of false innocence.

"Because I love you. Your life matters to me, Kathleen."

"Come on! You don't love me. You just say so. If it were true you wouldn't say it."

"I'm saying it because it is true."

"You're saying it out of pity. You don't need me. I don't make you feel good or happy."

These arguments had none of the results I hoped for. On the contrary, after each one, Kathleen let herself go still further.

Then one evening—the day before the accident—she explained to me at last why she couldn't believe in the integrity of my love.

"You claim you love me but you keep suffering. You say you love me in the present but you're still living in the past. You tell me you love me but you refuse to forget. At night you have bad dreams. Sometimes you moan in your sleep. The truth is that I am nothing to you. I don't count. What counts is the past. Not ours: yours. I try to make you happy: an image strikes your memory and it is all over. You are no longer there. The image is stronger than I. You think I don't know? You think your silence is capable of hiding the hell you carry within you? Maybe you also think that it is easy to live beside someone who suffers and who won't accept any help?"

She wasn't crying. That night she hadn't been drinking. We were in bed. Her head was resting on my outstretched arm. A warm wind was blowing through the open windows. We had just gone to bed. This was one of our rituals: never to make love right away; to talk first.

I could feel how heavy my heart had become, as if it were unable to contain itself. She had guessed correctly. You cannot hide suffering and remorse for long. They come out. It was true: I was living in the past. Grandmother, with her black shawl on her head, wasn't giving me up.

"It isn't my fault," I answered.

I explained to her: A man who tells a woman he thinks he loves, "I love you and shall love you forever; may I die if I stop loving you," believes it. And yet one day he sounds his heart and finds it empty. And he stays alive. With us—those who have known the time of death—it's different. There, we said we would never forget. It still holds true. We cannot forget. The images are there in front of our eyes. Even if our eyes were no longer there, the images would remain. I think if I were able to forget I would hate myself. Our stay there planted time bombs within us. From time to time one of them explodes. And then we are nothing but suffering, shame, and guilt. We feel ashamed and guilty to be alive, to eat as much bread as we want, to wear good, warm socks in the winter. One of these bombs, Kathleen, will undoubtedly bring about madness. It's inevitable. Anyone who has been there has brought back some of humanity's madness. One day or another, it will come to the surface.

Kathleen was sober and lucid that evening. I had the impression her old self had come to visit her. But I knew that it would leave again. That the visit would be short and that only the self that was trying to imitate it would remain. And someday even that one would stop searching. Then the divorce would be final.

That night I understood that sooner or later I would have to leave Kathleen. To stay with her had become meaningless.

I told myself: Suffering pulls us farther away from other human beings. It builds a wall made of cries and contempt to separate us. Men cast aside the one who has known pure suffering, if they cannot make a god out of him; the one who tells them: I suffered not because I was God, nor because I was a saint trying to imitate Him, but only because I am a man, a man like you, with your weaknesses, your cowardice, your sins, your rebellions, and your ridiculous ambitions; such a man frightens men, because he makes them feel ashamed. They pull away from him as if he were guilty. As if he were usurping God's place to illuminate the great vacuum that we find at the end of all adventures.

Actually it is good that this should be so. A man who has suffered more than others, and differently, should live apart. Alone. Outside of any organized existence. He poisons the air. He makes it unfit for breathing. He takes away from joy its spontaneity and its justification. He kills hope and the will to live. He is the incarnation of time that negates present and future, only recognizing the harsh law of memory. He suffers and his contagious suffering calls forth echoes around him.

One day or another I shall have to leave Kathleen, I decided. It will be better for her. If I could forget, I would stay. I cannot. There are times when man has no right to suffer.

"I suggest an agreement," Kathleen said. "I'll let you help me, provided you let me help you. All right?"

Poor Kathleen! I thought. It's too late. To change, we would have to change the past. But the past is beyond our power. Its structure is solid, immutable. The past is Grandmother's shawl, as black as the cloud above the cemetery. Forget the cloud? The black cloud which is Grandmother, her son, my mother. What a stupid time we live in! Everything is upside down. The cemeteries are up above, hanging from the sky, instead of being dug in the moist earth. We are lying in bed, my naked body against your naked body, and we are thinking about black clouds, about floating cemeteries, about the snickering of death and fate which are one and the same. You speak of happiness, Kathleen, as if happiness were possible. It isn't even a dream. It too is dead. It too is up above. Everything has taken refuge above. And what emptiness here below! Real life is there. Here, we have nothing. Nothing, Kathleen. Here, we have an arid desert. A desert without even a mirage. It's a station where the child left on the platform sees his parents carried off by the train. And there is only black smoke where they stood. They are the smoke. Happiness? Happiness for the child would be for the train to move backward. But you know how trains are, they always go forward. Only the smoke moves backward. Yes, ours is a horrible station! Men like me who are in it should stay there alone, Kathleen. Not let the suffering in us come in contact with other men. We must not give them the sour taste, the smoke-cloud taste, that we have in our mouth. We must not, Kathleen. You say "love." And you don't know that love too has taken the train which went straight to heaven. Now everything has been transferred there. Love, happiness, truth, purity, children with happy smiles, women with mysterious eyes, old people who walk slowly, and little orphans whose prayers are filled with anguish. That's the true exodus. The exodus from one world to the other. Ancient peoples had a limited imagination. Our dead take with them to the hereafter not only clothes and food, but also the future of their descendants. Nothing remains below. And you speak of love, Kathleen? And you speak of happiness? Others speak of justice, universal or not, of freedom, of brotherhood, of progress. They don't know that the planet is drained and that an enormous train has carried everything off to heaven.

"So, you accept?" Kathleen asked.

"I accept what?" I wondered.

"The agreement I suggested."

"Of course," I answered absentmindedly. "I accept."

"And you'll let me make you happy?"

"I'll let you make me happy."

"And you promise to forget the past?"

"I promise to forget the past."

"And you'll think only about our love?"

"Yes."

She had gone through her questionnaire. She stopped to catch her breath and asked in a different tone of voice, "Where were you before?"

"At the station," I said.

"I don't understand."

"At the station," I said. "I was at the station. It was very small. The station of a small provincial town. The train had just left. I was left alone on the platform. My parents were in the train. They had forgotten me."

Kathleen didn't say anything.

"At first I was resentful. They shouldn't have left me behind, alone on the platform. But a little later, I suddenly saw a strange thing: the train was leaving the tracks and climbing toward the smoke-gray sky. Stunned, I couldn't even shout out to my parents: What are you doing? Come back! Perhaps if I had shouted, they would have come back."

I was beginning to feel tired. I was perspiring. It was warm in the bed. A car had just screeched to a stop under the window.

"You promised not to think about it anymore," Kathleen said in despair.

"Forgive me. I won't think about it anymore. In any case, these days trains are an outmoded way to travel. The world has progressed."

"Sure?"

"Sure."

She pressed her body against mine.

"Every time your thoughts take you to the little station, tell me. We'll fight it together?"

"Yes."

"I love you."

The accident occurred the next day.

T HE TEN WEEKS I spent in a world of plaster had made me richer.

I learned that man lives differently, depending on whether he is in a horizontal or vertical position. The shadows on the walls, on the faces, are not the same.

Three people came to see me every day. Paul Russel came in the morning; Kathleen in the evening; Gyula in the afternoon. He alone had guessed. Gyula was my friend.

A painter, of Hungarian origin, Gyula was a living rock. A giant in every sense of the word. Tall, robust, gray and rebellious hair, mocking and burning eyes; he pushed aside everything around him: altars, ideas, mountains. Everything trembled, vibrated, at his touch, at the sight of him.

In spite of our difference in age, we had a lot in common. Every week we would meet for lunch in a Hungarian restaurant on the East Side. We encouraged each other to stick it out, not to make compromises, not to come to terms with life, not to accept easy victories. Our conversation always sounded like banter. We detested sentimentality. We avoided people who took themselves seriously and particularly those who asked others to do so. We didn't spare each other. Thus our friendship was healthy, simple, and mature.

I was still half dead when he burst into my room, pushed the nurse aside with his shoulder (she was getting ready to give me an injection), and, without asking me anything, announced in a firm and decided voice that he was going to do my portrait.

The nurse, needle in hand, stared at him aghast.

"What are you doing here? Who let you in? Get out immediately!"

Gyula looked at her with compassion, as if her mind were not all there.

"You're beautiful," he told her. "But mad!"

He studied her with interest.

"Beautiful women nowadays aren't mad enough," he went on nostalgically. "But you are. I like you."

The poor nurse—a young student—was on the verge of tears. She was stuttering.

"The injection— Get out— I have to—"

"Later!" Gyula ordered.

And taking her by the arm, he pushed her toward the door. There, she whispered something in his ear.

"Hey! You!" Gyula said after closing the door. "She says you are seriously ill. That you're dying! Aren't you ashamed to be dying?"

"Yes," I answered weakly. "I'm ashamed."

Gyula walked about to familiarize himself with the view, the walls, the smell of the room. Then he stopped near the bed and challenged me.

"Don't die before I've finished your portrait, do you hear? Afterward, I don't give a darn! But not before! Understood?"

"You're a monster, Gyula," I told him, moved.

"You didn't know?" he wondered. "Artists are the worst monsters: they live on the lives and deaths of others."

I thought he would ask how the accident had happened. He didn't. And yet, I wanted him to know.

"Do you want me to tell you about it?" I asked him.

"You don't have to," he answered disdainfully. "I don't need your explanations."

There was a circle of fondness around his eyes.

"I want you to know," I said.

"I'll know."

"It's a secret," I said. "No one knows it. I'd like to tell you."

"You don't have to," he answered contemptuously. "I like to discover everything for myself."

I tried to laugh. "I might die before you have a chance."

He was flaming with threatening anger. "Not before I'm through with your portrait, I told you. Afterward you can die whenever and as often as you like!"

I was proud. Proud of him, of myself, of our friendship. Of the tough laws we had made for it. They protected us against the successes and the certainties of the weak. True exchanges take place where simple words are called for, where we set out to state the problem of the immortality of the soul in shockingly banal sentences.

Gyula turned up every afternoon. The nurses knew they weren't to disturb us when he was there. For them he was an animal whose insults, in Hungarian, would have reddened even the cheeks of a black girl.

While he was sketching, Gyula told me stories. He was an excellent storyteller. His life was filled with innumerable adventures and hallucinatory experiences. He had died of hunger in Paris, handed out fortunes in Hollywood, taught magic and alchemy nearly everywhere. He had known all the great men of contemporary literature and the arts; he liked their weaknesses and forgave them their successes. Gyula too had an obsession: to pit himself against fate, to force it to give human meaning to its cruelty. But of course he only spoke of that mockingly.

One day he came as usual toward the beginning of the afternoon and, framed by the window, began to work. He was silent. He hadn't even said hello when he came in. He seemed preoccupied. Half an hour, an hour. He suddenly stopped moving, remained motionless, and looked me straight in the eyes, as if he had just torn asunder an invisible veil that covered them. For a few seconds we stared at each other. His thick eyebrows arched as he frowned: he was beginning to understand.

"Do you want me to tell you?" I was upset.

"No," he answered coldly. "I have no use for your stories!"

And again he was absorbed by his work, in which he found answers to all questions and questions for all answers.

A week later he told me something that didn't seem to have any relation to the subject we were then discussing. We were speaking of the international situation, the danger of a third world war, the important part that China would soon be playing. Suddenly Gyula changed the subject.

"Incidentally," he said, "have I told you the story of my unsuccessful drowning?"

"No," I answered mockingly. "Where did it happen: in China?"

"Spare me your comments," he said. "You'd do better to listen."

Good old Gyula! I thought. How do you tell a woman that you love her? You probably insult her, and if she doesn't understand that kind of love-talk, you simply stop loving her. Good old Gyula!

One summer he had gone to the French Riviera for his vacation, to get away from the heat. He often went to the seashore. That morning he swam out too far. Suddenly a sharp cramp paralyzed his body. Unable to use either his arms or his legs, he let himself sink.

"I began to drink the salt water of the sea," he said. "There was no fear in me. I knew that I was dying, but I remained calm. A strangely sweet serenity came over me. I thought: at last I'll know what a drowning man thinks about. That was my last thought. I lost consciousness."

He was saved. Someone had seen him sink and rescued him.

While watching the lines his brush drew on the canvas, Gyula went on, smiling imperceptibly.

"When I came to, I looked all around me. I was lying on the sand, in the midst of a group of curious people. A bald old man, a doctor, was leaning over me and taking my pulse. In the first row, a terrified young woman was looking at me. She put on a vague smile for me, but the expression of terror remained. How distressing: a horrified woman who smiles. I thought: I'm alive. I have outwitted death. One more time death didn't get me. Here is the proof: I'm looking at a woman who is looking at me and smiling. The horror on her face is there for death, which must still be very near, right behind me. The smile is for me, for me alone. I told myself: I could have been here, in the same spot, and not have seen this woman, who, right now, is more graceful and beautiful than any other. I could have been looked at by a woman who didn't smile. I must consider myself happy, I told myself. I'm alive. Victory over death should give birth to happiness. Happiness to be free. Free to provoke death again. Free to accept freedom or to reject it. This reprieve should give me a feeling of well-being. And yet, I didn't have it. I was searching conscientiously within myself: not a trace of joy to be found. The doctor was examining me, the people gave me mute expressions of sympathy like alms, and the young woman's smile was becoming more open—that's how one smiles at life. In spite of that, I wasn't happy. On the contrary, I was terribly sad and disappointed. Later, this unsuccessful drowning made me sing and dance. But there, on the sand, under the burning, purple sun, under the eyes of this unknown woman, I felt disappointed, disappointed at having come back."

Gyula worked silently for a long time. I think he was painting with his eyes closed. I was wondering if he was still disappointed. And if later on he had seen the young woman again. But I said nothing. Paul Russel came back to my mind. He is wrong, I thought. Life doesn't necessarily want to live. Life is really fascinated only by death. It vibrates only when it comes in contact with death.

"Will you listen to me? Gyula, will you?" I implored.

He jumped up as if I had just forced him to reopen his eyes. There was a little sardonic laugh.

"No, I won't," he said.

"But I'd like you to know."

"To know what?" he asked harshly.

"Everything."

"I don't need your stories in order to know."

Good old Gyula! I thought. What happened to the young woman on the beach? Did you insult her? Did you tell her, "You are a little bitch, a dirty little bitch?" Did she understand that these were words of love?

"Gyula," I asked him, "what happened to the unknown woman?"

"What unknown woman?"

"The one on the beach. The one who smiled at you?"

He was overcome by a loud laugh that must have been hiding a wave of tenderness surging up in him from the distant past.

"Oh, that one?" he said in a voice that tried to sound vulgar. "She was a little bitch, a dirty little bitch!"

I couldn't help smiling. "Did you tell her that?"

"Of course I told her!" He realized I was smiling. "You monster," he shouted at me in disgust. "Let me work. Otherwise I'll beat you up!"

The day before I was supposed to leave the hospital, Gyula came in surrounded by an aura of arrogance. He stood like a victorious general at the foot of my bed, between the river and me, and announced the good news: the portrait was finished.

"And now, you can die," he said.

Gyula placed it on a chair. He hesitated for a second. Then, turning his back to me, he stepped aside. My heart was beating violently. I was there, facing me. My whole past was there, facing me. It was a painting in which black, interspersed with a few red spots, dominated. The sky was a thick black. The sun, a dark gray. My eyes were a beating red, like Soutine's. They belonged to a man who had seen God commit the most unforgivable crime: to kill without a reason.

"You see," Gyula said. "You don't know how to speak; you are yourself only when you are silent."

He quivered slightly, unable to hide his emotion.

"Don't talk," he added. "That's all I'm asking you."

And to hide, he went to the window and looked at the playful waves of the East River moving elegantly toward their date with infinity.

He had guessed. It was enough to look at the painting to realize. The accident had been an accident only in the most limited sense of the word. The cab, I had seen it coming. It had only been a flash, but I had seen it, I could have avoided it.

A silent dialogue now took place between Gyula and me.

"You see? Maybe God is dead, but man is alive. The proof: he is capable of friendship."

"But what about the others? The others, Gyula? Those who died? What about them? Besides me, they have no friends."

"You must forget them. You must chase them from your memory. With a whip if necessary."

"Chase them, Gyula? With a whip, you said? To chase my father with a whip? And Grandmother? Grandmother too, chase her with a whip?"

"Yes, yes, and yes. The dead have no place down here. They must leave us in peace. If they refuse, use a whip."

"And this painting, Gyula? They are there. In the eyes of the portrait. Why did you put them there if you ask me to chase them away?"

"I put them there to assign them a place. So you would know where to hit."

"I can't, Gyula. I can't."

Gyula turned and all of a sudden I saw that he had grown older. His hair had become white, his face thinner, more hollow.

"Suffering is given to the living, not to the dead," he said, looking right through me. "It is man's duty to make it cease, not to increase it. One hour of suffering less is already a victory over fate."

Yes, he had grown older. It was now an old man talking to me and handing over to me the ageless knowledge that explains why the earth is still revolving and why man is still looking forward to tomorrow. Without catching his breath, he went on as if he had saved these words for me for a long time.

"If your suffering splashes others, those around you, those for whom you represent a reason to live, then you must kill it, choke it. If the dead are its source, kill them again, as often as you must to cut out their tongues."

A boundless sadness came over me. I had the impression I was losing my friend: he was judging me.

"What if it cannot be done?" I asked him, feeling very dejected. "What should one do? Lie? I prefer lucidity."

He shook his head slowly.

"Lucidity is fate's victory, not man's. It is an act of freedom that carries within itself the negation of freedom. Man must keep moving, searching, weighing, holding out his hand, offering himself, inventing himself."

All of a sudden I had the impression that it was my teacher, Kalman the Kabbalist, who was talking to me. His voice had the same kind, understanding accent. But Kalman was my teacher, not my friend.

"You should know this," Gyula went on without changing his tone of voice, without even blinking an eye, "you should know that the dead, because they are no longer free, are no longer able to suffer. Only the living can. Kathleen is alive. I am alive. You must think of us. Not of them."

He stopped to fill his pipe, or perhaps he had nothing else to add. Everything had been said. The pros and the cons. I would choose the living or the dead. Day or night. Him or Kalman.

I looked at the portrait and hidden in its eyes I saw Grandmother with her black shawl. On her emaciated face she wore an expression of peaceful suffering. She was telling me: *Fear nothing. I'll be wherever you are. Never again shall I leave you alone on a station platform. Or alone on a street corner of a foreign town. I'll take you with me. In the train that goes to heaven. And you won't see the earth anymore. I'll hide it from you. With my black shawl.*

"You're leaving the hospital tomorrow?" Gyula asked in a voice that sounded normal again.

"Yes, tomorrow."

"Kathleen will take care of you?"

"Yes."

"She loves you."

"I know."

Silence.

"You'll be able to walk?"

"With crutches," I answered. "They took off the cast. But I can't put any weight on my leg. I have to walk with crutches."

"You can lean on Kathleen. She'll be happy if you lean on her. Receiving is a superior form of generosity. Make her happy. A little happiness justifies the effort of a whole life."

Kathleen will be happy, I decided. I'll learn to lie well and she'll be happy. It's absurd: lies can give birth to true happiness. Happiness will, as long as it lasts, seem real. The living like lies, the way they like to acquire friendships. The dead don't like them. Grandmother would not accept being told less than the truth. Next time, I promise you, Grandmother, I'll be careful. I won't miss the train again.

I must have been staring at the portrait too intensely because all of a sudden Gyula started gritting his teeth. With an angry, enraged motion, he took a match and put it against the canvas.

"No!" I exclaimed in despair. "Don't do that! Gyula, don't do it! Don't burn Grandmother a second time! Stop, Gyula, stop!"

Gyula, unmoved, didn't react. His face closed and withdrawn, he was holding the canvas with his fingertips, turning it in all directions, and waiting for it to be reduced to ashes. I wanted to throw myself on him, but I was too weak to get out of the bed. I couldn't hold back my tears. I cried a long time after Gyula had closed the door behind him.

He had forgotten to take along the ashes.